"FRIENDLY CRITTER, AREN'T YOU?" HE SAID.

Struck by his rudeness, Leah stopped to gape at him. She set her hands on her hips. Too late she remembered her torn clothes. She quickly gripped the ragged edges and gave a little huff of air before answering him. "No one invited you to this town, mister. In fact, Defiance needs another gunfighter like a hole in the head. You've got no call to be rude."

A grin whispered across his hard mouth. "I was talking about your wolf. He's very protective of you."

Leah blushed, something she'd done about as many times as she could count on the fingers of one hand. She had grown up in Defiance with four-fifths of its population male. There was little men could say or do that shocked her, but for some reason, this stranger got her all riled up.

Also Available by Elaine Levine

RACHEL AND THE HIRED GUN

AUDREY AND THE MAVERICK

Published by Zebra Books

LEAH and the BOUNTY HUNTER

Men of Defiance

ELAINE LEVINE

ZEBRA BOOKS
KENSINGTON PUBLISHING CORP.
http://www.kensingtonbooks.com

ZEBRA BOOKS are published by

Kensington Publishing Corp.
119 West 40th Street
New York, NY 10018

All Kensington titles, imprints, and distributed lines are
available at special quantity discounts for bulk purchases for
sales promotion, premiums, fund-raising, educational, or
institutional use.

Special book excerpts or customized printings can also be created to fit specific needs. For details, write or phone the office
of the Kensington Special Sales Manager: Attn.: Special Sales
Department. Kensington Publishing Corp., 119 West 40th Street,
New York, NY 10018. Phone: 1-800-221-2647.

Zebra and the Z logo Reg. U.S. Pat. & TM Off.

ISBN-13: 978-1-4201-1866-7
ISBN-10: 1-4201-1866-8

First Printing: August 2011

10 9 8 7 6 5 4 3 2 1

Printed in the United States of America

This book is dedicated to my son,
Aaron,
who has taught me much about honor, loyalty,
and how one goes about being a lifelong friend.

It is also dedicated to his wife,
Michelle,
who has become a daughter of my heart.

Together,
they had the tremendous foresight to
make me a grandmother of two beautiful children—
bringing a whole new state of grace to my life!

Chapter 1

Dakota Territory, June 1868

Jace Gage rode slowly down the main street in Defiance, the leather of his saddle loud in the quiet stillness of pre-dawn. Expecting a sharp-shooter, he scanned the street, roof tops, and alleys. No shadows moved furtively. No sentries kept watch. His absence over the last few weeks had lulled the sheriff's men into complacency. Maybe ghosts were all that remained in Defiance.

The morning wind whistled around the empty buildings, disturbing the tumbleweed skeletons piled here and there. A couple of saloons were boarded up. A billboard sign hung askew over a bank's gaping front entrance. Several businesses had broken windows or missing doors. The few houses he could see fared no better; their weath-ered, wooden siding looked dingy in the faint morning light. A sway-backed porch on one house leaned over a collapsing stoop, its intricate fret-work forgotten.

He didn't like the feel of this town. He didn't like the looks of it, or the smell of it, or the sound of it either. Even Mother Nature wanted to forget this place, wipe it off the face of the Earth like the infected rat's nest that it was.

And Jace was happy to oblige.

He had two thousand dollars in his pocket for riding into town. The U.S. marshal in Cheyenne had a like sum waiting for him once Sheriff Kemp and his cohorts were gone.

Dead or gone, to be exact.

A commotion broke into his thoughts as he approached the general store. Two men and a boy were scuffling. A black timber wolf crouched nearby, a massive, growling shadow braced to join the fray. Jace dismounted and tied his horse to the hitching post. The men laughed low in their throats, their attention focused on the boy they shoved back and forth between them. The sexual overtones in the play turned Jace's stomach. The boy, trying to get away, pleaded with them. He had to be young—his voice hadn't changed yet.

Jace pushed the edges of his jacket back behind his holsters and flexed his hands beside his Colts. He'd never cleared a place as foul as this, where the outlaws had turned to the town's boys for their pleasure. He'd enjoy killing these two.

The sun crested the horizon just then, washing everything in its brilliant pink glow. As if sensing their time for play was ending, one of the men ripped the boy's shirt and vest open, revealing the sweetest pair of tits Jace had seen in a month of Sundays.

Maybe a whole year of Sundays.

And then all hell broke loose. The kid shouted for the wolf to attack. Instantly complying, the beast jumped at one of the men, clamping his powerful jaws down on a meaty forearm, yanking and twisting as if to separate limb from man.

Taking advantage of the second man's shock, the girl dug her fingers into the notch at the base of his throat and used it as a handle to yank him to his knees. Before he'd even hit the ground, she'd palmed her knife and pressed it to the soft flesh beneath one of his eyes.

"Take a long look, mister, 'cause it's the last thing you're gonna see," the girl warned softly.

The hairs rose on Jace's neck at the sweet sound of her voice, the harmony of it jarringly discordant with her actions. Whether his response was in warning or desire, he couldn't distinguish. She was fierce, lethal even. And she made no attempt to hide what she was—a killer.

"While you're on your knees, friend," Jace spoke up, "best ask the kid's forgiveness." The man's gaze shot to Jace, though he didn't move his head. The girl showed no reaction to his presence. "You see, this is my town now, and we don't treat women— or kids—like that here."

"Goddamn, Johnny! Listen to his voice! That's the Avenger!" the second man hissed. He was on his back, his bloodied arms thrown up to protect his face. The wolf's powerful jaws hovered near his neck, long fangs bared in warning as he awaited a single word from the girl.

Johnny swallowed hard. Careful of the knife,

he glanced up at his captor. "Our apologies, Miss Morgan. Don't know what came over us."

Miss Morgan? Jace cursed and gave the girl another look, watching while she considered her next move. After a tense few seconds, she released the man's hair and sheathed her knife.

"Wolf! Come!" she called the black beast to her side. He lowered his jowls over his teeth with a cough, giving his victim a last, one-eyed glare before trotting over to sit at her heels. The two men scrambled to their feet, eyeing Jace warily before scurrying away.

Leah finally felt her heart hammering against her ribs, in her throat, in her ears. She'd been afraid the third gunfighter had come to join the other two and had no choice but to make a move to keep them all at bay. Until that moment, she'd tried to keep the scuffle quiet, worried that Jim, the shopkeeper, would come out of the store to defend her.

She was shocked to discover the third man was the famed "Avenger."

The gunfighter walked toward her, his spurs making a chink-chinking sound with each step of his long stride. He was fortified like a one-man army with a rifle over one shoulder, two bandoliers loaded with rifle cartridges crossing his chest over his loose jacket. A gunbelt was strung across his hips with twin Colts strapped to his thighs. A Bowie knife the length of her forearm hung next to the buckle of his gunbelt. Her eyes traveled the long distance down his thighs to the boots that came almost to his knees. She wondered what other weapons he held concealed within them.

Folding her arms to close her shirt as best she could—and to hide her shaking—she studied his hardened visage—and disliked what she saw. A few days' growth of beard covered his square jaw. His lips were hard slashes between lines that bracketed his mouth. High cheekbones made hollows above his jaw. His eyes were by far the worst of his features. As blue as chicory flowers, they were windows into the blackest soul Leah had ever seen.

She remembered the rumor that this man had survived a hanging. Unable to curb her curiosity, she let her eyes dip to his Adam's apple and the scar that circled what she could see of his neck. He hadn't even attempted to hide the livid white twists burned into his skin. A frisson of warning rippled through her.

What kind of man could survive a hanging? She met his gaze again. His blue eyes held hers before sweeping over her hair and down the column of skin that her ripped clothing exposed, examining her as she had him. Her breathing quickened, but she resisted the urge to pull the torn edges of her shirt and camisole closer together. She did not back away.

He arched a brow at her. She lifted her chin. Wolf began growling.

"Nice pet, kid," he said in that desert-parched voice of his that made her thirst for an endless drink of water. He moved around her and headed to the steps leading up to the boardwalk in front of the store.

For two weeks, she'd hidden in her house, frightened of the monster the Avenger was rumored to be. It was said he had more kills than Cullen Baker, that no man could outdraw him. And his skill with a knife was legendary. The sheriff's men had bandied stories about town of the Avenger throwing a knife with such swift accuracy that he buried it deep in his opponent before the other could even cock his gun. Seeing him now, she felt foolish for her fear; he was just another gunfighter, like all of those in town.

Yet even as she thought it, she knew it was a lie. He was unlike any who had come for the sheriff. Jace Gage was a man who had already cheated death once. Perhaps he could do it again. Perhaps he would succeed here.

"Some avenger you are," she challenged him with a bravado she didn't entirely feel. "You might have stepped in sooner."

"Didn't look like you needed help," he rasped without breaking stride or looking back. Outside the entrance to the general store, he did pause and sent her a look over his shoulder. "A word of advice, kid. The next time you draw a knife on a man, you'd best use it. A dead enemy's a whole lot less trouble than a living one."

"I have no enemies in this town, mister."

The man nodded, contemplating her words. His eyes narrowed as he looked from her to the two men running for the sheriff's office. He let his gaze swing back her way as he answered, "I'm guessin' you do now." He entered the store.

Leah drew a long, calming breath. Wolf stopped

growling, but a lip was still snaggled up over one of his fangs. He watched her patiently through one golden eye and the milky one long ago ruined by an angry porcupine. He was a sorry sight, she had to admit. He'd been losing his winter coat for a month, and now the tufts of downy gray underfur pushing free of his black hair made him look like a half sheared lamb. She adjusted her clothes to cover their torn state as best she could, and then went inside Jim's store.

Everyone was standing around stiffly, staring at each other. "Leah, come with me," Sally, the shop-keeper's wife, ordered with a wave from the store-room. Sally always hid there when trouble came to the store. Leah ignored the invitation. She was done hiding.

Jim broke the silence. "Good day, stranger. What brings you to Defiance?"

"I have business with the sheriff," the Avenger answered in his gravelly voice.

"You a friend of his?" Jim asked.

"I don't count outlaws among my friends. I've come to take Kemp to Cheyenne."

"You with the law?"

"Nope."

"You the one they call the 'Avenger'?" Jim asked.

The Avenger winced and shook his head. "I'm just a man trying to earn his keep. Name's Jace Gage."

"I'm Jim Kessler, and this is my wife, Sally. Seems you met Leah Morgan already."

Gage tipped his hat to Sally but completely ig-nored Leah. "Is there a hotel or a room still to be had in this town?" he asked Jim.

"Maddie, down the street, runs a boardinghouse. Leah's heading that way. She can show you."

"Jim! No!" Sally complained in a whisper loud enough for all to hear.

"He ain't gonna hurt her, Sal. Besides, between Wolf and her knife, she can take care of herself," he said meaningfully.

Leah shot a glare at the Avenger, then headed for the door. He could follow or not; it was up to him. Wolf fell into step with her as she walked down the boardwalk and into the street. A bend in the road, then two short blocks separated Jim's from Maddie's. Leah lived across the street from Maddie, so Jim had been right—she was headed that way. She hadn't gone far when she heard the jingle of Gage's spurs as he caught up to her. She didn't slow her stride. He drew even with her, leading his horse. Wolf moved to walk between him and Leah.

"Friendly critter, aren't you?" he said.

Struck by his rudeness, Leah stopped to gape at him. She set her hands on her hips. Too late she remembered her torn clothes. She quickly gripped the ragged edges and gave a little huff of air before answering him. "No one invited you to this town, mister. In fact, Defiance needs another gunfighter like a hole in the head. You've got no call to be rude."

A grin whispered across his hard mouth. "I was talking about your wolf. He's very protective of you."

Leah blushed, something she'd done about as many times as she could count on the fingers of one hand. She had grown up in Defiance with four-fifths of its population male. There was little men could say or do that shocked her, but for some reason, this stranger got her all riled up.

As if he was aware of her confusion, his smile deepened. Leah resumed walking in stony silence, turning down Maddie's drive a few minutes later. It led around the boardinghouse to a small stable and carriage house. Right past the main building, she caught sight of a movement over by the stable. She stopped abruptly and dragged the Avenger back against the house—no small feat in itself, for he was much larger than she was.

"Wait! Don't move!" she hissed, caring little that he landed with his back against the house or that she now stood with one of his legs wedged between hers. She pressed a hand on his chest to hold him in place as she peeked around the corner.

"You got a shortage of men in this town, kid? Or do you wrangle all the newcomers this way?"

His words made Leah aware of several things— how tall he was, how close to him she was standing, and exactly where his leg was. His glance razed the pale skin of her chest. Her cheeks heated up again. She hastily took a step away from him and crossed her arms over her torn clothes. "I saw someone near the stable. You can't go over there. They'll kill you."

"They're likely to kill you, too, if you stay so near me. I think I can manage to get a room without your help."

"You know, I should let them blow your fool head off. You can't win against the sheriff and his gang. There's too many of them. Others have tried, and not a one of them left with the bounty he came for, if he was lucky enough to leave."

She looked up at the Avenger's granite face and crystalline blue eyes. "You should leave town, Mr. Gage, 'cause you're as good as dead if you don't." She slipped the reins of his horse from him and moved as if to head toward the stable.

"Whoa, what do you think you're doing?" He pulled her back. Wolf stepped on his boot, his one good eye glaring up at the man.

Leah frowned as she pushed against him. "I'm gonna buy you five more minutes of living by putting your horse up for you."

"No, you're not," he said with a lopsided grin. "You've come far enough. Just run along now. I'll take it from here." He eased the reins from her.

Leah peered into his eyes, studying him even as he watched her. He was so alive now, and he wasn't very old, late-twenties to mid-thirties, she guessed. It would be a shame to see him killed. But she'd learned how easily death came to anyone, in this town especially.

"Well, good luck to you, then." She moved away, walking backwards so she could give him one last warning. "If you're partial to being buried, I suggest you leave some money with Maddie to buy you a pine box and a hole in the cemetery. Otherwise, they'll dump your body a ways out of town for the scavengers to pick clean." She pivoted and walked down the drive, toward the street. She didn't look back—there was no point—they'd be burying him in the morning.

She wondered which of the sheriff's men would get his horse.

Chapter 2

Jace watched the hoyden cross the street and disappear into the shanty opposite Maddie's, one of several on that side of the road. His mind kept flashing images of her big blue eyes and dark sable hair. Hell and damnation. It would be his luck that she was the one he was supposed to keep safe.

Maybe she would do what most decent folks did when he cleared a town; hide in her home until he was done with what he came to do. Somehow, he doubted he would be so fortunate.

Leaving his horse in the drive, he went to Maddie's front door and knocked. No response. He knocked again. No response. He sighed and turned around to look at Leah Morgan's house. Her black wolf was lying across the threshold of the front door, still watching him with his one good eye. She and her mangy beast were a matched pair, he thought as he faced the closed front door of the boarding-house.

He couldn't very well break the door down. If Maddie wouldn't let him in, he'd make camp outside town, at the river—which was what he'd decided to do when the door opened. A slightly plump woman with graying brown hair glared at him. Her crisp white apron reflected the bright morning sun, making him squint.

"Hello, ma'am," Jace said, sliding his hat off the back of his head to let it hang by its thong. "I was hoping you might have a room I can rent for a few weeks?"

The woman looked him up and down, her lips pressed in a thin line, her gaze snagging on every piece of his personal armament. "I've got a room," she said with a nod, then stood back and let him enter.

Daylight from the windows at the front of the house lit the entranceway, brightening the beige and rose wallpaper. Salmon-colored velvet drapes separated two rooms from the foyer and hallway. The scent of beeswax was strong in the air, and the wood floor gleamed from a recent scrubbing. A wear path in the middle of the hallway was lighter and slightly indented from the outer edges. Maddie's boardinghouse saw plenty of traffic. He followed the path to a desk in one of the front rooms where the woman opened a ledger and inked a pen.

"You with the sheriff?" she asked.

"No."

"Well, that's something in your favor, at least. But you look like trouble, mister. I don't like trouble in my house."

Jace met her look. "I won't be starting trouble here, ma'am, but I sure won't walk away if it finds me. In fact, some of it's already waitin' for me out by your stable."

"That boy's been there since last night." The woman's eyes narrowed. He watched her gaze follow one of the straps of his bandolier down to a Colt. She flashed a look at him. "It's you! You're the Avenger."

"I'm no avenger, just a man tired of camping, looking for a room."

The woman frowned at him. "My normal rate is five dollars a week. But I'm charging you double. And if you break anything, you'll be charged for that too."

Jace nodded.

The woman made a disgruntled sound, as she gave him a sidelong glance. "Well, sign here. Pay for this week in advance. I don't want to be cheated out of my fee if you get yourself killed." She took his money, then returned the ledger to its drawer and locked the desk.

"My name's Maddie, Mr. Gage," she said, having picked his name up from his signature. She extended her hand, which he shook. "Meals are at eight in the morning, one in the afternoon, and six in the evening. If you're here, you'll be served. If not, you got to wait for the next one. I ain't waiting on you." She handed him a key to a room on the second floor. "I lock the front door at 10:00 p.m. sharp. There are unsavory types in this town. It isn't a good place to be out and about at night."

"Then I'll need a key. My work keeps me out late."

"What work is that?"

"I'm running the sheriff and his gang out of town."

Maddie blew a thin whistle of air and shook her head. "Avenger or no, it's good you paid in advance." She unlocked a drawer, took out a key and handed it to him. "Don't lose it."

Jace retrieved his saddlebags, then went to his room. The space, worn but clean, contained a narrow bed with an old quilt and a pillow in a crisp, white covering. There was a nightstand on one side of the bed and a washstand on the other. On the opposite wall was a small dresser. A faded wingback chair sat next to the room's only window, which, he noticed, looked out at the shanties across the street.

Jace turned his attention to the fellow out back. Leaving by the front door, he went around the side of the house, behind the carriage house and came up next to the boy, who was standing in the shadows by the stable.

"You seen him yet?" Jace asked, crossing his arms as he, too, looked at the house.

"He's inside Maddie's. He was with the Morgan gal," the guard answered. He looked at Jace, then nearly jumped out of his skin as he registered the fact that the man they were talking about was the very one standing next to him. He sidled back, slamming against the side of the stable.

"Holy Jay-sus, it's you!" he exclaimed.

Jace made a face. "Now there's a case of mistaken identity I don't get all that often."

"It's you—you're the Avenger."

"I don't like being called that," Jace warned.

"You gonna kill me?"

"You gonna kill me?" Jace countered, nodding

toward the gun the boy pointed at him with a shaking hand.

"No! No, sir! No, I'm not."

"Then maybe you should holster that piece."

"Yes, sir!" the young gunfighter said as he struggled to put his weapon away. When he was done, Jace reached over and set a hand on the boy's shoulder, peeling him away from the stable wall and leading him toward the front of Maddie's property.

"I'm gonna make you an offer, boy. You, and any of your friends you can gather up, you ride outta town. For good. If I ever lay eyes on you again, you better be living as a law-abiding citizen." Jace looked at the boy whose shoulder he still held. "I suggest you take this offer and get the hell out of town."

The boy's eyes were wary. "You killed the two sentries the sheriff posted outside of town. How come you ain't gonna kill me?"

"They didn't take the offer I'm making you. And I don't like being on the business end of a gun, especially once the shooting's begun." They reached the street. Jace dropped his hand.

"You just gonna let me go?" the boy asked.

"Yes, I am. As I said—I hope I don't see you again." Jace gave the boy a steely look. "I rarely give second chances; I never give third chances."

Jace watched the kid hurry away. It was time to visit the sheriff. He cut across Maddie's property, moving with a confident stride that wouldn't cause an observer to question his identity as he crossed the street and stepped onto the boardwalk. He reached for the door before anyone inside had a chance to ready for him. It took his eyes a second to adjust to the dim light of the front office—time afforded him since the element of surprise was his. He took a step to the right, out of the open doorway and into the protection of the adobe wall.

The room smelled like old sweat and stale spittoons. A man sat at a desk near the back—the sheriff, Jace guessed, based on his age and the star on his vest. Two other men were in the room, one sitting in a chair in front of the desk, the other lounging against the wall. At Jace's entrance, the one sitting stood abruptly, knocking over his chair. The man leaning against the wall moved forward a step.

"How the hell did you get in here? I told Johnny to guard the door," the sheriff growled as he quickly sat up.

Jace shrugged. "Johnny and I have come to an understanding."

The sheriff slumped back in his chair. "So, the mighty Avenger is finally here," he sneered.

"We'll take care of him, boss." The sheriff's men came forward slowly, their great size leaving little room in the small front office. One of the men grinned at Jace in anticipation of the coming fight, his crooked nose evidence of his violent nature. He lurched toward Jace, throwing a punch.

Jace ducked and drew the door closed so that the man's next swing connected with solid wood instead of flesh. He straightened in time to hit the other thug in the throat, dropping him to his knees as he fought to get a breath. The first thug came at Jace again, fast, leaning forward as if to pound Jace with his head—the door already forgotten in the heat of battle. Jace yanked the hardwood panel inward again, catching the man's skull at his temple and briefly laying him out.

When he staggered to his feet, the sheriff bellowed, "Get out, Hammer. Take Paul with you."

The giant of a man shook his head, weaving a bit on his feet before scooping up the still-coughing Paul with an arm under his shoulder. When they were gone, Jace looked at the sheriff, wondering what other nasty surprises he had up his sleeve. The older man rocked his chair back on two legs as he returned Jace's regard.

"I knew you would come, you or someone like you," he said.

Jace lifted the overturned chair and turned it around to straddle it. "You didn't make it hard to find you."

"So, Avenger, what's the plan?"

"I'm gonna take you to Cheyenne. I'll guarantee you a fair trial and a nice length of new rope."

The sheriff studied Jace, all humor gone from his face. "I don't want to hang."

Jace nodded solemnly. "I can't say as I blame you. Anytime you want it the easy way, all you gotta do is draw your gun," he offered.

"Why not shoot me and be done with it?"

"I got no quarrel with you, and I don't have a liking for unnecessary killing. 'Sides, there's something else I want."

"What would that be?"

"The loot you've been taking from the stage coaches," Jace announced.

"You think I'd be living in this shit hole if I had a bundle of gold lyin' around?"

Jace didn't answer immediately as he silently regarded the sheriff. "I admit to being curious about that, 'cause you've been here a while, haven't you? I'm gonna find your gold, Sheriff, and then I'm gonna take you and it and give you both over to the U.S. marshal in Cheyenne."

The sheriff's eyes narrowed as he regarded Jace. "Is that so? And what do you suppose the good marshal will do with this gold you think I have? You aren't thinkin' he'll give it back to the poor bastards I took it from?"

"It ain't my worry what he does with it. I was hired to do a job, and that's what I plan on doing." Jace got to his feet. "If you want your men to survive, you'll tell them to give me a wide berth and keep their guns holstered. And if I was you, I'd start talking sooner rather than later, 'cause no amount of silence is gonna keep you from that rope."

Jace turned his back on the sheriff and walked to the door, his senses fixed on the man behind him. Unsurprisingly, there was no sound, no movement; the sheriff wasn't ready to die. Jace paused on the threshold, making sure the way was clear as he filled his lungs with fresh air. He paused a minute, considering his next step. Defiance was a scrappy town.

He wondered if he would be its salvation or its ruin.

* * *

Jace watched Maddie bring serving bowls over to the long work table in the kitchen that evening. It was almost time to confront the sheriff and his entire gang at the saloon, an event he'd looked forward to for many weeks, ever since he'd begun stalking the town. Supper consisted of pan-seared T-bones, mashed potatoes, green beans, and rolls—a far cry from the camp fodder he usually ate.

She set a tall glass of cool water in front of him, along with a pitcher of the same. He waited impatiently for her to join him at the table, and once she had, he waited still longer while she said a lengthy and thorough grace.

". . . lend Your right arm of justice to those who know what to do with it, and give guidance to those who might falter without it. And Dear Lord, while You're looking down on this town, we pray You keep those who are innocent safe . . ." Maddie continued.

Jace sighed silently, watching the condensation collect like sweat on the glass water pitcher. When Maddie finally stopped, he was afraid to offer an "amen" lest that spur her to further elaboration with the Lord. It was a great relief to see her open her napkin and spread it on her lap. He did the same, then dug into his steak, which was tender and savory and might have been downright divine while it was hot.

When the first wave of his hunger was sated, he looked at his hostess and smiled.

"I met a friend of yours last month, Mr. Gage,"

Maddie said. "Julian McCaid. He told me you were coming to town, but he didn't say why."

"The government's gotten tired of Sheriff Kemp's trouble-making. The U.S. marshal in Cheyenne sent me to run him and his gang out of Defiance."

Maddie took a roll and broke it in half. "That man's been trouble for a decade. Don't see why anyone suddenly cares about him now."

"This country's building railroads everywhere. They're in desperate need of railroad ties, and it happens the Medicine Bow Mountains are a fine place to cut them. The logging camps need supplies and money, and the government's decided the road through Defiance is the best route to those camps. The only problem is—Sheriff Kemp."

"But they sent you. One man. Why not send a garrison of soldiers?"

"I've cleared over twenty towns since the war ended. Ain't a one that's beat me yet."

Maddie pressed her lips together and glared down at her plate. "I'm sure the government has great faith in you"—she looked up at him—"but they don't know Sheriff Kemp like we do. I mean no offense, Mr. Gage, but you're not going to win this town."

Jace slowly smiled. "No offense taken." He would defeat the sheriff, or die trying. He didn't particularly care which.

When night came, Jace headed over to the one watering hole still open for business—Sam's Saloon and Restaurant. He wanted to observe the sheriff, discover who his cronies were. He hoped to identify the weaker links in the sheriff's gang, find somebody willing to talk about him, which might lead to some clues about where he'd been hiding his gold. Jace had no idea if it was stashed in town or somewhere in the mountains, or even out on the Plains. Hell, it could be anywhere.

Light spilled from a saloon up ahead. Piano music and boisterous laughter filtered into the street, distorted by the evening wind. A familiar tension twisted through his veins. He wondered, as he always did when working a new town, if this would be his last night, the last saloon he would visit, the last pack of murdering roughs he would confront.

His spurs made their familiar jingle as he walked down the boardwalk. Stepping through the opened glass door of the saloon, he paused at the entrance, taking in the lay of the room.

It was as dusty inside as the street outside. Two large wagon wheels sporting lanterns swayed with the warm air that blew in, throwing shifting shadows about the room. A few whores brought spots of color to the saloon. Their high-pitched laughter sounded brittle, like the bawling of calves left motherless. A dozen men were scattered about, sitting at tables, drinking and gambling. Several stood at the bar.

It was as good a room to die in as any, Jace guessed, pushing his hat off the back of his head as he walked up to the counter. Keeping his back to the room, he observed the patrons in the long mirror behind the bar. The sheriff was at a table against the wall with a couple of men Jace hadn't yet encountered. He ordered a beer. The barkeep's gaze jerked his way at the raspy sound of his voice. Jace ignored him, but the man on his left didn't. He looked at the barkeep, then at Jace. His gaze took in the guns tied to Jace's thighs, the straps of his bandoliers.

"You're the one who beat up Hammer and Paul."

Jace downed his beer, then peered into the empty glass. "What of it?"

"You aren't welcome here, mister. They shoulda made that real clear to you," he said, shoving Jace's shoulder.

"Oh, they did," Jace answered before turning to slam his beer mug into the man's face, knocking him out, his nose bloody and broken. The music lurched to a jarring stop. Jace heard two guns being cocked, one behind him and one to his right by the saloon entrance. The mechanical clicking of the triggers echoed in the now silent room. Men jumped from their tables and backed away, clearing a wide circle around the three gunmen. Even the barkeep took several steps back.

Jace ordered another beer. Briefly, the barkeep stood paralyzed as his eyes darted from Jace to the two men holding guns on him. Hands shaking, he quickly filled a glass, then shoved it toward Jace. The scrape of the glass on wood was loud as the mug slid down the counter. Jace caught it, watching the men in the mirror.

"I don't know who you think you are, mister," the gunman behind him said, standing perhaps a dozen paces away, "but now would be a good time to leave."

Jace nodded at the man's reflection. "I'm fairly certain I know who I am, friend, but I'm guessin' you don't."

"Oh, I know, all right. You're the Avenger. And we got two guns trained on you right now. Ain't no way you're gettin' outta here."

Jace took a long draw of his beer, then put it down and rested his hands loosely on the edge of the bar. "Maybe," he answered, speaking to the man's mirror image. "The thing is, I ain't ready to go anyway. So you gonna shoot or stand there and yammer about it?" he asked the man who stood behind him.

The two men looked at the sheriff, who gave a nod. They raised their arms and took aim, but Jace had already pivoted, crouched, and palmed both Colts. His guns discharged before theirs, putting a bullet in the forehead of one and straight through the heart of the other. The shock on the face of the man who had spoken was nearly as gratifying as that on the sheriff's.

While the thunder of gunfire died, Jace straightened and holstered his pistols. He threw back the rest of his beer, then turned to the room. "Anyone else got an issue with me?"

In the deafening quiet, his hoarse voice carried. Silence was his only answer.

Jace locked eyes with the sheriff. The sheriff slowly smiled. It wasn't a happy smile. He shoved at the shoulders of the men seated on either side of him, clearing out the table, then gestured for Jace to approach. Jace ordered another beer. Taking it, he stepped over the man he'd downed with his mug. The sound of his spurs reverberated through the still-silent saloon. He stepped over the dead man who had been behind him.

"You're making an annoyance of yourself, Avenger," the sheriff commented as he motioned for Jace to take a seat. "What's it gonna take for you to move on, son?"

Jace remained standing and gave him a hard look. "You know what I want."

"We can't always have what we want."

"That ain't a problem I generally suffer from, Sheriff." Jace sipped his beer. "Now, if I was you, I'd cut my little gang loose and tell them to ride outta here."

"What if they don't want to go?"

Jace shrugged. "That's their call. It all works the same for me. Like I told you before, this ain't personal. I got no love for killin'. Besides, I get paid whether they're dead or just gone."

"Who's paying you?"

Jace grinned. He knew his expression was more a showing of teeth, like a dog's snarl, but he liked to do it in situations like this. "Aw, Sheriff, that's bad business. You know I can't tell you."

"So you gonna call me out in the street?"

"Would you accept?"

The sheriff shook his head. "I'm not stupid. I saw you're a fast draw."

Jace made a face as he shook his head and looked at the mug he held. "That's how it always goes. You'll send your boys after me, one by one, two by two." He looked at the sheriff. "I'll slowly whittle your team down. In the end, the handful of men you have left will decide to pack up and clear out. You're already down five, maybe more." Jace looked at the sheriff, all humor gone. "Let's get to the heart of the matter, Sheriff. You give me what I want, and I'll see you get to Cheyenne in time for your hangin'."

"That's a hard offer to refuse, Avenger."

Jace grinned. He downed his beer and slammed the empty glass on the table. "Actually, that's a promise, not an offer. Night, Sheriff."

Chapter 3

Rupert Hardin took his glass of whiskey and leaned back against the bar as he surveyed the smoky room. Cow hands, card sharks, local workers, business tycoons, and emigrants alike filled every seat in the house that billed itself as the best saloon in Cheyenne. A trio of women danced and sang on the stage, far to his left. It appeared musical talent wasn't a requirement for the act's success so much as bare legs beneath lifted skirts and the sheer volume with which they belted out the tune. It was payday, and the boys were anxious to drop their wages on cards and whiskey and women.

One of the U.S. marshal's men entered the saloon and navigated his way around poker tables to a place at the bar next to Rupert. Dean Lambert. Rupert did not take his eyes from his casual surveillance of the room, did not acknowledge his arrival, though he felt a quickening of anticipation. This man knew where he could find Jace Gage.

"You new to these parts, friend?"

Rupert turned and looked at him. "I am. So are half the men in this room."

The marshal's man smiled and held out his hand. "Name's Dean Lambert, U.S. Marshal's Service."

Rupert shook his hand and introduced himself. "Been waiting the whole damned night to talk to you."

Lambert's expression warned him to exercise caution. "Why don't we take our drinks and find a seat?"

Rupert had his whiskey glass refilled and followed Lambert to a shadowy corner where a man was being friendly with a saloon girl. "Take it upstairs," the deputy growled as he kicked the man's chair.

Lambert took the man's vacated chair, forcing Rupert to take one with his back angled to the room. Not his preferred position. He slipped his pistol out of his holster as he sat—just for insurance. "Get to it, Dean. Why'd you bring me here?"

"I know you've been after Jace Gage for a long time."

Rupert didn't answer, didn't feel the need to state the obvious.

"What I want to know is, why?"

"That's my business."

Dean met Rupert's glare with his own hard stare. When Rupert didn't offer more information, Dean sipped his beer and began to stand up. "Then we're done here."

Rupert cocked his gun and pointed it at Dean beneath the table. "Sit down."

Dean looked at Rupert's arm, then at his face. "Shoot me if you want. You can carry on your hunt for the Avenger until Doom's Day. I don't care. Or you can work with me and get to him a lot faster."

Rupert considered that statement. He released the hammer and Dean sat back down. "Gage killed my sister."

Dean's brows rose. "When?"

"March of '65."

"It was war."

"Not this. I was there. He shot her in cold blood. While she begged for her life." His sister had given her life for the cause. He had a blood debt to settle.

Dean studied him. "So you're going to kill him."

Rupert nodded. "He'll beg for his life like she did. Then I'll shoot him."

"That's what I wanted to hear. You want Gage. I want something the man he's after is hiding."

"What's that?"

"Gold."

"How much gold?"

Dean shrugged. "Hard to say. Could be fifty thousand."

Rupert leaned back in his seat. "So what's the arrangement?"

"You kill Gage and help me get the gold, I'll give you ten percent."

"Fifty percent."

"No."

"Then no deal."

"Twenty percent," Lambert offered.

"When I kill Gage, there will be no one standing between you and the gold. That's worth half."

"There is one other person. The sheriff. He's

the only one who knows where he hid it. Even his men don't know."

"So we'll get him to tell us, kill him, and split it halves."

Dean gave him a long look. Rupert saw him for the sidewinder he was, selling out his badge. Dean wouldn't live to see his half. "Deal."

"So where's Gage?"

"In Defiance, about three days' ride northwest of here."

"What's he doing there?"

"Marshal Riggins wants Gage to clear Sheriff Kemp and his gang out of town before a series of payroll wagons start rolling through Defiance on their way up to the Medicine Bow logging camps."

Rupert slowly grinned. This day just got better and better. "I'll ride out in the morning."

"No. Gage just got to Defiance. Let him clear out as many men as he can. Then, when the sheriff is desperate for some new guns, you go in. Give it a couple of weeks."

Rupert's grip tightened on his whiskey glass. He was but three days from meeting face to face with his enemy. He'd tracked Gage through four territories, Texas and California in the last sixteen months and resented having to pause here in Cheyenne, but prison had taught him many things—including patience. He had one shot at Jace Gage, one chance to make the bastard pay for what he'd done to Rupert's sister. He'd lay low here and bide his time.

Chapter 4

Jace stood on the corner by the stage depot, watching Leah cross the street toward him. She hadn't noticed him yet, so he was able to observe her without interference.

And what he saw set his teeth on edge.

If it wasn't bad enough that she'd been at the saloon already this morning—alone—she now crossed the street as if she had no concerns at all. Being a woman in a town overrun by thugs, she was always in imminent danger, as he had discovered yesterday.

And what a woman she was.

Her pants were cinched at the waist by her knife belt, emphasizing her curvy shape. Every step rotated her hips in an unconscious gyration that made his body tighten. Her vest did nothing to minimize the generous swell of her breasts. Why she wore the revealing garb of a boy instead of the properly concealing apparel of her gender, Jace couldn't figure. He wondered how the hell he was supposed to keep her safe as he rolled the cigar stump in the corner of his mouth. Best thing would be to get her out of town.

Jace's gaze moved to the black wolf walking beside her. His head came to the girl's ribs. His fur was scruffy, his pace leisurely next to that of his mistress. Jace had the clear impression that the wolf outweighed the woman by at least twenty pounds. More alert than Leah, the beast caught his scent. His lip curled up to reveal a hair-raising row of teeth and canines as he started a low growl. Reacting to the sound, Leah looked up abruptly. Seeing him, she set her jaw and changed directions, continuing in the street rather than using the boardwalk where he stood.

Two quick strides brought him into step with her. "Mornin'," he greeted cheerfully, ignoring the grouchy wolf as he tossed his cold cigar away.

She cast him a sideways glance. "You survived the night. I thought for sure we'd seen the last of you when I heard the gunshots yesterday."

"Guess I'm harder to kill than you think."

She stopped abruptly and frowned up at him. "Mr. Gage, don't you have somewhere you need to be?"

"Of course."

"Well then"—she nodded at him—"good day to you."

Jace couldn't help grinning at her dismissive tone. "Good day, kid." He didn't move away.

"Don't let me keep you."

"You're not. *You* are where I need to be." He crossed his arms and frowned at her. "I promised your friend, Audrey Sheridan, I'd look after you.

Seeing the trouble you ran into on your delivery rounds yesterday, I can't risk letting you be alone."

"Mr. Gage—"

"Jace—"

Her expression tightened a notch. "The day I need a man following me about is the day I need to find a new town."

"I agree."

She studied him a moment. "Well then—" She nodded again, indicating their conversation was concluded.

"Where do you want to go?" he asked, before she could continue on her way.

She raised a dark, delicately arched brow. "Go, Mr. Gage?"

"Jace—"

"I'm not going anywhere. I thought we were in agreement."

"We are. We agreed you needed to move out of town."

"We did no such thing. We agreed I don't need you following me about like a puppy."

A puppy? Jace sent a look over his appearance. The day was warm, so he'd left his jacket at Maddie's. He saw his pistols, knife, and bandoliers, felt the weight of the rifle that was slung over one shoulder. He had another knife in his left boot and a derringer in the strap of his right bandolier, but of course she couldn't see them. He stood a foot taller than she did and was easily a foot wider.

There was nothing puppyish about him.

He shook his head, shoving aside her insult. She'd begun moving toward her gate. "I can take you out to Hell's Gulch. Audrey and McCaid want you to come out there."

"No."

"Why?"

"I'll be under foot. They don't need me hanging around."

"She could use your help with the kids." He frowned, wondering at her resistance. "What exactly do you think's going on over there? McCaid's setting the property up as an orphanage."

Leah waved her hand. "I'm not going out there."

"I have friends up at the Crippled Horse and the Circle Bar ranches. I could take you up there. Sager and Rachel are far enough away that you'd be safe."

"No."

Jace's temper started to rise. "What's goin' on here in town ain't a game, kid. This is war. Folks are gonna die here. Could be a lot of folks. Your friends want you out of danger. And frankly, I don't have the time or the patience to be your duenna."

Her stubborn expression never wavered. "I have always done for myself—as I always will."

This was an argument he didn't intend to lose. He leaned closer to her, ignoring the warning growl her wolf issued. "If you decide to stay, I can sure as hell guarantee I'll know your every thought and every move. You won't be able to take a piss in the outhouse without me knowing about it. So what's it gonna be? McCaid, Sager, or me?"

If the pallor in her face was any indication, he'd

struck a nerve. To her credit, she didn't back down. She was a fighter, all right.

"I don't need anyone, Mr. Gage," she said in that sweet, quiet voice of hers, as different from his own voice as silk and sandpaper. "No one. I know my way around a gun and a knife. I can hunt, trap, and fish. I have a successful bakery business here, even now. I can support myself. Besides, I'm not alone. Maddie and the Kesslers are still here in town. So is Audrey's brother, Malcolm—he lives just next door. And I've got Wolf."

"They weren't any help to you yesterday morning." Jace clenched his jaw, hunting for the words he needed to convince her of the danger she faced if she stayed. "McCaid, Sager, or me?" he repeated.

Her eyes slowly shut. "I can't go. Don't you understand?" She looked up at him, searching for something he could tell she didn't find.

"No. I don't understand."

"If I go, it will all change. I can do for myself here—now. If I leave, I'll lose everything. I give it all up, all of my freedom."

"You can come back when it's safe."

"What if there's nothing to come back to?" Her words were a whisper. The moisture in her eyes hit him like a fist in the gut. How could she be so attached to such a wretched little town?

"Then it's me you choose. So be it. But you will obey my orders without question. I won't have you endangering me or anyone else in this town by your bull-headed thinking, is that clear? For starters, you're not to leave your house without

Maddie, one of the Kesslers, Malcolm, or me with you."

She drew a shaky breath and sent a long look over his shoulder, toward the mountains. He'd been watching them himself a few minutes earlier as he'd waited for her. He knew she was seeing rolling hills that crested higher and higher until they peaked in jagged ranges far to the west, the tips still snow-capped. It was as if something there called to her. He'd seen that look in many a prospector's eyes, but he doubted it was gold she was after.

He took hold of her arms and drew her up closer to his face, a mistake his body reacted to instantly. His jaw tightened until he spoke through clenched teeth. "I promise, kid, if you buck me on this, I will tie you up and haul you out to Sager's for the duration. Are we clear?"

She lowered her head so that her hat brim shielded her eyes from him. He could feel the tension in her rigid body. She was five feet and three inches of sheer rebellion. He hoped he hadn't imagined her slight nod. Deciding to leave it at that—for now—he set her back on her feet. She shoved through her gate with Wolf close on her heels, marched up to her house, then slammed her door behind her, never once looking back.

Jace shook his head. The girl was a massive complication he did not need right now. He pondered her desperate glance toward the mountains as he headed up the street to the general store. He had to replenish his supplies before he headed out to

Meeker's Pass. Time to give that old rock heap a closer look before the sheriff reinforced his guard there. He expected the pass would be heavily guarded one, maybe two weeks, prior to the first payroll shipment. That's what had happened last month with the false shipment Jace had setup to see how the sheriff played his men.

But what to do with Leah? Not for a minute did he think she'd follow his rules if he weren't here to enforce them. If something happened to her while he was away, it would be one more notch in the gun the Devil already pointed at him. Jace thought of her desperate glance toward the mountains and wondered whether she really was as self-sufficient as she claimed.

Maybe he'd best find out, he thought as he stepped onto the boardwalk at the store's entrance. Jace scanned the room as he moved across the threshold into the shadowy interior. Jim was behind the counter, in the telegraph office. Sally was near him, her dark hair in a bun, her apron white and tidy. On Jace's left was a kid who had been at the saloon last night. He straightened as he noticed Jace. In fact, all talk stopped, and all eyes turned to Jace as he crossed the threshold.

Jace dropped his hat off his head to let it hang at his back. "Morning," he greeted Jim, ignoring the boy. Unfortunately, the boy wouldn't be ignored.

He sauntered over to Jace, his hand already on his hip, fingering the butt of his gun. "The sheriff don't want you here. He put a hundred dollar bounty on your head, and I aim to claim it."

News of the bounty improved Jace's spirits; it meant that Kemp's boys wouldn't gang up on him. They'd try to hit him one by one so they wouldn't have to share the bounty. Sure, they'd try it clean or dirty, but it was better to face them individually than in a group.

He met the boy's gaze and held his silence. Out of the corner of his eye, he saw Jim give Sally a nod as he stepped over to the counter. Without argument, she disappeared into the shadowy storeroom.

"Boy, you pull that gun on me, you're gonna die," Jace warned. "You won't ever see that money."

"Maybe so. Maybe not."

Jace nodded, not taking his eyes off the kid, who was at most sixteen or seventeen. His cheeks were still soft looking. His hands shook. His face was white. A hundred dollars was a lot of money to him. Hell, it would be to anyone.

"Even if you did manage to kill me, the sheriff's likely not good for the bounty. Why throw your life away for a man like him when you could ride outta here? Any of you boys—you can clear out of town. That's all I'm here for. There doesn't have to be any more killin' than what's already happened. There ain't no shame in staying alive." The kid's gaze wavered.

Jace saw the flicker, but couldn't afford to ease up. "You go outside," he pressed, his voice low and calm. "Give it a good thinking. When I'm done here, I'll come out too. If you're there and you pull that gun, you'll die. If you're gone, I'll know you reconsidered the dying part, and I won't come after you."

The kid walked to the open door and sidled outside, never turning his back on Jace until he was several steps outside.

Jace moved toward the counter. Ignoring the black look the shopkeeper gave him, he rattled off the supplies he needed while Jim took down the list. When Jace was finished, Jim gave it a once over, then looked at him from beneath his brows. "This is a big list, Mr. Gage. You leaving already?"

"I'm heading out for a bit. Not too long. I'm taking Leah Morgan with me," he announced, having realized he'd warmed to that idea.

Sally gasped and clenched her collar more tightly against her throat. "Why are you taking her?"

"I gave my friends, Julian McCaid and Audrey Sheridan, my word I'd see to the girl's safety. That ain't a thing I take lightly. Besides, she said she can do for herself up in the mountains. I'd like to see that. I offered to take her up to Sager and Rachel's or down to be with Audrey and McCaid, but she wouldn't go. When things get bad, I may have to send her up the mountain, but I gotta see how she handles herself first. I'm having a hard time believing she can do what she says."

"She can," Sally insisted. "Sometimes I think it's unnatural, but we all rely on the fresh meat she brings in when we need it. Maddie's guests never go hungry, thanks to Leah. She's up there all the time. She found Wolf up there one summer."

Jim shot a warning glance her way. Sally quit

talking and set about gathering the supplies Jace had ordered. Jace paid for the supplies and started toward the front door.

"Mr. Gage—" Sally shot Jim a dark look before focusing on Jace. She came forward, her hands grasping a small sack of flour and another of beans. "Eddie out there, he's only a boy. You aren't going to kill him, are you?"

"He's a boy with a gun, Mrs. Kessler—that tends to even things out." Jace frowned at Sally. "I gave him a chance to leave, I can only hope he took it." He looked back at Jim. "I'll be back for those items after I saddle up."

Jace looked out to the street as he settled his hat on his head. No sign of Eddie. He stepped onto the boardwalk and paused, using all of his senses to test his surroundings. There was no sound of a gun being cocked. No furtive movements caught his attention.

He scanned the opposite side of the street, down a block to where the saloon was. A couple of men lounged around, but none looked ready for a gunfight. No one was on any of the roofs that he could see. No one was on the boardwalk on either side of the street. The tension eased out of his body as he realized the boy had decided to live another day. Hopefully, he'd moved on, maybe convincing a few others to head out as well.

Jace returned to Leah's house and entered her yard. Wolf rose to his feet on the porch and started a low warning growl. Jace continued up the path to the front stairs without pausing, though he felt his own hackles rise. He was more than a little relieved when Leah opened her door, sparing him a full confrontation with her beast—one he didn't intend to lose. Her gaze went from him to the fearsome wolf whose growl was louder now, his teeth exposed.

"Wolf, down!" she ordered brusquely. Wolf coughed, flapped his jowls, and dropped to recline by the railing on the porch. "Mr. Gage, is there something you need?"

"Yep." He started up the stairs. "You said you can hunt and fish, that you're good with a gun and a knife. I want you to prove it." Without the cover of her wide brimmed Plainsman's hat to shield her face, he could see more of her expression. He found it impossible to believe anyone with such a sweet face and petite stature could be as venomous as he feared she was.

Were women never what they showed themselves to be?

"I have nothing I need to prove and no reason to try. Good day, Mr. Gage."

He caught her wrist before she could turn away. His mind registered the feel of her, making him wish he hadn't touched her—not because he feared her knife, or her guardian beast, but because he was instantly aware of her femaleness. It was becoming increasingly difficult to think of her as a kid.

"You have every reason to prove it to me. There might be another option for you. If I think you're safe enough in the hills, I could send you there when things get bad here." She looked from her wrist to his eyes, but made no attempt to pull free. They stood close. He could see the rise and fall of her chest, feel the heat of her skin.

And he knew there was no other option. He would not let her out of his sight, unless it was to hand her over to the protection his friends could give her.

"How can you clear this town if you're not here clearing it?"

"I've made my intentions known. The sheriff's down half a dozen men already. Won't hurt to let the dust settle. My absence will give those who want to leave a chance to do so." He let go of her. "Are you up for a trip to the hills?"

She slowly smiled. Her eyeteeth were pointy, extending slightly below the line of her teeth. Unconsciously, he ran his tongue along his own teeth, wondering what hers would feel like if he were to kiss her.

When he kissed her, he corrected himself.

"I think the question is, Gage, are you ready for a trip to the hills? I'd like to see if you can keep up."

Jace couldn't keep the grin from his face. There was nothing he loved quite as much as a good challenge. "Collect your things, kid. I'll meet you out front in a half hour. We'll see which of us is more man."

Jace returned to Maddie's and saddled both his horse and the one Julian McCaid had left behind for Audrey's brother, Malcolm, to use. The big black stallion was magnificent and high spirited, an aggressive mount well suited to the outlaws McCaid had taken him from. He wondered if Malcolm could handle him.

Even more, he wondered if Leah could.

Chapter 5

Jace tied the horses to Leah's fence near where she stood waiting for him. Her bedroll, coat, and canteen rested on the ground. A saddlebag was thrown on top, half its fringe missing. She held a shotgun in its scabbard, the leather as scarred as her saddlebag. A sturdy fishing rod rested against the pile.

Jace watched her approach the outlaw's horse, which was looking a little white eyed now that he'd caught the scent of open air. The beast didn't want to be tied up, and he didn't like standing so near the wolf. She spent a minute rubbing his neck, her gloved hands sure and steady, speaking to him in a voice that made all the nerves along Jace's skin perk up. He couldn't make out her mumbled words, but they were low and rhythmic. Hypnotic. The horse calmed down while Jace stirred up. She checked the halter, tested the cinch.

So. She could handle the horse. That was good. But maybe not surprising. He crouched and began to dig through her saddlebags as Leah tied her shotgun scabbard to the saddle and settled her rod. He found a fish filleting knife, a scaler, a folded pouch of fishing tackle, a box of shotgun shells, and a gun cleaning kit in one side.

"What are you doing?" she asked with a frown.

"I'm checking to see if you know what to pack for the trip."

Her answer was an inarticulate grunt. She took the saddlebags from him and slung them over the back of her saddle. "I'd return the favor"—she looked at the packs his horse carried—"but I can tell from your rig what kind of a greenhorn I'm taking up the mountain."

Jace handed her bedroll and jacket to her. "You can thank me later. There's no way you can live on a pound of jerky and some oats for any length of time."

"Gage, Gage, Gage." She shook her head. "The forest is its own supply depot. I won't let you starve."

Jace glared at her. How could a girl not even as tall as her horse's withers sound so damned cocky? He untied his mount and swung up in the saddle. "I never took to eating twigs and leaves."

Leah mounted up using an old log she'd set by her fence for that very purpose. "I wouldn't know." She grinned at him. "I've never had the pleasure— or the need—to eat twigs." And then she was gone.

His heart jumped to his throat as he watched her. He kneed his mount, charging after her and Wolf, cursing up a blue streak for being stupid enough to give her that horse, until he caught a thread of laughter in the wake of her speed.

The nearly treeless foothills made it possible to go at a full run for quite a distance. They had crested two hills and were ascending a third before he caught up to her. Or rather, before she slowed down.

"What the hell was that about?" he shouted over to her.

"Blink likes to go fast. Something the outlaws taught him."

"'Blink'?"

She laughed and patted her mount's thick neck. "It's what I call him, 'cause he's always gone in the blink of an eye. I guess his outlaw owners had a frequent need to get out of town fast and taught him bad habits. He's got too much energy. I like him to run it out before we really start climbing. But so far, he's been as sure-footed as a mountain goat. I've come to rely on him." She looked at Jace. "I'm hoping I can convince Audrey to give him to me."

"Maybe she would, if you waited out this thing with her at Hell's Gulch."

The joy left her face, fast as water draining from a sieve. She looked away, and they continued on. Not long afterwards, when their ascent became increasingly steep, they took the trail single file. The path was narrow, but clearly defined. They left the barren hills behind and entered the cool forest. The wind grew stronger as they climbed. Jace listened to the sound it made against the ponderosa and lodgepole pines, hearing the aspen add their noisy clatter to the mix. Looking up at the blazing blue sky through the green boughs, he drew in a deep breath of fresh air and calmly followed Leah, curious to see what she would do next.

She pulled up at a clearing about an hour later and waited for him to come even with her. "What do you want for dinner, Gage? Fish, fowl, or small game?"

"Surprise me."

She nodded. "We'll camp here, then." She walked her mount over to the edge of the woods by an established campsite, then dismounted. After settling her gear, she strung a corral line for their horses near a wide patch of grass.

"I'll be back in a bit," she said as she retrieved some wire and twine from her packs. "Do me a favor. Stay here," she ordered Jace.

"And miss seeing you set snares? Nope."

"I don't need you traipsing through the brush, scaring off supper."

He shrugged innocently. "I might learn something."

She shook her head and walked into the woods, not waiting for him to settle his mount. When he caught up with her, she was arranging the third snare. Jace crouched to get a better look at her handiwork. He tested the ties, acknowledging that she knew what she was doing.

"Did your father teach you to set snares like this?"

"My father was a gambler, Gage, and quite possibly a drunk. I don't remember his helping my mother with anything useful, like putting food on the table. Course, I don't remember much before I was four.

And he died when I was ten." She straightened and swiped the dirt off her hands.

"How did he die?"

She looked at him, her gaze searching his eyes. "The sheriff came to town and shot him. Just like that. No how-do-you-do. No 'I caught you cheating at cards.' Just saw him and shot him."

Jace's lips thinned. "So the sheriff's been in Defiance for, how long then—ten years? How old are you?"

She gave him a glare. "Old enough to live on my own."

He gave her an arch look. "That's what we're here to figure out. So who did teach you?"

"A friend."

Getting information from her was about as easy as skinning a porcupine. "Where's that friend now?" Maybe there was another option for her safety. The sooner he could dispatch her someplace safe—in someone else's care—the sooner he could focus on what he'd come to Defiance to do.

Her eyes went flat. "Dead, I guess." She shrugged and headed through the underbrush toward a narrow stream, collecting kindling and small branches, which she handed back to him without even a glance.

When his arms were full, they returned to camp. A couple of heavy logs were drawn up on two sides of an old fire pit, making handy benches. The entire camp area was clearly a favorite stomping ground for her. If she frequented the same spots, she wouldn't be safe up here—not if she wanted to keep a low profile. He dropped the kindling and told her to mount up.

"Why?"

"We're gonna do some target practice."

They rode a few ridges to the northeast until they came to a long, narrow clearing along the bank of a creek where an old lodgepole pine had fallen across a few boulders. They dismounted and tied their horses within the line of trees. Jace pulled his rifle from its scabbard, then moved a bit farther into the clearing. The spiny branches of the rotting tree made perfect targets a hundred yards away.

Jace handed her his rifle, watching how she handled it. The gun was heavy, but she'd been expecting its weight. Bracing the butt against her ribs, she checked that it was loaded then lifted it to her shoulder. She fired one shot. It nicked a piece of bark off the wide base of the tree.

"Shoots low to the right."

"It does."

She sited and fired again, missing the tree completely as she hit the boulder behind the tree. "That's too bad," Jace said, feeling disappointed. "I guess I thought you really could shoot." She lifted her head to give him a glare, then sited and fired again. Again she missed the tree. "What the hell are you shooting at?"

"Those pebbles on the boulder between the rotten ends of the tree. There's two more left." She fired and picked another one off.

Jace grinned down at her. There was a two inch span between long, jagged spikes at the broken end of the tree. "Good. Now see those broken branches at the top of the tree toward the middle? Shoot them off." The old branch stubs were about six inches long.

Leah sited them. "One shot or three for each?"

"One."

Leah fired. One of the stubs shattered at its base. "Now the rest."

Leah fired, shaving the tip from the next stub. Her next shot halved it. The final shot cleared it from the log. She handed the rifle back to him. "Satisfied?"

"I'm impressed."

Leah folded her arms. "Let's see you do that."

Jace repeated her four shots on the next two stubby branches. His shots were too fast for her to gauge his accuracy, but the end result was the same. He returned his rifle to its scabbard and picked up a heavy branch, which he broke into a few six-inch segments.

"Now let's see what you can do with your shotgun."

Leah retrieved her shotgun and a box of cartridges from her saddlebag. She put two shells in the chamber. Then gave him a nod. He tossed a branch section up into the air high in front of them. She shot it. He tossed the second one almost instantly after the first. She shot it, too.

She lowered the shotgun and looked at him. He grinned at her, pleased with her ability. She gave him a bored look and shook her head. "I told you I'm a good aim, Gage. You can't eat something you can't shoot."

He handed her the remaining branch section and took the shotgun from her. He emptied out the chamber and loaded two more shells into it. Then he nodded at her to toss the wood. He fired once and split the stub into one large and one small chunk, then fired at the small piece, shattering it.

She gave him a dark look. "That kind of fancy shooting isn't going to do me any good. You can't eat a bird if you obliterate it."

Jace handed her the shotgun. "It's all about control and hitting what you aim for." He unholstered his pistol and held it out to her, butt first.

She stared down at it for a long moment without reaching for it. When her eyes met his, they'd gone dark, like a midnight sky. "I use guns to hunt for food, Gage, not for the fun of killing. I don't know how to shoot a revolver, and I don't intend to ever learn." She walked back to the horses and put her things away, then mounted up and left without looking back.

Jace turned back to the fallen tree, and shot every last protruding branch from its spiky surface.

Not once could he ever remember killing for fun.

"Do you always use the trail we took to get up here today?" Jace asked later that evening as they sat by the campfire where Leah cooked their supper—rabbit seared over open flames.

She set more kindling on the fledgling fire and blew into the flames. "I used to come up on the north end of town, until the loggers took that path and clear cut a road. They made it nearly impassable in the winter and spring, and anytime it rains or snows." She looked at him. "There's dozens of ways to get up here. I came the easy way since I had you with me."

"I can get along fine without a woman smoothing the way for me. This is supposed to be a test for you. How about you showing me what you're really able to do?"

"I told you I've got nothing to prove. And until I know what you're capable of managing, I won't risk putting you in a situation you can't handle. I've come down the mountain on a travois myself. It ain't much fun."

"What happened?"

"I broke my leg. I was deer hunting. The doe startled as I fired. The shot wounded her, but it wasn't enough to bring her down. I ran after her, slipped on some aspen leaves and went down on a boulder. Snapped my leg at the shin. It was stupid."

"How did you get back to town?"

"My friend was up here hunting, too. He set my leg and splinted me up. Then he and Wolf went after the doe and finished the job. She took my saddle on the ride down and I got the travois. I'd rather have walked down, broken leg and all."

"How old were you?"

"Sixteen."

Jace was dumbfounded. "Your mother let you come up here alone with a man when you were sixteen?"

"I'm alone with a man now," she paused, studying him. "Am I in peril?"

He ground his teeth, feeling she might, indeed, be in danger. When he didn't answer, she continued. "Joseph was my friend, not a lecherous old man. He taught me everything I know about hunting and fishing, tracking and fighting."

Jace watched her stir the beans in the pot, sensing she was at her threshold for answering his questions. The problem was, for every one she answered, several more arose.

Chapter 6

The sun slipped behind the mountain, coloring the pasture in a soft, gloaming light. The forest was alive with the loud chatter of birds settling in for the night. Jace and Leah sat on opposite sides of the fire after supper, cleaning their guns. Jace had finished his first Colt and was starting on his second when Leah finished with her shotgun. "Hand me your rifle. I'll clean it."

"Nope. No one touches my guns." He looked at her. "I let you shoot it because you didn't bring your own rifle, but normally no one comes near my weapons."

Unperturbed, Leah put her cleaning utensils away and headed down to the stream to clean the oil off her hands. While the day had been lovely and warm, the evening was cooling down fast—the mountain held no heat at night. She put her coat on, then poured two cups of Jace's coffee and set one near him.

Taking a seat opposite him, she leaned back against the log and let the fire warm her toes as the coffee heated her hands. She watched the gun-fighter's concentration on his task. The fading light made shadows on his cheeks and emphasized his hard jaw. Something about his rough features made her stomach feel fluttery.

Jace looked up from his task. She met his gaze, then looked away, uncomfortable with his percep-tive eyes.

He sipped his coffee, watching her briefly, then went back to his Colt. "Talk to me."

"You talk too much, Gage."

He smiled, but did not look away from his pistol. "We live alone, you and I. I got all the silence in my life I want. It's nice to have someone to talk to. Tell me about you. Before. When life was normal."

Leah didn't immediately take the bait. She watched the fire dance between them, admiring its insensibility. The fire appeared when it was sum-moned and left when it had consumed its fuel. It knew no remorse. No fear.

So much had happened in the year since Logan's brother, Sager, had come home. He'd brought Rachel out to the Crippled Horse ranch, married her, and they now had a son. Leah's mother had sickened over the winter and never made it to spring. Sager's friend, Julian McCaid, had followed him out here and setup a sheep ranch. He'd taken Leah's best friend out to his spread, with all of her foster children. And now Jace had come to town, bringing with him the threat of constant violence.

Everything was changing. Leah hated change. Maybe she should come up here for a while, get away from it. But she couldn't bear the thought of Defiance becoming more of a ghost town than it already was. A town needed people, else it died.

"Years ago, when Defiance was still thriving, my mother made a decent income with her bakery business. Enough to buy a big new iron stove. But after my father was killed, things changed. Fewer people came to town, and then those who were there started to move away. We began to rely less on her bakery business and more on my food forays. When the war came, more people left. Audrey's mom started taking in stray children. There was more need than ever for me to bring in meat."

She looked at him. "I know what I do isn't normal for a girl, but I like doing it. And I'm good at it—folks depend on me. I couldn't see living any other way. It's why I can't leave Defiance. I can't do what I do in a larger town."

He met her look over the fire. Muscles knotted and flexed in the corner of his jaw as he studied her. He finished the Colt and took up the rifle. "Go on."

"That's it."

"Who was the man you met up here?"

Leah pulled her knees up and leaned her chin on them. She missed him almost as much as she missed her mother. "His name was Joseph. He was a trapper who worked this area. I was eight when I first met him. He thought I was a runaway."

"Were you?" He looked up from his task again.

"Maybe."

"What were you running from?"

"I don't know." She'd been six when they moved to town—too young to go exploring by herself. But when she was eight, the call was too loud. "I think I wasn't running from, but running to. I'd always wanted to go exploring up here. But when I finally did, I got lost. I'd spent several days wandering around. I didn't have any food or any way of finding any. And then I saw Joseph."

She smiled. "He was an enormous bear of a man, with a heavy black beard and a huge coat of buffalo hides. When he laughed, the forest shook, or so I thought at the time. He moved like a bull through the woods. I always wondered how he could be a successful trapper.

"He fed me and scolded me for running away. It took us two days to come down to this area. He showed me how to find trails that other animals frequented, information he used to set his traps or hunt the type of animal he wanted. He walked me to the edge of the forest and ordered me to return home.

"I was in so much trouble." She remembered that homecoming vividly. "My mother didn't let me out of the house for a week. All the while I wondered what Joseph was doing, if he had moved on, what else he could teach me."

She looked at Jace and smiled. His gaze sharpened on her. She lowered her eyes and continued her story. "As soon as she let me out, I went back up and found Joseph again. That's when he taught me to set snares. That week, when I came back down, I brought some rabbits for a dinner stew. From then on, my mother never argued about my forays up the mountain. I went often that summer. Every time I did, Joseph was there and I learned something new."

She listened to the fire, trying to distract herself from Jace's intense regard, but she couldn't ignore his low, rough voice. "I'm sorry about your losing Joseph. We have so few true friends in life, it's hard not to bond with the ones we meet."

Leah swallowed hard, then took a sip of her coffee. "Well, story time's over. I'm turning in." She tossed the rest of her coffee into the pasture, then settled down on her bedroll.

Jace watched as Wolf came over to share the narrow space with her, taking up most of it. The beast stretched nearly from Leah's chin to her feet. Leah rested her head on her folded elbow and slowly rubbed a hand through Wolf's black fur. Her caresses soothed the wolf, but stirred something in Jace. His gaze moved up her arm, her shoulder, to her face. She was watching him. He was glad darkness had come, glad for the cover it gave him. "Tell me about Wolf."

"Tomorrow." Her eyes closed. Her hand stilled. Sleep came instantly to her, though not to Wolf. He watched Jace, his one yellow eye unblinking.

Jace shoved his Colts back into their holsters and packed up his gun cleaning kit. Slinging his rifle over his shoulder, he went for a walk around the small clearing, then down the trail a ways, feeling too edgy to sleep. Leah was unlike anyone he'd ever met. Keeping her safe was looking, more every hour, as if it might be the hardest thing he had ever done.

* * *

Silence woke Jace the next morning. The fire was cold. The wind was still. And Leah was gone.

He sat up, rubbing a hand over his face, forcing himself to focus. He cursed and got to his feet. Her horse was gone, too. She'd left him. How the hell had she done that? Saddles made noise. Horses weren't all that quiet, either. He cleaned out the coffee pot and their cups at the thin creek, then packed up his bedroll and cleared their campsite.

She'd left a quarter of one of their roasted rabbits from last night on a spike near the fire pit. He yanked it off the spit and took a bite, glad he didn't have to go without breakfast and irritated she'd seen to that as well without waking him. It was her fault he'd been so tired. He'd watched over her long into the night.

The growing light of dawn made it possible for him to see a clear track across the pasture. A dew had settled in the thin mountain pasture, and her trail cut right through it. He followed it to the woods, where it met up with a narrow deer trail. He smiled and rocked back on his heels. He would catch up to her in no time he thought as he returned to camp to fetch his horse, his mind playing through several different scenarios about what he'd do when he caught up with her.

Chapter 7

He followed her tracks for a few miles, moving deeper and higher into the Medicine Bow range. The trail gradually changed from a dirt path that clearly showed her horse's hoof prints to a rocky slope of crumbling shale. Up to that point, her trail had climbed steadily, but something warned him it had been too easy. The sun was high when her trail grew faint. He dismounted and took a closer look at the signs he'd been following. Small rocks were newly disturbed, but a hoof print belonging to a Big Horn sheep was cast on a clear patch of dirt. She'd changed direction. *When? Where?*

Jace stood and set his hat back on his forehead with a curse. She'd covered her trail, alright. He pulled his mount's reins over his head and dropped them. Time to regroup. He drew a cigar out of his pocket and sliced off the end, mulling over the situation while he lit the tobacco. He leaned against a boulder and considered their conversations yesterday, searching for a clue.

Yesterday she'd mentioned needing to discover

the extent of his ability to navigate the wilds of the mountain range. She was definitely challenging him. Yet it was unlikely she'd take him up much higher until she had a handle on his abilities. Then he remembered she'd asked him what he wanted for dinner. Fish, fowl, or small game. They'd had small game for supper. And she'd demonstrated her ability to hit her mark with her bird gun.

She'd gone fishing.

He walked his mount a ways down the steep hillside to the small stream that flowed toward a sharp ravine. He'd lost her at the water. He'd gone up, while she'd gone down.

He followed the water, vaguely remembering a mountain lake he'd seen when he'd perused maps of the area before taking the job. The closer he got, the angrier he became. The way was steep, far too dangerous for a girl to face alone. And she'd had the gall to lecture him about being safe out here.

Clearing the trees, he came to a ridge above the lake. The water was an impossibly blue color, reflecting the sky and the dark secrets of the woods. He started a circuit of the wide mountain lake, wondering if she was even here. He spotted a bit of shoreline in the distance and took a chance that she'd found a likely fishing spot there.

Cresting another small ridge, he looked down to another cozy campsite and found her. Rage and desire fused, stiffening his body. *Good Christ.* She was naked. Or nearly so, dressed only in her camisole and drawers. She sat on a boulder at the lip of the lake, drenched in sunshine. Her hair was damp, but drying. The wind tousled loose tendrils as if stroked by an invisible lover.

He tore his gaze away from her to survey the area. She had a small campfire going in a ring of stones. Another old haunt of hers. She wasn't safe up here if she continued to frequent her routine locations. Wolf scented him, alerting her. She cast a glance toward the wolf, her hair sweeping off her shoulder. Her camisole was loose, one strap slipped over her shoulder. Jace clamped his jaw shut, waiting for her to see him. She followed Wolf's posture, her gaze rolling up the hill until it connected with him.

She straightened. "Gage! What are you doing here?"

He didn't answer her. He couldn't with his jaw locked shut. She climbed off the rock, jumped down to the one below it, and then below that until she was on the ground. She walked barefoot through the shallow water, wild like a wood nymph.

He dismounted and started toward her. She moved with a lithe ease, her steps fluid and light. She had even finer curves than he'd guessed at in her boy's garb. Goddamn, he wanted her as he'd never wanted another woman. Not even his wife.

"You left me." His voice was rougher than usual.

She cocked her head. Her lips tilted up in a slight smile. "I left you food. And a trail even a novice could follow."

"Bullshit. You led me up to the sheep runs, then back-tracked."

She did grin then. "You mind turning around? I

thought you'd be hours yet—I'm not dressed for company."

He didn't want to turn away. He swept her with his gaze. *Lace.* She wore lace beneath her britches. He cursed, wishing he didn't know that. He turned stiffly sideways. He heard her rustle through her things, but kept his eyes averted.

"You can turn around now." He didn't need to be asked twice. Her feet were still bare. She'd wrapped a blanket around her shoulders. A red union suit covered half her calves. "I wanted to dry a bit more before I got dressed again."

He moved toward her, ignoring Wolf's cautionary growl. The girl didn't back up, didn't even know when she was in danger, though her wolf knew it. The breeze fingered her hair. He watched its restless movement, his hands aching to reach for her, to repeat the wind's touch.

"I've caught dinner for Wolf and me. The rod and tackle are on the bank. The trout are thick. You shouldn't have any problem getting one of your own. That is, if you know how to fish."

His nostrils flared; he was breathing hard. The breeze brought him her scent, sweet and lemony. He drew it into his lungs greedily, like a predator scenting dinner. He took his hat off, then held her gaze while he began disarming himself.

He slipped his rifle off his shoulder and propped it on one of the logs skirting her little campfire. He unbuckled his gunbelt, then shrugged free of each bandolier, setting each item in a growing pile at his feet. He drew the straps of his suspenders off his shoulders and pulled his shirt from his waistband, unfastened a few buttons, then yanked it over his head. He wore an old knit undershirt. Not what he would have worn if he'd known he'd be stripping in front of a woman like Leah. He drew it over his head, then tossed it by his things.

While she watched, he took his time untying his kerchief, exposing the scar about his neck in its entirety. He glared at her as he sat on the log to remove his boots. He pulled the knife out of his boot, then kicked off his boots and removed his socks.

She watched him still. He took a step toward her, reading more into her interest in him than he was certain was there. "Maybe you could see to my horse while I look after my supper?"

She grinned. "I'm allowed to touch your tack?"

Jace clenched his jaw. He glared at her another minute, then shoved his hat back on his head and stomped down to the bank. Snatching up the rod, he checked the lure.

Leah drew a deep breath as she watched him head toward the lake, her first full breath since he'd arrived. How the devil had he found her so fast? She shrugged free of her blanket and went to unload his things. She set his bedroll on the opposite side of the campfire from hers and moved his pile of gear there. Her gaze strayed down the way at him as her mind replayed the image of him undressing.

She'd seen nearly naked men before. She'd grown up surrounded by men. She and Audrey had been the only girls in their group, but they had all played together in the river, fishing, swimming, exploring their way through the long, hot summer months. None of the boys had looked like Gage. He was a massive wall of muscle and sinew. Seeing him made her uncomfortably aware of the differences between them—his height, his size, his strength were all greater than hers. He could, at any moment, use them against her, as the sheriff had done with her mother.

But unlike her mother, she would stand and fight, should such a thing come to such a pass. Joseph had taught her tricks, ways she could use her natural advantages. She retrieved her knife belt and strapped it over her union suit, just in case, then went to tend his horse. Once she'd removed his tack, she brought him down to the lake for a drink, then tied him up to the picket line near Blink by a patch of sweet meadow grass. Taking up a perch on the hill directly above the lake, she wrapped her blanket about her shoulders and watched Gage. His movements were hurried, jerky. And he kept walking around. He'd never catch anything at this rate. She set her hands on her knees and rested her chin on them. He didn't really need to catch anything. She already had two good sized fish— more than enough for the two of them and Wolf, but she wanted to be sure he had an appreciation for her efforts.

"You're doing it wrong," she called out to him. She pushed the blanket off her shoulders and showed him the smooth movements he should follow with his arms. "And quit moving around," she called out helpfully.

He looked over at her, lowering the rod as he stared at her. He grunted something she couldn't quite make out, then jumped to a boulder a little farther out and resumed what he'd been doing.

Leah watched him battle with the rod and line a short while longer. If he didn't stop soon, he'd have to pick another part of the lake to fish. She dropped her blanket, then walked down the hill to stand at the edge of the water. She pulled the legs of her long underwear up above her knees. With any luck, she'd stay fairly dry. She didn't dare take her union suit off, not with Gage there.

He glanced at her, then looked again. "What are you doing?" he called over to her.

"I'm coming to help you."

"I don't need your help."

"Gage, there are so many trout, you could catch them with your boots. If you haven't hooked one yet, it's because you don't know how. I'll show you."

She walked over to stand near him. "Toss your line." She showed him again the gentle motion he should be making with his arms.

"My feet are so goddamned cold, I can't feel them."

"Concentrate, Gage. The sooner you catch something, the sooner we can get out of the water. Do like this with the rod. Set the lure between those boulders and dangle it, gently." All this talking was not helping either. Trout could be skittish.

Leah closed the distance between them and ducked beneath his arms. If he could get the movement right, he'd catch something. She put her hands on his forearms, guiding his movements.

"Like this, Gage. Tease the fish. Make it want to nibble." She felt his chest expand with a deep breath, and wondered suddenly if it had been wise to come so close to him.

Jace let himself absorb her scent, the feel of her in his arms. "Are you—standing on my feet?" he asked, confounded.

"I'm trying to hold them still. Move only your arms. And quit talking," she whispered.

Jace had never been in so precarious a situation before. Leah had drawn that ridiculous union suit over her lacy underclothes, but the knitwear did little to preserve her dignity. It was stretched tight over her hips and bosom, leaving little to the imagination. God, if the men in town knew what they had moving so carelessly among them, they'd tear her apart like a pack of dogs.

She was directing his arms in gentle bounces, causing them to brush against the sides of her breasts. Was she really unaware of the effect she was having on him? Thank God he'd left his denims on, though her soft bottom pressing up against his thighs was still a brutal temptation. He leaned in closer, hoping to catch a bit more of her heat, wanting to feel more of her. Her unbound hair tickled his chest. He looked down the front of her union suit. Her nipples were puckered to tight points from the cold. Christ. He shut his eyes and rested his face against her hair. He drew her scent in with each pull of air. Lemony. He hadn't imagined it. Must be the soap she used.

"What are you doing?" she asked.

"Nothing," he responded, perhaps too quickly.

"You're smelling me."

"No, I'm not."

"Well, concentrate, Gage. I think you almost have it now."

He had it, all right. The itch to touch her, to feel her soft curves against his body, skin to skin. He opened his eyes, seeing the bit of lace that peeked out from the top buttons of the red knit she wore. He nuzzled aside her hair, touching his mouth to the sensitive area behind her ear.

"Gage?"

"Mm-hmm?"

"You're not concentrating."

"You have no idea how focused I am." He moved his mouth a little lower. Her grip on his arms tightened as her breathing sped up. He watched the rise and fall of her chest, mesmerized.

"Leah—" He paused. He needed to step away from her, now, if he had any hope of preserving her dignity. Or his. "I think I'll eat from my supplies tonight." He reeled in the fishing line, locking her between his arms. Taking the rod in one hand, he pulled his arms away, setting her free, though it was the very last thing he wanted to do. He wanted her to turn in his arms and face him. He wanted to pull her against him, wanted to taste her lips, see if she tasted as sweet as the rest of her looked and smelled.

She didn't leave. Instead, she slowly turned, stepping off his feet to stand between his legs. Her tongue darted out to moisten her lips, pink and wet. His dick responded, like a fish to a lure. He clamped his jaw shut and locked his eyes on hers. She glanced at his chest. Her lips parted. He tensed, wondering what she would think of his body, scarred as he was from battles, ambushes, and bar fights.

She lifted her hand and touched a jagged scar that was a remnant from a knife fight in Nebraska. His abdomen tightened as her fingers lingered. Her hand was small, her nails trim, her palm calloused. She stroked her fingers against his skin, crossing to another scar, this one thick and puckered. A barber in South Pass City had had to dig out a bullet, but the knife he used wasn't clean and the wound had festered. Her eyes moved up his chest to another scar, a thin mark left by a riata wielded by a particularly skilled vaquero in New Mexico Territory.

He couldn't take any more. "I concede, Leah. You win this challenge." His voice was a rough whisper, raw even to his own ears.

She didn't appear to hear him. Her other hand touched him, her thumb brushing across an old knife wound from a confrontation in Colorado. Her eyes moved up his chest, catching on each scar they passed. Almost every town he'd cleared had left its mark, and he remembered every single one of them. She skipped over the scar at his neck. He didn't blame her for not looking at that one. It was hideous. Like a brand, marking him, showing everyone what had happened the day his wife had ripped out his heart.

Her gaze moved over his chin, pausing at his

mouth. He drew in a breath, wishing he had the strength to beg her to stop. Or to step away himself. When her eyes met his, he saw their sapphire color had gone violet. A reflection of the water, no doubt.

Watching him, she reached up and covered the rope burns on either side of his neck. "Does it hurt, Gage?" she asked, looking at his neck.

He sucked in a breath. "More than you would believe."

"What happened?"

"My wife hanged me."

She drew her hands away and took a step backward. Revulsion chased away the empathy in her eyes. "What did you do to her?" Her voice was a whisper.

As he stood there, more than three years after the event, the memory was still razor sharp. "I loved her." He watched Leah's expression harden. She took her fishing rod from him and climbed back down the line of boulders to the shore.

Jace closed his eyes, overwhelmed by the flood of memories Leah's questions evoked. How many times had he slipped away from his unit to spend a few precious hours with his wife, time spent making love, sharing dreams for their future— a future she never intended to see created. He'd put the men in his unit in jeopardy again and again, for her. For a spy.

Jace walked to the shore, shucked his denims, then waded into the lake. He dove under when the water was waist deep, felt the water close over him, welcomed its mind-numbing cold. He broke to the surface and stretched out, cutting through the lake with strong, sure strokes, letting his mind dwell on nothing but the cold.

The breeze that evening was steady and warm, unusual for the high country that time of year. The pines swayed and whispered as the air moved through them. When Jace had finished swimming, he'd gone for a long hike, taking mental notes about the location of the lake so he could find it again, should he ever need or want to. Who else from town came up here to Leah's campsites? The sheriff? Was his gold hidden somewhere up here?

He was surprised to see, upon his return to camp, that Leah had supper well in hand. Two large trout sizzled over a fire, next to a pan of cubed potatoes and the fluffiest batch of biscuits he'd ever seen come from a campfire.

He sat on the log near the fire, watching her, gauging her mood and her reception of him. She looked up from the fish she was cooking. "You look surprised. I told you yesterday I wouldn't let you go hungry. I'd already caught your fish when you rode in earlier." She grinned then bit her lip to keep the smile contained. "I wanted to test you."

He held her gaze. "Joseph did a good job training you."

"So you acknowledge my ability to survive in the mountains, that I can come up here if things get bad in town?"

"If they kill me, you can come up here—until Sager or McCaid come for you." He studied her, wondering at her extraordinary self-sufficiency. "Leah, you're not a mountain man. You're a woman. You don't belong up here. You belong in town, with a husband and a family. It's the way of things—why do you fight the natural order of life?"

She handed him a plate, filled with his portion of fish, a couple of biscuits, and most of the potatoes, "I won't argue the part about the town. I like living in Defiance. But marriage isn't a requirement for every woman. I could do without it. I'm quite capable of seeing to my own needs."

"Marriage is all there is for a woman."

She laughed, but there was an edge in her voice that made it sound joyless. "I'm not most women. Plenty of us do fine without a husband. Maddie's running her own business in town—and quite successfully. My mother never remarried after my father died." She paused, her gaze on the water pitcher. "Many widows don't remarry." She handed him a tin cup of cool water. "A man isn't a requirement for a woman's life, Gage."

He took a bite of fish. It was delicately seasoned and cooked to perfection. In truth, it was the best fish he'd ever had. He tried to figure her out, tried to find where she fit in the various categories he had for women, but it was like trying to force a square peg into a round hole. Nothing fit. She cooked like a woman. She looked and smelled like a woman. But she dressed like a man and had the courage of a seasoned fur trapper.

He changed tactics, feeling again for the limits of her bravery. "What happens if a mountain lion takes exception to your hunting in his territory?"

She palmed her knife, flipped it so she held the tip of the blade, and tossed it right past where he was sitting. He didn't even have time to move away. The whine it made as it flew by his face made the hairs go rigid on his neck. He cupped a hand to his cheek, checking to see if she'd shortened his whiskers. Unable to help himself, he looked behind him and saw the handle of the blade vibrating in the dead center of an inch-wide sapling fifteen feet away. Had a mountain lion been standing there, the knife would have cleanly pierced his heart.

"Then I guess I'd have me a warm mountain lion coat come winter," she answered as she dished out her plate and sat at the opposite end of the log. "I've been stalked by a mountain lion before. She followed me around one whole summer. Usually, I couldn't hear her. I couldn't smell her. But there was a silence in the woods when she was near. Some nights, when the wind calmed, I was certain I could hear her panting."

"How do you know it was a mountain lion?"

She gave him a pained look, as if she'd explained something obvious and still he didn't understand. "I can track any animal, Gage. Joseph saw to that. When I began to suspect I wasn't alone, I circled around on my own tracks and found hers following me."

Jace took a quick bite of a biscuit, though it was too late to cover his shock. "You really aren't afraid out here, are you?"

"These woods are alive, but they're not evil. The plants and animals do the things God set them to, in ways that are knowable and familiar. I'm not greedy. I don't take more than I need, more than the town needs. We fit together, me and the wild."

Jace began to see that containing her would be like holding a fistful of water. He ate in silence until he cleared his plate. When she was finished, he gathered up the dishes and started down to the lake to wash them. He hadn't gone but a few steps when he stopped, not yet ready to walk away from the point he'd been trying to make.

"Leah, when I'm done with the sheriff, you can go back to doing what you want to do. Until then, I expect you'll do as I tell you. And anytime you want to go up to Sager's or out to Julian's, you let me know. Are we clear?" He looked at her over his shoulder.

She didn't answer his question. Instead, she retrieved her knife. "While it suits me to have a protector, Gage, I will have one. When it doesn't, there's not a thing you or anyone can do about it. Is that clear?" She wiped the blade on her thigh and sheathed it.

He was glad he would be done with both the woman and the town in short order. "That sounds like another challenge." He couldn't help the grin that followed those words.

"And you did so good with the last one."

His grin became a full smile. "It ain't over yet."

She met his smile with her own lopsided grin. Her eyes were shining, glowing with mischief. He continued down to the lake. She could do whatever she wanted up here. As long as she didn't distract him in town, they'd be just fine.

How he was going to keep that from happening was another matter altogether.

Night had come, stilling the wind to a gentle whisper in the trees surrounding their camp. In the near distance, an owl hooted. The night hunters were at work. Jace picked up his bedroll and laid it out next to hers, putting her between him and the fire.

"What are you doing?" She eyed him warily.

"Preparing for bed." He had no intention of waking up alone in the morning, wasting another day looking for her or worse—risking her returning to Defiance alone.

"Is it necessary for you to sleep on this side of the fire?"

"After the way you disappeared this morning? I'd say so."

The look she sent him confirmed his thinking. She had had no intention of being around come dawn. Jace settled on his bedroll and lay back, then threaded his fingers behind his head as a pillow.

"You said last night you would tell me about Wolf tonight."

"It isn't a story for a man like you. It isn't something you would understand."

"A man like me? A killer, you mean?" Leah remained silent. "Even killers enjoy a good story."

"It's a long story."

"I got nothing but time."

She sighed and looked into the fire. "My father was at Sam's Saloon, playing poker when Kemp came to town. Folks who saw it said he just walked into Sam's Saloon and shot my father. Didn't accuse him of cheating. Didn't give a reason of any kind, just shot him. After that, my mother changed. Everyone in town changed. Bill Kemp made himself sheriff and imposed his own law on the town. He hovered around our house. I didn't like him and I didn't understand what had happened. My mother grieved too deeply to deal with the sheriff or to help me. She just kept warning me about marrying the wrong man."

"What kind of wrong man?"

"A gunfighter. A gambler. Any of the men we have in town. I came up here, hoping I would see Joseph, hoping he could make sense of things for me. But it was his time to trade for his winter furs, so he wasn't here. I built a small lean-to as he had shown me and set my snares. I stayed up here for a month, until I could no longer hear my mother crying in my mind."

"Was he a good father? You said before he was a drunk."

She considered that and was a little surprised to realize that she hadn't been terribly sad about her father's passing. "I mourned him because my mother mourned him." She poked the fire.

"I was making a final round of my snares, taking them down, when I came across Wolf. He'd stolen a rabbit from one. He looked as if he'd been in a terrible fight—the left side of his face was swollen and infected. He was very lean and was too weak to eat the rabbit."

"Were you scared? An animal that injured is dangerous."

"Of course. Even lean and ill, he was a sight to see, big as he is. I'd come too close before noticing he was there. I froze, watching him. He didn't move. I realized he couldn't rip through the fur to get to the meat with his jaw so swollen. I skinned a rabbit I'd taken from another snare and cut a small piece of meat for him, which I threw his way. He sniffed it, but didn't eat it. I threw him another. Then several more.

"When I returned that evening, I saw he'd eaten the meat. I fed him again, two more times. The next night, I brought him water. Though he'd eaten, he'd gotten worse. He was lying on his side. I came as close to him as I dared, then slowly moved closer. When I was near enough to touch him, I could see the tips of porcupine quills covering the side of his face from his eye down the side of his jaw.

"I touched his paw, his neck. He didn't move, didn't growl. I went around behind him, thinking it might be safer to work on him away from the business end of his mouth. Still, he didn't move. I hoped, if I could get close enough to pull the quills out, then I might be able to tackle the infection."

She met Jace's gaze. "I'd had enough of death, you see. I was determined that he would live. I pulled the first quill out of his cheek. When he didn't growl or whine, I spent the next hour removing all of them. His eye on that side of his face was ruined. I made a poultice that Joseph had shown me that fights infection, then covered his face with it and laid a cold cloth over that. I kept the cloths cold on the infection throughout the night. When dawn came, I couldn't stay awake any longer. I shut my eyes for a minute, but several hours passed. The sun was high when I woke. Wolf lay next to me, like this, but with his head on my arm.

"The swelling had gone down. I fed him for two more days. His face began to scab over in a healthy way. I thought it was safe to leave him. It was as if in healing him I'd restored balance somehow, though I had no idea whether he'd be able to live. That part wasn't up to me, I figured.

"When I returned home, my mother still mourned, but in a more subdued way. She didn't punish me for being gone so long. Maybe she knew by then there was no point. The morning after I came home, she went out to gather eggs from our chicken coop. She screamed and came running in for the rifle, saying there was a wolf in our yard."

She looked at Jace and smiled. "It was Wolf. He'd followed me down the mountain. He was trying to get into the coop. I was never so happy to see anyone as I was to see him. My mother made me take him back up to the mountain and leave him. Which I did. Twice. He wouldn't stay. The second time, Joseph was there.

"He told me that Wolf had bonded with me as his new pack leader, and that I had better find a way to teach him how to behave in his new world, for he couldn't survive in his old." Leah dragged a hand through Wolf's thick fur. "I asked Joseph what I should name him. He said every living thing already had a name, that I must listen to his spirit tell it to me and then I would know what to call him.

"So I did. His spirit talked about running fast through cold woods, the power and cunning he used in hunting, the rules kept among his pack. His name was long and had no human equivalent. And so I settled for its short form. I called him what he is. Wolf."

Jace listened to the last of her words. The fire crackled. He didn't want her to stop talking. He loved the sound of her voice. It was like a song well sung. "How long have you had him?"

"Ten years now."

It did not need saying that that was old for an animal like Wolf. Jace rolled to his back and thought about what life would be like for Leah once Wolf passed. Perhaps it would be for the best. It would be impossible for her to settle in a larger town with a pet like Wolf. And she couldn't stay in Defiance much longer.

A sharp tug at his arm woke him a few short hours later. Leah crouched over him, holding up her arm and his, tethered one to the other. He'd waited for her to sleep after her story last night, then bound the two of them together so that she would not leave without waking him.

"Where is my knife?" she asked.

"I took it. I'll give it back in the morning. Lie back down. There's hours yet until dawn."

"You want me to sleep? You've bound me like a dog."

"Not a dog. Dogs do what they're told. Lie down." She resisted, tugging futilely against the string. When she brought their wrists to her mouth and began gnawing on the rawhide, he pulled her forward and into his arms.

"Enough. Settle down and go to sleep." He rolled on his side and moved her to her side, giving her his arm as a pillow. Her heart was pounding, her thoughts buzzing—he could almost hear them.

"This is sneaky and underhanded, Gage. I expected better from you."

"Did you? From a killer? I told you this afternoon the challenge wasn't over."

"How can you sleep with someone who hates you?"

He drew a long breath, smelling her hair and the soft feminine scent of her. "You wouldn't be the first, trust me."

"I won't sleep."

"Of course not. Just lie still so I can." As if that was possible with her body spooned against his. He didn't know what to do with his free hand. It was too intimate a gesture to touch her more than he had to, so he rested it along his own hip. But when she tried to wiggle away, he wrapped it about her waist and pulled her against him once more. "Stay put. I don't want to waste half the day tomorrow looking for you. I've learned what I needed to know. We're heading back to town in the morning.

Unless, of course, you've decided to go to Sager's or McCaid's?"

"No."

She didn't speak further, and she didn't move. Tied to his wrist, her clenched fist had nowhere to be except against the open palm of his hand. Her shoulders were set in a rigid line, but her body was warm against his.

It was a long time before sleep claimed him.

The smell of coffee and the sizzle of frying bacon woke Leah late the next morning. An early riser by habit—and necessity—she rarely slept past sunrise. For a moment, she was twelve years old again and Joseph had breakfast cooking for her. But when she opened her eyes, and saw the gunfighter slinging bacon, her dream world receded and reality took hold.

She quickly looked at her wrist, remembering the binding that had tied them together. It was gone and had left no marks on her wrist. She lifted the corner of her bedroll and found her knife. She didn't look at Gage, didn't want to remember the way it felt being held in his arms. His hand had stayed still on her stomach, holding her back against his warmth but not taking further advantage of her vulnerability. Despite her best intentions, she'd actually fallen back asleep for several hours.

"Why didn't you wake me?"

"We're in no hurry this morning."

She did look at him then. His raw voice, spoken

in that low, quiet way of his, made her stomach somersault. She crossed her arms, bracing herself against the emotion packed into her mother's warning, whispered from her death bed: *"Trust no one. Always do for yourself. And never, never love a gunfighter."*

As they approached town later that day, Leah noticed the change in Jace. His posture wasn't relaxed, though to look at him she wasn't sure how she knew that. Maybe it was the way his eyes swept the town, his gaze covered by the brim of his hat. Maybe it was the way he kept one hand free to reach for his gun should he need to. Maybe it was the muscle that worked in his cheek. He was a target, and he knew it. And she was one, too, whenever she was near him.

They pulled up outside her house and were about to dismount when a commotion outside the general store caught their attention. Jace turned his tired horse in that direction, moving in a controlled trot. Leah followed him, too curious to stay behind. She tied her horse by the water trough outside the store. A woman she didn't recognize was backed against the wall outside the store, a sheaf of papers clutched tightly in her grasp. Two of the sheriff's men flanked her, standing too close for polite conversation. Jim had come outside too, and held a shotgun pointed at the men.

"What's going on, Jim?" Jace asked as he slowly approached the tense group.

The woman sent Jace a soulful look, answering

before Jim could. "They think they can bully me into not covering your triumph here, Jace."

Jace sighed. "I'm disappointed, boys. I thought I made myself clear about the new rules in town."

One of the men turned and stalked toward Jace, his face folded into a look of pure aggression. He shoved a finger into Jace's shoulder. "You don't own this town yet. You can't outgun us all, and we don't cotton to her writin' up her lies. That camp follower of yours is gonna twist this all around, making you a hero when you're nothing but a hired gun, like all the rest of us."

"Don't worry about her. She's not staying. You've said your piece, now move on."

The first man shouldered past Jace. The second one stopped when he came even with Jace and looked right at him. "You're a dead man, Gage."

When they were gone, Jace confronted the woman. She looked about to faint. Her face had gone pale, and her gloved hands gripped her papers in a tight embrace. Her strawberry-blond hair was pinned up in a lovely arrangement of twists and curls, all tucked beneath a trim cap. She wore a green linen traveling suit and somehow managed to look cool even in the heat of the summer afternoon. Perhaps she was in shock, but Leah doubted it. She cast a jaundiced look at the woman, seeing her behavior for the performance that it was.

Jace, however, must have believed in her weakened condition, for he took hold of her arms to steady her. "What are you doing here, Felicity?"

"I had to come, Jace. Marshal Riggins in Cheyenne said this was the worst town you've ever cleared. I've documented all the others, since your very first town—how could I miss this one? Please don't be angry. I know you said to stay away, but I had to come!"

Jace drew a deep breath and slowly released it. He began stroking her arms, as if to warm her. The woman's color returned. "You can't stay here. The marshal was right."

"I can't leave. Not by myself. And the next stage is a week away. I'll be on it, I promise. I'll use this time to get a sense of the town and your enemies." A slow smile lit her face as her eyes pleaded with Jace. Leah watched Jace's hard expression ease up. He actually began to grin at the woman. And still his hands stroked her, slowly, soothingly.

Leah turned, too disgusted to continue observing their intimate reunion.

"Wait!" Jace called to her. Leah turned to glare at him, but he only had eyes for the lovely blond. "Go with the kid. Stay at Maddie's. We'll talk about this tonight."

Heat flooded Leah's face. She turned and saw Jim watching her. Giving him a disgusted glance, she stomped down the store's front breezeway to the steps and her horse. Images of Jace stripping to go fishing, memories of sleeping in his arms, flooded her mind. She had little doubt what he and Felicity would be doing tonight—after their talk—and hated that it bothered her. She'd never before thought about what happened behind a bedroom door. And she had no claim on Jace.

None—other than the fact that he had set himself to protect her.

She heard footsteps behind her, quick, dainty little steps. She didn't greet the woman.

"So—kid—tell me, are you a boy or a girl?" the woman asked, eyeing Wolf warily.

Leah took up the reins for both her and Gage's horses. Starting toward Maddie's, Leah flashed the woman a dismissive glance. "I am what I am."

Miss Conway laughed and straightened her cap. "Well, that's a relief. A boy would have given a clear answer." She smiled at Leah in a way that chipped at the wall she'd put up. "And it would have been a shame to waste such beautiful violet eyes on a boy."

Leah looked away, unnerved. "Gage is right. This town isn't safe. You shouldn't have come."

"Every town he works is a dangerous place. Without exception. I've documented all of his exploits. My publisher says his stories are the best selling of any he's printed."

"You write about Gage?"

"No. I write about the 'Avenger'!"

"So you're the one who gave him that nickname."

Miss Conway grinned at Leah. "I did. Very appropriate, don't you think? The west has never seen a bounty hunter as fierce as the Avenger."

"It's all fiction?" Leah stopped and stared at the woman.

"Well, fiction that's rooted in truth."

"Is he ambidextrous?"

"Yes."

"Is he a fast draw?"

"Yes."

"Has he killed a hundred men?"

The woman shrugged, looking a little disgusted. "Well, probably not. Don't tell anyone, but he talks most of them into not fighting. I do have to embellish his endeavors. I have to make an income you know." She studied Leah. "You're very curious about Jace."

"Not just me—the whole town is. We've been on pins and needles waiting for the Great Avenger to come in." They walked a few steps in silence. "He's going to die, isn't he?"

The humor left the woman's face. "I hope not. He cheats death at every turn." She held her hand out to Leah. "I'm Felicity Conway. It's nice to meet you."

Leah started to take her hand, then realized how filthy her old leather gloves were. She gave the woman a sheepish look and dropped her hand. "Leah Morgan. Welcome to Defiance."

"Glad you showed up when you did." Jim grinned.

Jace cast a distrustful glance around town. "Jim, you better get inside, and stay away from the windows. I'm guessing things are going to take a turn for the worse pretty soon." Jace watched the two men saunter down the street toward the saloon. They stopped and turned to face in his direction.

"In fact, right now." Jace pushed Jim toward the door of his store.

"Jace Gage! Get out here and face us. We ain't scared of you," one of them hollered.

Jace stepped off the boardwalk to face them. "Two against one. You consider that fair odds?" Jace called back as he stalked closer, his spurs clinking with each step. The wind had calmed to a breeze in the hot afternoon sun, letting his raw voice carry the distance.

"You got two guns. It's fair," one of the men assured him.

"I guess you boys are figuring on splitting the reward?"

"We are," the other man answered.

"You ever lay eyes on the money Kemp is offering?" Jace doubted Kemp would willingly part with a dime of his ill-gotten money.

"Kemp's good for it."

"Sure he is." Jace grinned.

"Shut-up, Harlan. Let's just do this." As one, they drew their guns and aimed at Jace. Their aim was off, however, for they were dead before they finished pulling their triggers.

Jace spun his Colts around his fingers and holstered them—not to be flashy, but to expel the excess energy throbbing through his body as he waited for the next challengers. He scanned the saloon entrance, seeing that the bench outside had been vacated. So, show's over for now, he guessed.

He walked into the saloon and calmly ordered a whiskey, as if there weren't two dead men lying in a heap outside. He took his drink and sat at a corner table, facing the room, meeting the eyes of each and every man who would look at him. Most wouldn't. The only sound in the saloon was the creaking of the rope suspending the unlit wagon wheel chandelier as it swayed in the breeze from the open door, a sound that was etched into Jace's soul as deeply as it was burned into the skin of his neck.

The devil was coming for him. It was only a matter of time.

Leah and Miss Conway were a block away from Maddie's when they heard the gunshots. Perhaps it was only one shot, one that echoed, but the sound stopped them in their tracks. *What did it mean? Who'd fired? Who was hit?* Leah needed to know.

Miss Conway turned to Leah. "Let's go see!"

"No! There's no telling what's happening over there. I'm supposed to get you to Maddie's."

"We're missing it, standing here arguing, Leah! You go to the boardinghouse if you want. I have to see what happened—it's why I'm here!" She started away, but Leah grabbed her arm.

"You don't understand this town."

The woman glared at her. "You don't understand Jace. Something comes over him, changes him. He's a sight to see in these confrontations."

"He's a killer."

Miss Conway glared at her, but said nothing else. She pulled away and hurried down the street. Leah tied the horses to Maddie's fence, then quickly followed.

Ever alert to the sound of more gunfire, the two

women cautiously peeked around the corner of an empty storefront, a block down from the saloon. The town was silent. No one stood with guns at the ready. In fact, no one was outside at all, except two dead men lying in the middle of the street in front of the saloon.

Miss Conway gave a disgusted sigh. "We missed it. All of it." She turned to Leah and froze. A chill rippled down Leah's spine as she watched the woman's eyes grow wide, watched as she looked in fear at something behind Leah. Steeling herself for what she would find, Leah slowly turned around.

Sheriff Kemp stood not two feet from her. His beard was scraggily, his face greasy as he leaned toward her. His eyes were always disturbing to Leah. They were so black that, even this close, she couldn't distinguish his pupils from his irises. She held still. Wolf came close, ever on guard.

"So you cheer the Avenger's lawlessness? He's killed six of my men, chased others away." Kemp stepped closer to Leah. She could smell the stench of aged sweat on him. "Get off the streets, girl. And take that camp follower with you."

Leah didn't wait to be told twice. She grabbed Miss Conway's arm and dragged her away.

After a little while, calm returned to the saloon. The piano player resumed his seat and pounded out a jaunty tune. Jace looked around the room at the collection of hard-bitten men the sheriff had gathered. The only common traits among them were their hunger for violence and their greed.

They had been grumbling of late about the back pay the sheriff owed them. The hold Kemp had on them was weakening. He'd better not wait for the stage to get Felicity out of town.

Sipping his whiskey, he wondered at the sheriff's uncanny ability to strike only the stages worth hitting. Somehow, he had to be forewarned. But how? Riders from Cheyenne, even riding hard and changing horses, would take too long. Unless the message wasn't being delivered in person. Maybe Kemp had a man in the telegraph office in Cheyenne. And that could only mean Jim was one of the sheriff's flunkies, too.

It didn't seem a man like Jim would help a criminal like Kemp, but knowing how the sheriff had blackmailed Leah's friend Audrey into distracting Julian McCaid, Jace figured anything was possible. What hold did Kemp have on the shopkeeper? Maybe he'd threatened Sally. They certainly lived in fear, those two, and Jim was ever protective of his wife.

Jace had watched the town from the hills for a while. Never once had Kemp left town. And he always stationed a man by the store at night. Maybe Jim knew where Kemp's gold was. Maybe it was hidden in plain sight, stacked among Jim's store goods. Jim had only recently hired help in the store—Audrey's brother, Malcolm. He was another player Jace couldn't quite figure out. The boy attended the regular meetings the sheriff held with the ranchers here at Sam's Saloon. Why? Whose side was he on?

Jace left the saloon, deciding to pay Jim a visit.

The wind was calm, the heat cloying. The late afternoon sun blazed down on the dirt of the main street, magnifying the temperature. Jace walked down the boardwalk past empty storefronts and businesses, his senses attuned to movement or sound. No one was about. Even the two dead men had been taken off the street.

He rounded the corner and crossed to Jim's store. As he stepped inside the open double doors, there was immediate relief from the sun, but not the heat. Sally was dusting shelves, and Jim was working through a stack of papers on his counter. The store was filled with the pleasing scent of heated burlap and licorice. A quick scan around the room showed him the three of them were alone in the store. Jace nodded in response to Jim's greeting, but something in his eyes put Jim on edge.

"What's on your mind, Jace?"

"I need to get Miss Conway into that supply wagon when it leaves for Cheyenne in the morning."

Jim looked at Jace, then over to Sally. "She can't wait for the stage?"

"Nope. Sam said Kemp got some of the boys set to make trouble for her. He knows she'll tell the newspapers what's really goin' on here."

"I don't like it. If the sheriff sees us slipping people out of town, he'll kill her and the teamsters. And us."

Jace arched a brow, his expression making it clear that the transportation was not optional.

The shopkeeper made a face. "We'll have to hide

her. Get her over here first thing in the morning. They leave after an early breakfast."

"Thanks. Oh, and Jim—suppose you tell me about the telegrams."

Sally sucked in a sharp breath and looked at her husband. "What about them?" the shopkeeper asked, his eyes flat, devoid of anger or fear.

"Why are you helping Kemp?"

Jim leveled a hard look at him for a long moment. "A man does what he has to do. Those telegrams were innocent enough in the beginning. News from his sister."

"He doesn't have a sister." Jim didn't blink, but Sally gripped the edges of her collar and held them tight against her throat. "Do you keep a log of the telegrams you receive?"

Jim nodded and fetched a notebook from his telegraph office. Jace flipped through the pages, seeing the sparse entries that were logged to area residents. "This doesn't show any of the sheriff's telegrams."

Jim put the notebook back beneath the counter. "The sheriff didn't want any of his recorded. But I kept a separate log." He flipped to the back of his ledger and turned it around.

Jace whistled low between his teeth. The dates of the sheriff's telegrams corresponded to almost every hold-up in the last year and a half, including the Army payroll headed for forts west of the Rockies. He looked at Jim. "Are you willing to testify against Kemp?"

"I'll answer that when he's behind bars. Until

then, I've got to do what I have to do to protect me and mine."

"Even at the cost of other lives, other people's loved ones?" Jace's eyes went hard. "You're generous with your sacrifices."

"Jim—" Sally whispered, her voice urgent.

"What do you want from me? What else can I do? Kemp's got a stranglehold on this town."

"He's gonna be getting a telegram in about ten days. I want you to delay delivering it for twenty-four hours. And I want to know about it before you tell him."

The shopkeeper studied Jace, gauging the risk before slowly nodding. "Twenty-four hours. If he or his men aren't in here when it comes, I'll do that."

Jace left the store, angrier than ever. The sheriff had passed his stink to everyone within his reach, ruling the town with the tight fist of a tyrant. He'd forced Audrey to seduce Julian and now he was sucking her brother into his corruption. Jace wondered what the bastard had on Maddie, for she had to be owned by him as well.

A movement down the street caught his attention. Leah. She'd changed her clothes since their return. She now wore a loose white shirt tucked into a slim pair of tan homespun trousers. Her back was to him, and her dark braid hung below her hat's brim. The garden was fenced with the same raw wood pickets that circled her and Audrey's homes. It was neat, weed-free, thriving. An oasis of order in the middle of chaos.

He wondered if the sheriff had something on Leah, if that was the reason she was so intent on staying in this wretched little town. But he'd no sooner thought it than he dismissed the idea. Leah wasn't a woman run by anyone, least of all a man like Kemp.

Leah's house was the last in a row of tumble-down shacks. Though weathered and badly in need of a coat of paint, her house was in fairly good repair. Her front yard, from the gate to her steps, was filled with a colorful herb garden, making her meager shack feel like a home. Something inside of him twisted.

He reached the fence surrounding her garden. His spurs announced him. Wolf, who was dozing in the middle of the street, didn't move, didn't even open his eyes from his lazy spot in the sun.

"Gage," Leah greeted him. Her white shirt caught the light and reflected it against her face. She was kneeling next to a bean pole, collecting pea pods. Jace didn't answer her. He looked down the street into the hazy prairie, shimmering in the heat. It felt good standing near Leah, in a nice way that was utterly foreign to him. She had brought this little patch of dirt alive. She maintained her home. She fed the town.

She did it alone.

"Miss Conway was sorry to miss your gunfight earlier," Leah said as she worked.

He watched her, but still didn't speak. He was what he had been in the war and since its conclusion: a killer. Here, in the sunshine, standing near her, he knew he was unworthy of her. "Leah." She looked up at him. "Come to dinner."

"Oh, no." She shook her head and gave a little

huff of laughter. "Your lady friend did not come all this way to dine with me."

"Felicity and I are old friends, nothing more."

"Well, maybe you need to tell her that."

"I have."

Leah brought the bowl of peas over. "Please give these to Maddie. She needed them for supper."

Jace lifted his hand, but he by-passed the bowl to touch her face. He moved slowly, giving her a chance to pull back. The skin of her cheek looked soft as a peach and smooth as polished marble. She didn't move away. He watched his fingers touch her face and sucked in a breath at the contact. Her skin was like silk beneath the pads of his fingers. He drew them down her cheek to the line of her jaw. His hand was dark against her face. He stretched his thumb along her chin.

"Come to dinner. Please."

Her head dipped as she lowered her gaze. "I have nothing to wear."

"You're wearing something now." He lifted her chin with his thumb. "Please." He looked into her eyes, watched them darken from sapphire to violet. Her lips parted. He bent toward her. Somewhere behind him, a door closed. The sound broke into the moment. Leah drew back. He felt her withdrawal as if something had been taken from him. He dropped his hand, but couldn't look away.

"Bring those peas over, Jace," Maddie called. "We're almost ready for supper! Leah—you're coming, too, aren't you?"

Jace didn't breathe while he waited for her response. She opened her mouth as if to answer, but didn't speak. She nodded. He smiled down at her.

"I'll be there, Maddie," she called.

Leah stepped into Maddie's kitchen a short while later feeling very much outside of her element. Why had Jace wanted her here? The way he'd looked at her moments ago still left her feeling warm and tingly. Something had changed in him, something that scared and thrilled her. The look in his eyes as he'd touched her cheek was unlike any she'd ever received from a man. She'd seen lust, derision, and competition when men looked at her, but never *reverence*.

Leah forced herself to ignore the nerves tightening her stomach. She'd dined often with Maddie—when there were stagecoach visitors and when it was only local folks she knew. It was ridiculous to be nervous now. She'd probably misread what she'd seen in his eyes.

Miss Conway was in the kitchen, helping Maddie set the table. When she smiled a greeting, Leah tried to return the gesture, but her response was more a raw baring of teeth than a smile. She'd been around Wolf too long. Leah busied herself with folding napkins and helping bring food to the table. She wished, for the first time in a long time, that she had a dress to wear. She'd never be as lovely as Miss Conway was in her pink cotton skirt and ruffled white blouse. Her hair had been brushed and rearranged in coils and braids pinned atop her head like a crown. Leah felt foolish for wearing the simple yellow ribbon she had tied at the top of her braid.

Jace entered, and the energy in the room shifted, as if he absorbed all the air. A strange heat filled her cheeks. She resisted the urge to look at him, though she felt his eyes on her. He took a seat next to Miss Conway, and Leah refused to acknowledge the slash of disappointment that he didn't sit next to her. Maddie called for grace and joined hands with Miss Conway and Leah. Jace reached his hand across the table. Leah looked at it, then at him.

That look was still in his eyes, as if she were an answer to a long ignored question. She put her hand in his, felt his fingers close over hers. She didn't hear the prayer Maddie spoke over the meal and only knew it was finished when Jace pulled his hand away from hers.

"So, Miss Conway"—Maddie opened the conversation—"you said you are a writer. It isn't often we have such an estimable visitor. What do you write?"

"Adventure stories." She looked at Jace. "About the Avenger."

Maddie's eyes widened. She looked from Miss Conway to Jace with an eyebrow lifted. "You started the legend."

"The stories are very popular with Luc and Kurt," Leah said, glancing at Jace, who appeared uncomfortable with the conversation. She turned to Miss Conway. "My friend has two foster boys who work hard to earn the money for stories like yours. They devour the ones with the Avenger—and then reenact the stories in their play."

"It's a myth," Jace argued. "Pure fiction. The Avenger doesn't exist."

"He's based on the exploits of a real man—you." Miss Conway looked at Jace. "You've become a legend."

"It's unrealistic what you have the Avenger do. The odds he faces would destroy a real man."

"And yet, look what you are doing here, Jace," Maddie said quietly.

A tension banded Leah's chest and arrested her breathing. Jace was the wrong man for her. For so many reasons. He had no intention of staying in town, if he even survived his work here. He'd said it himself: a man like him didn't expect to live. It was why her mother had warned her away from gun-fighters. She would only end up a widow with a broken heart.

She took a bite of braised rabbit Maddie had made from rabbits Leah had snared that morning, wishing Jace had never given her the look that had sent her mind on a flight of fantasy, causing her to yearn for something that could never, would never, be.

Chapter 8

It was midnight before Jace heard the scratching at his door. He sat on top of the covers, in the dark, wearing only his denims. Waiting. The door was unlocked. Felicity peeked inside. The faint light from the hallway silhouetted her as it illuminated his room.

"Why are you sitting in the dark, Jace?" she asked as she entered and closed the door behind her.

"Maddie's house is watched. Kemp's boys don't need to know anything more than they already do about my activities."

She lifted two glasses and a bottle of amber liquor. "Whiskey?"

He nodded. She poured two glasses. "I knew you'd come," Jace said as she settled next to him on the bed, leaning up against the headboard. Her robe slipped from her shoulders in tempting invitation.

"I couldn't stay away. We've been together for three years, Jace. I haven't missed a single town."

"This one's different. Usually the towns I clear are still populated by decent citizens, and there's enough regular folks for you to hide among. Not so here. You gotta leave, Felicity. I talked to Jim. He's got a supply wagon coming through tomorrow that could take you to Cheyenne before the stage comes back."

Felicity set her glass down and turned to her side, running a hand slowly up Jace's chest. He lifted her hand and brought it to his mouth. He kissed her knuckles, then released her. "Don't. I told you in Denver that we're through."

"Why? We're good together. We can give each other what we each want, what we each need."

A breeze blew in through the window, billowing the lacy panels flanking the curtains as it spilled into the room. A dark part of him wanted to roll her over, lift her nightgown and shove into her. No prelude. No effort. She'd be wet, ready for him. She always was.

It just wasn't enough anymore.

He sat up and set his feet on the floor and his elbows on his knees. "You have no business traipsing after me, putting yourself in danger. You can't keep doing it, Felicity."

"You are my business, Jace. I write about you. We could get married."

"I'll never marry again. You know that." He stood up. Looking at her leaning against his headboard, warm and open and waiting for him, he questioned his sanity in denying himself what she offered. If only she didn't want more than he could give. If only he didn't want more than he had a right to.

He gulped the rest of the whiskey in his glass. "Time for you to go."

She scooted across the bed and moved to stand angrily in front of him. "I've given you three years of my life. I made you a hero." She thumped her chest. "I made you what you are. You can't do this to me. You can't leave me like this! You can't dismiss me."

Even in the room's dim light, he could see the sense of betrayal that ravaged her face. "I'm sorry," he whispered. "I never meant to hurt you." He thought they'd been good together, neither asking more than the other could give. But, while she'd been only a diversion for him, he'd become her goal.

She gave a strangled laugh and wiped her fingertips across her eyes. "Hurt me," she scoffed. "As if I'd let you. But I can hurt you. The Avenger will go bad. On this job. He'll throw in with the sheriff. You'll be hated, Jace. I have that power."

"I never interfered with what you wrote, Felicity, though I never approved of it either. I have no control over you. I never did." Jace opened the door, regretting having made an enemy of yet another lover. "You do what you have to do. You've seen Defiance—now you can write about it from the safety and distance of Cheyenne. Good night."

When she was gone, he refilled his glass and guzzled its contents. Twice. He went to fill it a third time, but decided it was easier to drink straight from the bottle. He sat in the chair at the window, feeling the warm summer breeze roll over him.

The whiskey changed his sense of smell, heightened it. The air bore the scent of melting snow from the mountains to the west. He closed his eyes and breathed in, listening to the wind whistle as it passed the window frame.

Snow. Wide open land. Room to ride. Room to be alone.

When he opened his eyes again, he looked across the street, to Leah's house. Her wolf lay across the front stoop. She was alone in her shack. He'd never known another soul, besides himself, who sought out isolation as much as she did. He wondered if it fulfilled her, or if it left her empty, as it did him.

He pulled a shirt on but didn't bother to button it, then stepped into his boots, and buckled up his gunbelt. Moving silently, he walked through Maddie's quiet house and out into the night. The cool night air did little to soothe his raw nerves. He didn't care if Kemp's man watched him. He had to see Leah. He crossed the street and went through her gate. Wolf sat up and growled.

"It's me, Wolf. You know me," Jace announced as he approached the front steps of Leah's home. Wolf came to his feet. The growl changed to a sharp bark, then a high-pitched yap. It wasn't a sound Jace had heard from Wolf yet. He paused on the stairs, where five steps above him, Wolf faced him. He shouldn't have come, shouldn't bother Leah.

Before he could leave, the front door opened. Leah stood there, in a voluminous white nightgown, holding her rifle. She took one look at him, then set the gun inside the door and crossed her arms. "What are you doing here, Jace?" Wolf dropped to his haunches beside her.

Jace came up the stairs, drawn to her like a river streaming toward a fall. "I don't know." He stared at her, drinking in the sight of her. "I had to see you." He stood on the threshold, looking down at her, feeling as if she might be the last tether connecting him to his sanity. He should not be here, intending to do what he was. But he'd wanted to kiss her since his first morning in town.

"You're drunk."

He nodded. "Probably." He touched his hand to her cheek, picking up where they had left off this afternoon. A sharp breath hissed between her teeth, but she did not pull away. "Leah"—he looked at her lips, then at her eyes—"do you ever feel alone, so alone that your bones rattle about in the emptiness inside you?"

"I like being alone."

He lifted his other hand to her cheek, cupping her face with both hands as he bent toward her. "Have you never wanted to connect with another human being? To bond completely. To be as one, even briefly?"

He felt the sweet exhalation of her breath as his lips took hers. The kiss was gentle, closed mouthed. He didn't want to frighten her, didn't want to lose the connection to her. He'd hungered for this, for so much more than this. He drew the sweet, soft scent of her into his lungs, holding her essence locked inside him until his chest burned.

Slanting his head, he kissed her from the other direction, then moved back. His mouth opened. He used his jaw to open hers. And then his tongue was inside her mouth. A shiver trembled through him. She gripped his wrists, pinning him in place as he held her.

When he broke the kiss, he kept his forehead against hers while he caught his breath. He wanted in. He wanted in to her home, her body, her life.

For the first time in years, he didn't want to be alone.

Leah released him and moved back a step. "I think you should go." Cool air rushed between their bodies. The moonlight made the white linen of her nightgown glow until the shadows of her home swallowed her behind her closed door.

He drew a ragged breath, then shoved a hand through his hair. Moving blindly down the steps, he cursed himself. What the hell had he done? He was supposed to be protecting Leah, not assaulting her. If he wanted a quick tumble, he could have taken Felicity and been done with it.

He slammed through her gate and crossed the street back to Maddie's. He'd wanted more than sex from Leah. He wanted what he hadn't allowed himself to want since his wife had betrayed him. He wanted to belong. It wasn't real, the life he yearned for, and wanting it weakened him. He'd locked this feeling away for years, but somehow Leah had unhinged him. He wouldn't let her that close again. He'd clear this goddamned town and move on. Sooner the better.

* * *

Leah gathered her loaves and rolls into a couple of baskets for her deliveries. Now that she was down to a few customers, she could manage the deliveries in a single trip. Hopefully, when Jace was finished in Defiance, families and businesses would return, and her business would thrive as it had before.

A knock at the door told her Maddie was ready. When Leah stepped outside, it wasn't Maddie waiting for her, but Miss Conway. She smiled a greeting and reached for one of Leah's baskets. "I told Maddie I would give you a hand."

"It isn't necessary. I can manage on my own."

"But we wouldn't want to anger Jace, now would we? Besides, it gives me a chance to visit with you before I have to leave."

"You're leaving? But the next stage doesn't come in for days yet."

"Jace is running me out of town. Says it's too dangerous. He's made arrangements for me to leave with the Kesslers' supply wagon that returns to Cheyenne today."

Leah made a face and looked away. "He's so bossy."

"Maddie has already taken my things up there. She thought it would be less conspicuous. I understand I have to hide in the wagon until I'm out of town." Miss Conway was silent for a few moments. "He's infatuated with you, you know."

"Of course he isn't. We only just met."

"Really? And yet you went with him on an intimate trip up the mountain, the two of you, alone?"

The blood rose to Leah's cheeks. She gave the woman a dark look. "There was nothing intimate about it. I told him that while he's in town I would rather wait up there away from the violence. He didn't believe I could manage for myself. I've been hunting and trapping for years on my own up there."

Miss Conway gave her an assessing gaze. "Have you? By yourself? That's incredible. Maddie told me you were to be thanked for our supper last night, that you brought her the rabbits she prepared."

"I did."

"Well, they were divine, so I do thank you." Miss Conway paused outside the back gate to Sam's Saloon. "Maybe I will make you the heroine of a new adventure series."

Leah laughed. They entered the kitchen yard at Sam's. An empty basket hung from a hook. Leah replaced it with the full one she carried, then led them back to the street and up to Jim's store. "Jace would love that. I suspect he never took to being the hero of your stories."

"No, he didn't." She grinned at Leah. "But a girl's got to earn an income, and he was such a perfect source for tall tales."

Leah heard someone behind them. She turned to see who it was and found two of the sheriff's men trailing them. She wrapped her hand about Miss Conway's arm and urged her along at a faster pace. It was awfully early for the men to be up and about. Did they know Miss Conway was leaving?

"What is it? Are we in danger?" Miss Conway asked.

"Let's get to Jim's. I don't think Jace is up yet, and I don't want to face this alone."

"He's gone."

Leah frowned at her. "What do you mean? Where did he go?"

"He rode out late last night."

That news left a sinking feeling in the pit of her stomach. One of the men behind them was the same one who ripped open her shirt that fateful morning that Jace had arrived.

When they rounded the corner, she knew her fears were well founded, for a third man started toward them from the boardwalk in front of Jim's. Leah and Miss Conway continued toward the store, trying to behave as if nothing were out of the ordinary. Wolf began a low, persistent growl. The man in front of them blocked their access to the boardwalk as the two men behind them came to a stop a few feet away. Leah's heart began a desperate beat. She pulled Miss Conway to the right to go around the man, but he stepped in front of them.

"What do you want?" Leah asked.

The man laughed, baring stained teeth. "Hear that, boys? She wants to know what we want."

The raw chuckles from the men behind her made Leah's skin tighten. Her mind rushed through several scenarios that included fighting, surrendering, and running. Not one outcome was reassuring.

"Johnny there"—he nodded to one of the men behind them—"told me what you got under here."

He touched the bottom edge of her vest. "I wanna see for myself."

Leah stepped back. "No."

"Oh, I'm going to. And if you sic that wolf on me, I'll shoot him. See, girlie? We got you outnumbered and there ain't nothin' you can do about it." He reached forward and grabbed her breast as the other two men yanked Miss Conway back.

Leah reacted instinctively. She gripped the man's palm, pinching it between two pressure points that Joseph had shown her years ago and twisting as she pulled it away from her. He crouched reflexively, resisting the pain. She kneed his groin. When he bent over, she jammed the heel of her palm against his nose, straight up and back, hard and fast. He lost his footing, and she followed him down, palming her knife as she went so that she held it in her right hand, blade to the bristly skin of his throat as she gripped a fistful of hair.

"There is one thing I can do about it, mister. I can carve you up and feed you to my dog like the rattlesnake you are."

"Goddamn, Turner!" Johnny sounded gleeful. "She got you, too. I told you you couldn't take her."

"Tell your friends to let go of Miss Conway," Leah warned.

"You ain't gonna kill me. If you were, you would have done it by now."

Leah heard again Jace's warning about a dead enemy. If she'd killed Johnny when he'd first attacked her, they wouldn't now be in this predicament. But then, things might have been much worse. Who could know? If she killed the man lying beneath her knife, she would be no better than he was. A murderer. She pressed the knife deeper against his skin. He winced.

"My hand's getting shaky. Call off your friends."

Jim came barreling out the door to his store, shotgun aimed at the man beneath Leah. "Leave the women alone, all of you. Get the hell out of here."

Out of the corner of her eye, Leah saw Miss Conway pull free and hurry over to the steps behind Jim. Leah released Turner and stepped back, shielding Wolf.

Turner leaned forward and spoke into Leah's face, close enough that his breath pummeled her cheek. "This ain't over yet, girl. You better watch your back, 'cause I'm gonna have you on it before I kill you."

The men stalked away. Leah took hold of Miss Conway's wrist and dragged her up the stairs and into the general store. Maddie and Sally hurried over to them, and Leah pushed Miss Conway into their care. They pulled her into the backroom, where Sally had water heating for tea.

Leah leaned against the door jamb and folded her arms, shoring herself up against the shaking that was starting through her body. She'd almost killed a man. And worst of all was how easy it would have been. There were now two that Jace would say she should have killed. She let out a shaky breath as she realized that here, in her town, a woman had to be able to kill to survive. Defiance had lost its soul. How had it come to this?

Sally brought a cup of tea over to Miss Conway, whose hands trembled as she reached for it. "It's good that you're leaving today, miss. Defiance is a bad place to be right now, under siege as it is."

Maddie offered Leah a cup of tea, but Leah refused it. She was shaking as badly as Miss Conway and didn't want anyone to see it.

"You should go too, leave with Miss Conway, Leah," Sally said as she sat next to their visitor, her hand on Miss Conway's knee.

"Go where—and do what, Sally?"

"Go to Cheyenne and be safe. Go up to Sager's ranch or out to Hell's Gulch. Even go up to the mountain."

"A woman alone in Cheyenne is no safer than any of us are here. At least knowing how bad the danger is here keeps us all prepared for whatever might happen."

"Then you'll stay at my house tonight, and I won't have any arguments about it," Maddie ordered, her face set. Leah had no intention of hiding at Maddie's. She had her guns. And she had Wolf. No one would dare bother her.

The teamsters arrived with the horses. Miss Conway came over and reached for Leah's hands. "You saved my life today. I wish you would come to Cheyenne. You could stay with me."

"I'm not leaving."

Miss Conway's hands tightened on Leah's. "He doesn't think of you as a kid, you know. I saw how he looked at you last night." Leah's mind slipped back to Jace's late night visit to her house. She wished it was true almost as much as she wished it weren't. She sent a quick look to the other women, hoping they hadn't heard Miss Conway, but knew from the way they watched her that they had.

"Promise me you'll write me if anything exciting happens here that I should include in the story."

Leah offered her a nonchalant grin. "Miss Conway, nothing exciting ever happens here."

Miss Conway dropped her hands and spun around to face the other women. "I should stay."

"You should go." Maddie pulled her toward the back door as Sally grabbed her satchel. Malcolm was there, holding a tarp. They hid Miss Conway in the wagon bed under the canvas. When the team was hitched and empty crates arranged in the back, Jim gave the drivers a warning.

"Keep her covered until you're an hour out of town. Then hide her again before you hit Meeker's Pass. An hour outside of the pass, you should be safe through to Cheyenne." He handed the man riding shotgun a box of cartridges—just in case.

"We'll get her there safely, Jim. Don't you worry. It's an honor to sneak the Avenger's ladylove out of town." He grinned at the driver. "We won't have to buy drinks for a year in Cheyenne!"

The wind blew along the ridge from the west, bringing Jace the faint scent of a campfire. Men had trailed him from Defiance, but when he'd reached the ridge that rimmed the valley, he'd slipped into the woods and lost them. Smelling the wood smoke now, Jace circled around to observe them. Dawn was still a half hour away, but already the birds were chattering noisily.

Jace dismounted. Moving stealthily, he climbed over a series of boulders, then lay flat on the highest one, presenting the least silhouette possible. Peering over the edge, he could see three men lying on their bedrolls around a small fire. Three men, but five horses.

Before he could even consider where the other two men might be, he noticed the noisy birds had grown silent. The hairs lifted on his neck, a reaction that had happened when he felt himself being sited down the barrel of a gun. He rolled to his side, slipping over the edge of the boulder and down to the one below it as gunshots ripped into the cool stillness of the morning air. Palming his pistol, he took aim at the man who was shooting, dropping him before he could fire another shot, and then gunshots blasted from every direction.

Jace scrambled for cover. Slipping beneath an overhanging rock, he dropped to his stomach and peered around a small boulder. The three men dozing by the campfire hadn't moved—they weren't men at all, but an arrangement of boots, hats, and blankets. Well, the five horses didn't lie. There might be others tied up out of sight, but he'd only counted five men trailing him from town. A movement to his left, a flash of dark against the tan of the rocks, had him rolling and firing. His mark tumbled from the outcropping to the camp below.

Jace heard the scraping of boots against gravel, unsettling loose stones. Three men scrambled down the pile of boulders, hurrying to the far side of the horses, using them for cover. There was an argument. Two of the men mounted up and rode off, heading in a direction that would take them down to Meeker's Pass. The third, hatless, bootless, glared up toward where he thought Jace was. He stomped into the center of camp and picked up his gear.

Jace stood up, his pistol gripped loosely in one hand. "You ridin' north or south, mister?" he called.

The man held up his hands and skittered back down to the camp, one boot on, one boot half on. "I ain't gonna shoot."

"That's not what I asked. You heading back to Defiance?" The man nodded. "Then take your friends with you." Jace shoved the body of the first man he'd shot down to the camp below. "Tell Kemp I own this pass." Jace leaned against the boulder behind him and watched the man hoist the dead gunmen onto horses. He packed up his gear, then rode out to the north, taking his dead cargo back to Defiance.

Jace edged his way around the rock outcropping to his horse. He dug a cigar out of his pack and lit it. Two more dead. Two more run off, he thought as he watched the smoke dissipate. The odds were improving every day.

He took up his horse's reins and headed higher on the ridge, going on foot when the path became too steep, climbing to an outcropping that faced the southern opening to the pass. The deadly area known as Meeker's Pass was formed by millennia of wear from wind and water, bitter cold winters and blazing hot summers that had worn the red sandstone walls into pebbles, rocks, boulders, and cliffs. The cut through that ridge was the only road into Defiance from Cheyenne. Nestled between the Medicine Bow Mountains and this pass, Defiance was the perfect hole in the wall for a band of outlaws like Sheriff Kemp's gang.

Jace sat on the ledge. A faint trail of dust could still be seen where the sheriff's deserting men rode hell bent for leather to Cheyenne. The supply wagon should be coming through soon. The best place to watch for it was on that promontory, where the sheriff's men had waited to ambush the loggers' payroll last month for the shipment that Jace had faked.

He didn't have long to wait today. The wagon, its load of empty crates, and two drivers came barreling through at a breakneck speed. Jace waved his hat at the men, who waved back at him. As the wagon passed, the rolled up tarp in the back moved and a woman's pretty face looked up at him. Jace smiled and waved to Felicity, glad she'd gotten out of town. He figured that ride home should be good fodder for her work.

Chapter 9

"I'm done, Sheriff. This ain't workin' out like you said it would. It ain't quick and clean. There's sure as hell no money—the payroll run last month was a sham. You let the Avenger set us up. He's gonna do it again, I can feel it."

Bill Kemp's nerves tightened as he watched Pete's white knuckled grip on his hat. The Avenger had killed more than half a dozen men, run off a like number, and played them all for fools. All of his men were getting nervous, scared of one god-damned bounty hunter, same as Pete.

"Then quit messing around and kill him. Gage ain't no saint. He bleeds red, like you and me."

Pete shook his head. "Can't be done. That man won't die."

"Bullshit. Set up an ambush."

"We did. Wilson planned to take care of him up on the ridge with a few other men."

Bill frowned. "Where is he?"

"He's at the barber's with Hal . . . gettin' fitted for

pine boxes. The others, they quit then and there. But me, I come for the money you promised."

"You'll get your money, when you've earned it."

Pete slapped his hat on his head. "Then I'm through."

"Leave now, you're a dead man," Bill warned.

Pete gave a dry laugh and turned toward the door. "I think I'll take up with the Avenger. He's got better odds."

Bill nodded to his two ramrods. He couldn't tell whether it was Paul's or Hammer's knife that did the job, but Pete's days ended on the sheriff's threshold.

"Get rid of him. Make sure the others know what happens to anyone who wants to leave. And bring me three or four of the best. I'm changing strategies."

Chapter 10

Jace moved slowly toward Defiance, his senses on alert. There shouldn't be too many men up and about now, a couple of hours before dawn. The sheriff's gang usually drank their pay—the whiskey Kemp had Sam provide—until the saloon closed. Kemp thought it kept them content while he waited to make a move on the loggers' payroll, but Jace knew the men were getting restless. The first payroll was scheduled to come through in less than two weeks. It couldn't be soon enough for Jace. He would have this whole damn thing wrapped up by then, and he could move on to a new town, a new challenge.

The moon ducked behind thick clumps of clouds. His horse's head came up as he tested the air, his ears pricked forward. Jace scanned the road and the houses. Leah's light was on, but that wasn't surprising, as she had to rise early to get her dough going. But then shadows moved between the light and the windows. Big shadows. Leah wasn't alone.

Jace covered the distance between him and

Leah's home at a gallop. He leapt from his horse, then vaulted the gate. Wolf lay sprawled across her front stoop. Jace paused, thinking he'd overreacted. The beast wouldn't be sleeping so peacefully if Leah were in jeopardy. Jace drew a relieved breath. He moved toward the stairs. He could see Wolf more clearly now—and he wasn't sleeping. His head hung off the top step at an odd angle, his tongue lolling from his gaping jaw. Blood soaked the stoop and spilled down the steps.

Jace took the stairs three at a time. He entered Leah's home silently and became aware of several things simultaneously. The room was lousy with five or six of the sheriff's men, all crowded around the kitchen table, where Leah lay spread-eagled, her shirt and drawers ripped open. Men held her legs. Another her arm. Another had her other arm hooked above her head. He gripped her jaw shut, her head against his belly to keep her from screaming. Everything that was sacred about her lay open and exposed for the sheriff's men.

"Hurry up, Turner! I want a go at her!" one of the men snapped at the man fumbling with his pants. He licked his lips and grinned down at her.

Something in Jace broke. Shattered. He moved behind the man about to rape Leah, grabbed his shoulder and head, then twisted, killing him instantly. The man to his right drew a knife. Jace grabbed his wrist and yanked him forward, spinning him around fast as he brought the man's wrist up to slice his own throat. The other man released Leah's leg and jumped to grab the knife from Jace. Jace's foot lashed out, catching him under his chin, crushing his windpipe. A fourth man ran out the front door, smashing through the banister.

And then, there was only one; the man who had been holding Leah's jaw shut ran toward the back of the house, into the curtain that separated the small storage space from the main room. It draped over him, catching him like a phantom. He snatched the blanket away from the last thug and planted his fist in the man's face, in his gut. He kneed the man's groin and followed him down, slamming his head against the wood floor, over and over, until he, too, was gone.

The house was silent then, except for the roar of his heart and the rasp of his breath. On all fours, he scanned the room. Leah was hiding beneath the table, her folded limbs white in the dim light. Even several feet away, he could see that she was shaking. She clutched her knife in one hand and the shredded ends of her clothes in the other. Behind her was the prone body of yet another man he hadn't noticed before. Johnny.

She hadn't gone down without a fight.

He met her gaze. His hands were still fisted in the hair of the man whose skull he'd just smashed. She stared in horror at him. He'd killed four men in the space of two minutes, most of them with his bare hands. He slumped against the wall opposite Leah and stared at her. As the battle fury drained away, he saw himself as she must—the monster he truly was.

The woman who feared nothing in the wild, who befriended fearsome mountain men and had bravely come down the mountain on a travois—the woman who had shown how calmly and effectively she would dispatch a rogue mountain lion, now trembled and hid beneath a table in her own home. Hid from him.

He cursed silently, shredding himself for not sending her to stay up in the mountains. But the surrounding area was crawling with men fleeing Kemp. It wasn't safe. Nowhere was safe anymore. He reached up and drew the old quilt from her bed. Slowly, careful to keep it out of the puddles of blood, he crawled to her side.

She pulled into a tighter ball.

"Easy now," he whispered. Her eyes were unfocused, her fist wrapped in a white-knuckled grip around the hilt of the knife with the business end up. "Easy now. You know me, Leah. I'm not one of them." He worried that shock was setting in, stealing her mind. He eased his hand around her fist to keep her from lashing out at him with the knife. "You don't need this now. Let me put it down. Easy." He pried the knife free and set it on the table above them. "I have your quilt here. I'm going to put it on you. That's all." He eased the blanket around her, completely covering her.

"Leah, honey, I'm gonna take you to Maddie's. I need to get you out of here." Slowly, carefully, he pulled her out from under the table, worried she might try to fight him. He lifted her in the tight ball she held herself in and carried her out the door.

He'd forgotten about Wolf.

"No. No-no-no-no." She pushed free of his hold and dropped to the ground. "Wolf. Not Wolf." She lifted her pet's limp shoulders and held his big head against her chest. The quilt fell away, exposing her to the cool air. She rocked Wolf and wept, a deep, mournful keening. Jace lifted the quilt once again and draped it over her shoulders. He cast an anxious look around them, concerned that the one man who had gotten away might bring back reinforcements. He only saw Maddie hurrying across the street toward them.

His steps were heavy as he moved down the stairs to greet her. This wasn't the way things were supposed to go. He'd bungled this whole thing. He was supposed to have protected Leah. He'd failed her. And the goddamned devil had carved another notch in the gun he pointed at Jace.

"I was putting coffee on and saw you out here. What happened? Did Wolf pass last night?"

Jace shoved his hand through his hair. "Wolf was killed. And Leah was attacked."

Maddie's hand flew to her face as she tried to cover her gasp of shock. She started toward Leah, but Jace stopped her. "Is she hurt?" she asked in a lowered voice, leaning toward him.

"I don't know. There were six of them. She killed one before I got there. I took care of four of them, and one got away—Hammer."

Maddie cursed. "Bring her over to the kitchen. I'll get water boiling for a bath."

She started to turn away, but Jace stopped her, catching her arm in a tight grip. "I wanted her to stay with you."

Maddie gave a sad shake of her head. "She was too stubborn—she refused."

Jace released her and shoved a hand through his hair, watching as she hurried across the street to get things ready, trying to pretend that Leah's soft sobs didn't slice at his heart. But no amount of wishing things were different could undo what had been done. He climbed the lower steps and leaned forward to touch her face. "Leah, sweetheart, Wolf's gone. He's not feeling any pain where he's at, but you aren't safe out here. Let me take you to Maddie's. She's getting a nice bath going for you." He tried to ease Wolf from her grip as he spoke, but she shoved him away.

"No! He was my friend, Jace, my only friend. Don't you understand?"

"I do. Truly, I do." *I know all about being alone.* He stood up and moved down the stairs, wanting to give her the room she needed to grieve, if only for a few minutes. He crossed his arms and leaned against the house. He would guard her here. So long as he lived, not another goddamned bastard would harm her. He steeled himself to the sound of Leah's sobs, but they hammered his brain. His soul. When they slowed, he went to the base of the stairs and looked up at her.

"I'll bury him. I'll take care of it." He moved up the steps and lifted her into his arms. "Where do you want me to put him?"

"Here, at the front stoop. That way he can guard this house forever."

He carried her down the steps, through the gate, and over to Maddie's kitchen door, which opened as he approached. He shared a long look with her. Setting Leah in one of the many chairs at the long table, he swiped an arm over the dampness on his cheeks. She folded her legs in front of her and wrapped the quilt tighter about herself. He looked at the top of her head, then at Maddie, then turned on his heel and headed for the door.

Maddie stopped him before he could leave. "Jace, you should get some rest, too. You look like hell. I put some fresh water up in your room."

"There's blood all over her place, and five dead men I gotta deal with." He put his hands on his hips and dipped his head, searching for the words that needed to be said. "I don't know what happened before I got there, Maddie. I don't know what they did to her." He looked at her. "I gotta go clean her place up."

"I'll take care of her. Don't you worry. Check on us when you get back."

Chapter 11

The sheriff left his apartment and went down the back stairs, heading through the alley toward the street, wondering where Paul and Hammer were. He tucked his shirt in, hitched up his britches and straightened his suspenders. Wiping a hand against the back of his mouth, he wished he had a cup of Sam's coffee right about now. He'd gotten a late start on the day, which was unusual. Things had been quiet overnight. Too quiet. Maybe the boys were reacting to how he'd dealt with Pete.

A few of his men were standing around at the front of the building, staring at something by the door to the sheriff's office. They backed away as he approached, revealing five prone bodies on the boardwalk. Flies already swarmed them, their buzz loud in the calm morning air. One of Kemp's ramrods, Paul, lay in the middle.

"What happened? What the hell happened?" He looked around. No one spoke. "Hammer! Goddamn it, Hammer! Get out here!"

Bill's sole remaining ramrod walked out of the sheriff's office. "Who did this?" Bill asked, careful to speak each word slowly and clearly, trying to keep his anger at bay.

"The Avenger."

"Why?"

Hammer shrugged. "We roughed the girl up, like you asked. Guess he didn't take a likin' to that fact."

"I thought he was out of town."

"He came back. Caught us at Morgan's house."

Rage pumped through Bill's veins as the gates of his self-control broke. He charged at Hammer, forcing him back against the wall. "What have you done? Jesus Christ! What have you done?"

"You said rough her up. That's what we done."

"I said rough up the writer whore. Not Leah Morgan."

"The girlfriend was gone, boss. Took off on a supply wagon returning to Cheyenne yesterday morning. The Morgan girl was our only other choice. What difference does it make?"

Bill pulled his gun and put the muzzle against Hammer's heart. He cocked it. "That wasn't what I told you to do," he said, "that's the difference." He pulled the trigger.

As Hammer slumped to the ground, Bill looked at the men gathered around him. "Who else was there last night? Who else!" No one spoke. No one moved.

He wiped his sleeve against his forehead, all thoughts of breakfast lost in the churning of his stomach. He looked from face to face. He was down to less than a dozen men now. "Where's the Avenger?"

"I seen him head over to the livery."

"Pin him down there. I don't want him to leave, leastwise, not alive." He grabbed the sleeve of one of the younger men and pulled him aside. "You, go to Jim's store and wait for me there. Tell him there's gonna be a wedding."

"Who's gettin' married?"

"You are." Bill stormed off the boardwalk and headed straight for Leah's.

Chapter 12

Leah sat at Maddie's table, her hands cupping a mug of hot coffee. It was a warm June morning, but she couldn't shake the chill surrounding her. She had scrubbed at herself so fiercely in her bath that Maddie had forced her from the tub before she could rub off all of her skin. She couldn't stop crying. Even now, when she thought there could be no more tears to shed, she would remember something silly or fearsome or wonderful about Wolf, and the tears would come again. No matter how she tried to think of other things, she couldn't escape the fact that his passing had left a hole in her heart as big as the Territory.

A plate of cold eggs sat before her. Maddie moved about her kitchen, washing dishes, sweeping, busy as if it were a normal day. Sunlight inched forward on the floor, slowly sweeping over Leah yet doing little to dissipate the cold covering her body, freezing her mind.

Jace had spent the rest of the night and the entire morning at her house, Maddie told her. He'd taken the bodies of her attackers over to the sheriff's. He'd buried Wolf, right where she'd asked him to. Maddie helped him scrub the inside of the house, returning a little while later with a fresh outfit for Leah and the good news that her carpet had not been spoiled.

Leah shuddered, thinking about the men who had invaded her home. Johnny had underestimated her willingness to use her knife. He'd been the first to die. But Turner had known it would take a group of them to overwhelm her, and he'd come prepared. If Jace had arrived any later, Turner would have made good on the threat he'd issued outside Jim's store the other day.

A heavy banging sounded on Maddie's front door. Loud and insistent. Maddie wiped her hands on her apron and cast a worried look at Leah. "Stay here, dear. I'll see who that is. You don't have to talk to anyone today. It's probably Sally. I'll let her know you're not up to seeing visitors yet."

Leah watched her coffee as she listened to Maddie hurry down the hall.

"Sheriff! What brings you here this morning?"

"Where is she? Where's Leah?"

"She's resting, Sheriff. She's had a hard night."

"I want to see her. Don't you think you can hide her from me."

"Please, you'll have to come back later—" Maddie's voice trailed off as Leah quit listening. She pulled on her boots, then moved through the kitchen door into the sunshine. She shoved her hands in her pockets. The breeze whispered over her bruises and tear swollen eyes, ruffled her loose hair. She started down the driveway toward the stable, ignoring the sheriff and Maddie in the front yard. One of them called her name. The sheriff probably. She kept walking. The world had gone silent, just as the sun had gone cold.

It didn't matter. Nothing mattered. She made it to the stable door, thinking of the mountains, of finding peace there. And then there was pain in her arm as someone grabbed her and spun her around. Sheriff Kemp leaned toward her, his eyes angry, searching over her face, her body. His mouth was moving. A vein was swollen in his neck, his face reddening. Odd that he didn't scare her, odd that she felt nothing, heard nothing.

He took hold of both of her arms and shook her. Maddie was hurrying over to them. Leah wanted to warn her away, but she wasn't in control of her faculties. It was as if she stood outside of herself and watched this happening to someone else.

The sheriff backhanded Maddie, dropping her to her knees as a volley of gunfire erupted down at the livery end of town. With it, all sound returned to Leah, the wind, crickets, shouts of men a block away. Leah covered her ears. "No!" Her voice sounded distant and odd. "No!" she shouted.

The sheriff grabbed her arm and started dragging her toward Jim's store. The gunfire continued. Jace was there, at the livery. Maddie had said he'd gone to ask the livery owner about borrowing the tools he needed to fix her front door. Leah wanted to be ill. This was wrong. It was all wrong. How could people live like this? She was sick of the blood and fear and violence.

She tried to pull free of Kemp's grip, but his hold was relentless, his fingers digging into her arm. They stepped onto the boardwalk and suddenly there was silence. Not the strange silence that she'd experienced moments earlier. She could hear the breeze. The gunfire had stopped.

"Why have you brought me here, Sheriff?"

He released his grip on her arm and shoved her inside the store. "You're getting married."

Leah planted her feet. "No, I'm not."

"You are." He gripped her chin and lifted up. "Look at you. Look what they did to you. You can't live alone."

"No."

His grip tightened. "How many more nights like last night can you take, girl?"

Why would he care what happened to her? It was a farce. He'd never cared about her and her mother. He'd always hung around nearby, leering at them when they went about their business in town, inviting himself over for supper. He'd say considerate things like that, then chase Leah out of the house and beat her mother to a pulp. Leah would hide at Audrey's next door, but even the short distance and closed doors couldn't drown out the sound of what was happening. Kemp was most dangerous when he was nice. "Leave me alone!"

The sheriff cupped the back of her neck and propelled her deeper into the store. She ducked out of his grip and reached for her knife. Her hand touched her empty waistband. God, she had no knife. No Wolf. In a panic, she looked around the room, seeking help. Sally stood at the entrance to the storeroom, her apron bunched in her hands, half covering her face. Jim stood behind the counter, one hand on the shotgun he always kept in close reach under the counter.

One of the sheriff's men stood near him, his Colt still holstered. In a flash it would all change. Jim would be shot if he lifted that shotgun, and then what would happen to Sally and the shop? How would she get on?

Run. The command whispered through her body, again—louder the second time. *RUN!* Leah did an about-face and bolted for the door, intent only on getting to Maddie's stable and Blink. If she could get to the horse, she'd ride bareback up the mountainside. Once there, no one would catch her.

She never made it to the front door, for three of the sheriff's men stepped inside, blocking her escape. Leah's gaze shot around the room. She was trapped and desperate. God, this couldn't be happening. The newcomers exchanged a look with the sheriff that could only be interpreted as triumphant. He nodded in acknowledgment.

She knew what that meant. They'd finally gotten Jace. Her knees almost gave out. He'd killed for her. Protected her. And now he'd been slaughtered, cut down in cold blood.

"Go stand next to Sean, girl."

"No." Leah straightened, wrapping her arms about herself.

The sheriff drew his revolver and pointed it at Sally. "Do it now. I'm not playing games."

She saw Jim's arm tense, but he didn't lift his shotgun. "A wedding ain't a place for guns, Sheriff.

What do you say we all put our weapons down?" His calm voice broke into the tension in the room.

Leah quit resisting. She couldn't bear to lose anyone else, anyone she loved. She walked in front of the sheriff, moving between his line of fire and Sally as she stepped over to the man he'd selected for her from among his gang. This marriage didn't mean anything. She would run. As soon as she could, she would flee to the mountain where no one would find her. She would go and never look back. The sheriff holstered his gun.

"Sally, wait in the storeroom," Jim ordered. Sally retreated without hesitation, but returned only seconds later, flanked by yet another of the sheriff's men.

Jim made a face. "Sheriff, hold on while I get my log book and seal."

"No games, Jim," Kemp warned.

Leah's heart was pounding. She chanced a look at the man the sheriff called "Sean." He was tall and not particularly fierce looking. In truth, he appeared as off-kilter as she was. He had a few days' growth of beard and thinning blond hair. A well-worn holster hung by his right hip; he wasn't as innocent as he appeared.

Jim returned with a notebook, stamp, pen and ink bottle. He was moving so slowly, Leah feared the stress would undo her. He opened the journal and flipped through the pages.

"Now then, I'll need your complete names. You first, Leah."

"Jim, you know my name."

"So I do. But I don't know if you have a middle name."

"Allison."

"Leah. Allison. Morgan," Jim said aloud as he jotted her name in his book. "And you, sir? Your name?"

The man cleared his throat, and cast a wary look over his shoulder at the sheriff. "Sean Flanagan O'Neill."

Jim jotted the name down. "Well, then." Jim looked up and scanned the room before letting his gaze settle on Leah. "Leah Allison Morgan, do you, of your own free will and intent accept Sean Flanagan O'Neill as your lawful wedded husband?"

Leah drew a breath to answer that question, but before she could speak, it was answered for her.

"No. She does not," Jace rasped, elbowing his way into the room.

The sheriff cursed and flashed an angry look at his men. "What are you doing here, Gage? This doesn't concern you."

"All the good citizens of Defiance are my concern, Sheriff. You know that. It's not nice of you to have a shotgun wedding and not invite me." He leaned toward Kemp and offered some friendly advice. "You shoulda trained your boys better. They took it for granted that they got me once I stopped shooting. Guess they weren't brave enough to come see for themselves. By the way, Gart didn't like having his place shot up. I expect your stable fees will be goin' up."

Kemp's face reddened. "Get on with it," he ordered the shopkeeper.

"I wouldn't, Jim," Jace warned.

"Leah's got to be married. She needs protection."

"She has my protection."

"Little good it did her last night. If the men know she's got a man at her house, they won't make that same mistake twice."

Jace gave a grim smile. "Losing control of your boys, Kemp?"

"Get on with this, Jim," Kemp ordered.

Jace glared at the boy named Sean. The kid sent a nervous glance beyond Jace to the sheriff, then back again. Jace arched a brow, and the boy decided to back away.

"If Leah's marrying anyone today," Jace said as he took Sean's spot, "she's marrying me." He leaned down and whispered to Leah, "This ain't real. It ain't for keeps. Don't go gettin' panicked. I'm gonna get you outta here, then we'll figure things out."

Shocked, Leah looked up at him. It should have been a relief that he wanted this no more than she did, but it wasn't.

He nodded at Jim. "How about you scratch off that name and write down Jace Holden Gage."

Leah dropped her gaze and stared at the counter, unable to make eye contact with anyone in the room. As slow as Jim had been proceeding before, he now hurried through the steps of the ceremony, quickly coaching them through their vows. There were only two words needed from her, and they fell from her mouth like a condemned woman's farewell. "I do."

More words and the whole thing was over. Jim turned his logbook around for them to sign. Jace signed his name in a compact, precise script. She stared at his signature.

How odd it was that she had come to this point in her life. Without even trying, she had made her life everything her mother had warned her against.

Jace pressed the pen into her hand. "It'll be all right. You'll see. Let's get through this and get outta here." He spoke the words in a whisper against her forehead. Somehow, his strength gave her strength. She signed her name beneath his. *Leah Morgan Gage.*

The room was silent when they turned around. Jace met the eyes of each man, daring him to say or do anything to make this worse than it already was. The men parted to give them room to leave. He set a hand at Leah's waist and guided her from the store. He didn't see Hammer, and the thug's absence made him nervous. Leah was outside and Jace was at the door when one of Kemp's men snickered a comment about which one of the newlyweds was going to wear the pants in the family. Jace dropped him with a right hook to his jaw.

Hearing the man crash to the floor, Leah looked back and caught Jace rubbing his knuckles. He stopped the motion. She turned away without a word. It was strange walking without Wolf moving between them, Jace thought.

As they moved down the boardwalk and out into the bright sunny morning, Jace broke the silence between them. "We're not keeping this marriage, Leah. When I take the sheriff to Cheyenne, I'll file for a divorce. You'll be free of him—and me—as soon as I'm done here." She said nothing in response to that statement, for or against it. He lifted his hat and shoved a hand through his hair. He wasn't sure she was listening to him and didn't know how to break through to her.

He thought about what had happened last night. He didn't know how many of the men had taken a turn with her before he'd gotten to her, didn't know how bad her injuries were. "Leah—you shouldn't be up and about today."

She released a harsh breath. "The sheriff didn't give me much choice."

It wasn't the answer to the questions plaguing him, but led him to another matter on his mind. "Why is he so all-fired interested in you, anyway?"

She shrugged. "I don't know. He's always been like that. First with my mother, now with me."

They had reached her gate. Jace turned her to face him. "Nothing changes, Leah. I'm still your protector. And I still need you to do what I say, for a little while longer."

"Let me go to the mountains. Let me go, Jace."

Jace sighed. His gaze took in her bruised face and tear-swollen eyes. "I can't. You won't be safe there. The sheriff's men are thinning out, leaving town every direction they can. They'll find you up there. You'll be alone. I can't do it, Leah."

She entered her small front yard, where two steps brought her in front of Wolf's grave. Her flowerbed had been turned over. Jace had had to dig up her daisies and flax to bury Wolf, and the shock of being disturbed had wilted the flowers. She stared at the slight mound, where Wolf, her constant companion, would forever lie. Her body stiffened.

Jace wondered if she was even breathing. He reached a hand out to touch her shoulder, wishing she'd had him put Wolf someplace less visible. By the woodpile, perhaps. She was cold beneath his touch, despite the heat of the blazing June sun.

A tear slipped down her cheek. Watching her mourn was like watching a statue weep, so still did she hold herself. His hand tightened on her shoulder as he pulled her into his embrace. "Wolf was a proud beast, Leah. He wouldn't have wanted to die an old dog's death. He died protecting you."

She relaxed against him. He cupped her cheek and pressed his lips against her forehead, holding her while she cried. She wrapped an arm around his waist and her hand touched his chest. He felt her stiffen. She sucked in a breath. She lifted her head and looked at the cartridges in his bandolier. Pushing away from him, she stared at the crossed leather straps that marked his trade as a vigilante. He watched her and waited, willing her to look beyond the leather and bullets to the man beneath.

Look at me, he silently begged her. *See me.* She didn't look up.

Jace raised his gaze to the brilliant blue sky. The light was so bright, there was nowhere to hide the ugliness of his soul. Leah was smart to reject him. She took a step toward her home, but stopped when she saw her front door still hanging in pieces in its frame.

"Leah," Jace said, not daring to touch her again, "please—go to Maddie's while I get your door fixed." He walked her to her gate and watched her cross the street to Maddie's. He was about to turn away when he saw Malcolm, Audrey Sheridan's brother, coming up the street. In his hand were the tools Jace had gone to borrow from the livery master.

Jace leaned on the fence and waited for him. "Thanks, Malcolm. You were a big help today. If you hadn't warned me what was happening at Jim's, I wouldn't have made it there in time."

"So you stopped it then?"

Jace made a face. "She got married, all right. To me."

"You and Leah are married?" Malcolm scoffed. "Oh, this is a fine day. Is Maddie making a big dinner to celebrate?"

"No. It isn't something any of us is very happy about. I think we better hold off on the celebrating—we're not keeping the marriage. Leah is still shocky about the attack and Wolf's death. I'll write McCaid and let him know what's happened. He can break the news to your sister."

Chapter 13

Leah stood in the middle of her home that night, her stomach in a knot. A cold sweat clung to her skin, making her nightgown feel clammy. Nothing in the small space of her home had been spared the violence of the attack. The kitchen table, her knife, the floor, the walls. Jace and Maddie had scrubbed the room clean, and her front door had been repaired. But the echoes of what had happened slithered about the shadows and chilled her skin.

A loud knock beat against the door, startling her, causing instant panic as her mind spun her back to the early morning hours. The men had pounded on both of her doors then, breaking in from the front and the back. She'd barely had time to grab her knife before they spilled into her home, surrounding her.

The knock sounded again. "Leah, it's me. Open up," Jace said from the other side of the front door. For a moment, she couldn't move. She grabbed her shawl to cover her nightgown, then opened the door a crack.

"What do you want?"

"I want to sleep with my wife."

"No!" Leah tried to push the door closed, but he maneuvered it open and entered her house, closing it behind him. "Jace Gage, you said this marriage wasn't real. You can't sleep here."

He set his saddlebags down and hung his hat up on a peg behind the door. "I can't protect you from across the street. I'm going to sleep here. And sleep is all we're gonna do, 'cause if we consummate this marriage, we're keeping it. And I sure as hell don't intend to do that."

Leah's heart was pounding. No man had lived in this house since her father, ten years ago. The room became uncomfortably small with Jace in it. She yanked a coverlet from the foot of the bed, grabbed one of the pillows, and handed them to him. "Then make yourself at home, Gage." She climbed on the bed and pulled the sheet up around her as she kept an eye on him.

Jace frowned as he set the bedding on one end of the kitchen table, feeling exceedingly unwelcome. He put his rifle on the table, pulled out his two Colts and set them next to the rifle, then withdrew his derringer and laid it next to the others, conscious all the while that Leah watched him in wary silence. He unbuckled his gunbelt and removed it, then slipped his bandoliers over his head. From his bags, he withdrew cases of rifle cartridges and bullets, then refilled the slots in his bandoliers and gunbelt.

When he brought his gun cleaning kit over, Leah jumped out of bed and confronted him. "You can't do that there! I need to keep the table clean so that I can make bread in the morning." Jace forced himself to keep contact with her eyes, refusing to let his gaze take in the strangely female garb she slept in. But his eyes had a mind of their own and dipped down her face, past her jaw, to the lacy collar that was buttoned tight, right up to her chin.

He thought of the underclothes he'd seen her wear on their camping trip, and realized while his wife wore men's clothing on the outside, against her skin, she loved lace and frills. It was an insight that made his body tighten. Blood heated a part of him that had no place in this marriage.

"Where do you clean your guns?" Jace asked, for once glad his old injury provided an excuse for his rough voice. She shook her head, giving a huff of surrender before going to a cupboard and pulling out a heavy canvas sheet.

"Here. Put this down."

He looked at her and couldn't help his grin. "Thank you, again." He didn't watch her get into bed, didn't once look at her, although his peripheral vision showed him she was lying on her side, watching him. By the time he'd finished cleaning his guns and had put his kit away, she was soundly asleep, her breathing deep and even.

He stripped down to his drawers, then went to Leah's dresser and poured water into the bowl so that he could wash his hands and face and brush his teeth. When he was finished, the bowl of brown water sitting on the pristine white, linen runner was an ugly reminder of his unwelcome presence in her home. He dumped the water outside and refilled the pitcher from water on her stove. Then, before getting into her bed, he arranged his weapons for the night, putting his knife hilt-out between the mattress and frame, setting one Colt under the pillow she'd given him, draping his gunbelt over the headboard with the other Colt's holster near at hand, and setting his rifle on the floor next to the bed. He wrapped himself in the blanket she'd given him and lay down on the bed next to her.

Her scent filtered up to him from the blanket and the pillow and her own warm body next to him, sweet and lemony. He drew the blanket up to his face and filled his lungs with the smell of her. The sun had set long ago, but twilight lingered in the room, cool and ethereal. He looked over at Leah, sleeping soundly next to him, blissfully unaware he'd joined her in bed. He rolled onto his side to watch her as the light retreated from the room. Her dark hair was drawn over one shoulder in a thick braid, the widow's peak at her forehead accentuating the heart shape of her face.

He wondered, as he drifted to sleep, what would become of her after their divorce.

A scream woke him—minutes or hours later, he didn't know. Even before his eyes opened, he'd rolled from the bed and gripped his knife, braced to defend Leah. It was still dark outside, but the moonlight gave enough of a glow that he could see inside the small space of her home. No one moved stealthily—there was nothing but shadows. He looked over his shoulder at her on the bed, wondering if he'd dreamt the scream or if Leah had had a nightmare.

She was cowering against the wall, the sheet pulled to her chest and clutched in her fists. He dragged his hand down his cheeks as he drew a calming breath, trying to keep from blurting out that she had scared the bejesus out of him, screaming like that. He sighed and set the knife back beneath the edge of the mattress, then wrapped himself in her blanket and lay down on the bed. The way she held herself from him, he knew the last thing she wanted was for him to offer her comfort.

"Why are you in this bed?" she asked, her voice barely a whisper.

He looked at the dark ceiling. "It was the only bed I saw."

"You were supposed to sleep on the floor. I gave you the pillow and a blanket."

"I've lived long enough to know a soft bed is a helluva lot more comfortable than the hard floor. There's plenty of times when I got no choice, but when I do, I pick comfort."

"You don't have a choice. You can't sleep with me."

"Why? We were sleeping just fine till you screamed."

"No! No!" She shoved at him, kicking and pushing. "Let me up! Let me go!" He sat up, trying to figure out how to wrestle her to stillness so that he could reason with her, but she scooted past him and off the bed before he got the chance. Hurrying several steps away from the bed, she spun around and faced him. Her hair was mussed, her mouth open as she panted. She was feral, like an untamable barn cat, cute but full of claws.

And then, he had a terrible realization. The brave woman who feared no mountain lion feared him.

In a flash, he was torn between reality and hope. Did he take the time they had together to try to teach her that not all men were like the sheriff's men? Or did he leave her her fear as a protective force? He knew a person couldn't tame an animal without being there to see to it for the rest of its life, as she had with Wolf. And he had no intention of sticking around once he took care of the sheriff.

In the end, he decided to let her make the choice. He held out a hand to her, palm up. "Leah, put your hand on mine."

"No. You'll grab me."

"I won't. No tricks. Please, just your hand."

"Why?"

He released a long breath. "Because we have to get through the next few weeks together. We need to trust each other. I am not going to hurt you. I need you to be comfortable around me."

She stepped nearer and reached out. She watched him, regarded his hand warily. And then, as if fearing it would hurt, she set her palm on his. A frisson sheared through him at the contact. He wanted so much more than this simple touch. He craved the feel of her body against his. He held perfectly still until she pulled away.

And when she did, he knew with stunning clarity, their marriage wasn't going to end well.

Chapter 14

Jace held the match to the end of his cigar and drew air through the tobacco into his mouth, releasing puffs of smoke as the embers began to glow. It didn't take long for the sheriff to come out of Sam's and head straight for him. The man hated unexpected behavior, and Jace's standing out there in the dark made him nervous.

"What are you doing out here, Gage?"

Jace squinted at him above the smoke from his cigar. "I'm bidin' my time, Sheriff." He pulled the cigar out of his mouth and gave it a critical look. It was the last of his stock. He hoped Jim got his order in from Cheyenne with the next supply run. "I'm curious about something."

"What's that?"

"What's your interest in my wife?"

"She's a resident in my town. Why wouldn't I be interested in her?"

"Beyond the fact that she's the only one you care about? You even had your men open fire on the livery master and smithy—two people you actually do need. Who the hell's going to see to your horses if you kill them? Makes a man curious."

Kemp sighed. "I was fond of her ma, and Mary died before she could see Leah settled. My only thought was to see to her welfare. I think Mary knew that her daughter, or the mannish thing she's become, could never live anywhere but Defiance."

"She likes her life the way it is." Or was, before their marriage.

Kemp cast a surreptitious glance around the street. His posture remained unchanged, but his voice came low and urgent. "If you win, if you beat me, you gotta promise to keep her here. This is her town, where she belongs."

Jace took a long draw on his cigar as he considered the growing mystery of Kemp and Leah. If there was one thing he didn't like, it was a mystery involving the woman he was married to. Even if it was a temporary marriage.

"I'll tell you two things that are true, Sheriff, to put your mind at ease. Leah ain't your business. And I am gonna win. Beyond that, unless you want to surrender or give up your gold stash, you and I got no need for further conversation. Night, Sheriff." Jace walked away, heading down the street to Leah's house.

He stepped inside her darkened house. Moonlight spilled into the room from the opened door, illuminating a pile on the floor—a lump of sleeping woman. Jace shook his head and scooped her up, then carried her to her bed.

He disarmed himself at her kitchen table, then stripped and washed up. After arranging his weapons as he had the previous evening, Jace settled in for the night. He folded his arms and crossed his legs, focusing on staying on his side of the bed. Maybe he should sleep on the floor. The thought of a soft woman, with curves like Leah's, sleeping an arm's reach from him was a brutal temptation to break the vow he made himself that long ago night, when he had stared into his wife's eyes as she and her brother had slowly stretched his neck. They needn't have hanged him. If Jenny wanted him dead, he had no use for life anyway.

He closed his eyes and breathed the lemony scent of the woman next to him. He would never again love a woman, no matter how sweet she smelled. No matter how well she could ride, how straight she could shoot, or how good a cook she was. His stomach growled, making him remember the scent of fresh baked bread that had filled the shack this morning.

He rolled onto his side, his back to Leah. This job couldn't be done soon enough.

Leah had a perfect sense of time—an internal clock, her mother had called it.

She always woke at the right hour to get her dough rising so that her customers had fresh bread for their morning breakfast. Usually, once she was awake, she was awake for the day—there was no going back to sleep for her. But this morning was different. She was snuggled up against the hard chest of a man, her head on his arm, his other arm wrapped around her back, her legs twined with his.

She was warm in the cool morning air and wanted to doze a bit longer.

And that realization yanked her out of her dreamy state.

Jace Gage! Her eyes flew open, but she didn't move the rest of her body, did not want to give him any clue that she was up. What was she doing in her bed? She'd gone to sleep on the floor. How could she have slept through being moved? What else had she slept through?

Remembering his reaction yesterday when she had startled him awake, she didn't want to repeat that disaster. She eased herself away from his body, careful not to jostle him. She slowly scooted to the end of the bed, watching him warily the whole while. She climbed over his feet and slipped off the mattress. Only then did she allow herself to draw a full breath.

She made a mental check of her body, but she couldn't tell if he had taken liberties while she slept. She didn't feel anything beyond the bruises Kemp's men had left her with a few nights ago. She glared down at Jace, her hands on her hips. She was sorely tempted to wake him and give him a piece of her mind.

No sooner had that thought crossed her mind than Jace lurched forward and grabbed her. She landed on her back on the bed, her wrists in his steely grip, his body half on hers. Her mind struggled to catch up to her changed circumstances.

Instinctively, she fought his hold on her, bucking and writhing beneath him, determined to dislodge him. His grip on her wrists kept her from reaching for her knife or his gun. She lurched forward to bite his ear, fighting him with all the raw skill Joseph had shown her to use.

"Stop it!" He pulled back. "Damn it, Leah, stop it! What the hell were you doing, looming over me like that? I might have shot you." He blinked, as if just coming fully awake himself. "You gotta quit spooking me, woman!"

"Why did you move me into this bed last night?" she asked through clenched teeth, still resisting him.

"Was there another bed you wanted to sleep in?"

"If you had left me on the floor, I could have gotten up without disturbing you."

"But leaving you on the floor while I slept in your bed was already disturbing to me." He bent to brush a kiss over her neck. She gasped at the shocking feel of his moustache on her skin and grew still, becoming aware of other things about him. His chest was bare. She could smell his skin, a musk of leather and man, a strangely pleasing scent. He wore only his underdrawers—and she only her nightgown and pantalets. He lay half on her, his thigh across hers. Her breasts were crushed between their bodies. She was breathing heavily from the exertion of resisting his hold, and the friction pressed her hardened nipples against him. The blankets were wedged in a painful ridge at her hip. She shifted her position and quickly realized the blankets were at the foot of the bed. That could only mean . . .

She stopped breathing, stopped all movement.

He was heavily aroused, and she didn't know what might send him over the edge. His moustache moved across the center of her throat, against the soft underside of her chin. Unable to hold her breath a moment longer, she released it and sucked in a deep breath, which pressed her throat against his face. She felt light-headed and was glad to be lying down. No, no she wasn't! she quickly corrected herself. Her heart beat rapidly. She fought the rising panic of being trapped within his arms.

He lifted his face, his mouth a whisper from hers. She couldn't stop the involuntary pant that broke from her lips. "You lied to me," she said with her very next breath.

The tension that rippled through him at her words rolled through her own body as well. He grew still. Even in the faint morning light, she could see his expression harden. His nostrils flared.

"When did I lie to you?"

"You said we would not keep this marriage. You said we would not consummate it."

"We haven't consummated it."

"Then why are you lying on me? Kissing me?"

He looked at her eyes, then let his gaze sweep over the rest of her face. "Because I like the way you feel. And I like the way you smell. And I love the way you taste," he said, his lips a breath away from hers.

She was tempted to touch her mouth to his, to feel what she had the night he stood at her door and kissed her, before her life had taken such a wrong turn.

"I don't like kissing."

A slow grin spread across his mouth, though his eyes didn't soften. In fact, the look he gave her poured heat through her veins like sips of brandy, warm and tingly.

"You don't like kissing," he repeated. "Now who's lying?"

"Men can't simply kiss. They're slaves to their baser urges."

"Are we? Slaves? Mm-Hmm." He bent his head, nibbled at the line of her jaw. "I could make love to you every night for the next month and still leave our marriage unconsummated."

She considered that for a moment, worried he might try. The heat that had seeped down to her toes, doubled back up into her face. Without Wolf, or her knife, or strength equal to his, she fought back with the only weapon left to her: words.

She tugged at her wrists. "Would you leave your bruises on me, too, like Kemp's men?"

His hold loosened some, but not enough for her to break free. "Honey, don't play me. You know I wouldn't hurt you."

"How can I know that? I'd never even heard of you three weeks ago. I know nothing about you."

"You know about all of my scars."

"Not all of them, I don't think. I don't know why you do what you do. No sane man would take a job like yours."

He regarded her for a long, silent moment. "I never claimed to be sane. And now, *Mrs. Gage*, I figure you got two choices. You can lie here and let me make love to you, or you can get out of bed and start your day. Your choice. But either way, I'm done talking."

"Then let me up." When he sat up, she scooted off the bed. Blood thundered through her body. She had an overwhelming urge to run, to light out of the house in a full-out charge as she did sometimes when she was on the hunt. Except now she was the hunted.

And her hunter lived with her in her cage.

Chapter 15

Maddie showed up promptly at 7:00 a.m. to walk with Leah on her rounds to deliver her bread a few days later. She had only three main customers left; Maddie, the Kesslers, and Sam's. Sam was her largest account, since all of Kemp's men tended to congregate there for their two meals a day. Perhaps even that account would be cutting back soon. The number of men in Sheriff Kemp's gang was rapidly dwindling as Jace staked his claim on the town. The sheriff had lost six men in just the attack on her.

Involuntarily, she angled her jaw back and forth, testing its soreness today. Memories rose violently within her, like a hot summer wind, threatening to suck the life from her. Jace, the very man she was married to, had dispatched four men in less than that number of minutes. God, she had married a killer, the worst in the whole lot of the men in town—the very thing her mother had warned her against. A chill scraped down her spine, followed immediately by a wave of cold, clammy panic. She was glad they had finished their deliveries, for she suddenly was nauseous.

"Leah? Are you feeling well? You're looking a bit pale, dear." Maddie frowned at her, pulling her out of her wretched thoughts. They were back at Maddie's now. The older woman took hold of her arm and dragged her inside the kitchen for a glass of the cold tea she'd had chilling overnight.

"How are you and Jace getting along?"

Leah sighed. Maddie, who had been her mother's closest friend and was now the nearest thing Leah herself had to a mother, would not let this go. She shrugged.

"Good enough, I guess. It's no marriage at all, though. He's never home, he doesn't take meals with me. He comes in after I'm asleep and leaves when I make my deliveries. I don't know where he goes. I don't know what he does. I don't care. We're not keeping the marriage. When he takes the sheriff to Cheyenne, he'll be filing for a divorce."

Maddie's face settled into a frown. "Does he think you'll be any safer then, when he's gone and Defiance is left once again without any law, a big, vacant town waiting for the next band of thieves to move in?"

"Neither of us wants this marriage. We were forced into it. And Jace isn't the 'law.' He's only another hired gun, worse really—he's a vigilante."

Maddie brushed that argument aside. "He's a vigilante working for the law. That's close enough. Have you consummated your marriage yet?"

Leah gave the older woman a steely glare, wishing the heat in her face didn't reveal her continued innocence. She had lived by her own rules long enough to have a healthy dislike for anyone meddling into her life. "No. And we're not going to because we're not keeping the marriage."

"Maybe you ought to keep it."

"Maddie! He kills people for a living. He holds himself above the law."

"Honey, there is no law out here. Soon, I hope there will be. But right now, we're all on our own. He's man enough to protect you—and gentleman enough not to press his advantage over you. And his friends are decent men, too—Julian and Sager. You could do a lot worse than sticking with Jace Gage—like living alone for the rest of your life."

Tears distorted Leah's vision. "I'm not keeping my marriage, Maddie. I promised my mother. She was dying and I promised her."

Maddie's face hardened. "Promised her what, Leah?"

"She made me swear that I wouldn't marry a gunfighter. But I did. I broke that promise. I'm not keeping Jace."

Maddie looked away, as if she were battling demons of her own. "Your mother had no right to make you give that vow. Your views on men were already skewed the wrong way." She got up from the table and started clearing dishes, her movements jerky with anger. "You make a big argument for law and order, Leah, but you don't live within society's rules for young girls. You never have. You can't have it both ways. Life isn't always black and white. Sometimes it's gray. Sometimes you have to go with gray because that's all there is."

Leah got up and helped clear the remaining few dishes from the table. "Are you saying I have to settle for Jace because he's the only man who will have me?"

Maddie grasped her shoulders, forcing Leah to look at her. "No. I'm saying Jace *is* the right man for you."

Leah thought about that conversation a short while later as she gathered up her week's laundry. She looked at Jace's saddlebags, trying to decide if she should wash his clothes too. Instead, she stripped the bed and remade it with fresh sheets, resisting the domestic intimacy that doing his laundry implied. She bent and gathered up the pile of dirty linens and started to walk out the back door, but got no farther than the corner by her dresser where his gear sat. She put the laundry down and knelt before his packs. She kept her hands in her lap as she stared at the scarred leather, wondering about the stranger she'd married, a man who carried on his horse everything he owned. He had no roots, no future. Even a marriage wasn't enough to bind him to a place. Or a woman.

She reached forward and opened one side of his saddlebags. It held various packs, bundles, and rolls, but no clothes. She opened the other side and pulled out a pair of denims, several underdrawers, a pair of long johns, some undershirts, and a couple of shirts. As she lifted the clothes out, something dropped to the floor. A picture. It was mounted in a heavy cardboard folder. The crease was so worn that the front flap was attached to the half with the picture in only two frayed spots. The photograph it held was breathtaking—a beautiful woman looked back at Leah. It was a close-up shot showing her face and neck in an oval cameo. She wondered what color the woman's eyes were in real life.

She must have been Jace's wife. The woman who had hanged him. The woman he loved still. He'd nearly worn the cardboard out, opening it to look at her. What had happened to her? Was she still alive? Had he divorced her as he would Leah? She set the picture back in his pack. Taking up his clothes with hers, she tried to put the first Mrs. Gage out of her mind. Whatever had happened, it wasn't her business.

Pinning the last piece of clothing to the line a short while later, Leah lifted her face to the morning sun, loving its heat. The weather hinted at a perfect day—warm and dry, with a slight breeze. How she wished she could spend it on a long walk in the mountains or an extended ride on Blink.

"Well, I never expected to see you mooning over my unmentionables." Jace's voice cut through her reverie. Focusing again on the line of drying clothes, she realized her hands gripped a pair of his underdrawers, and her cheek was resting against his waistband.

She sent him a glare and caught up her laundry basket. "Shouldn't you be out killing people?"

"Sadly, the streets are empty of anyone worth shooting. I came to see if you wanted to go fishing. Maddie offered us a fish fry this evening—if we bring the fish." His grin was hesitant. His smiles never quite reached his eyes, but they always caught at her heart. "And since I'd like to eat tonight, I thought I'd better bring you with me. She said you know the perfect fishing hole."

"I do." Leah couldn't help returning his smile. "I'll get my gear while you get the horses."

"They're already out front waiting." He stopped her as she hurried toward the house. "Bring your rifle and hunting gear, some food supplies and your bedroll."

She gave him a dark look. "Why? What's happening?"

"Nothing that I'm expecting. But it's what you don't expect that always gets you."

Leah stored her gear in an orderly fashion out of habit, and she was grateful now for how quickly she could load her packs and meet Gage out front.

Blink had none of the wild-eyed look he usually had when she first took him out of Maddie's stable. In fact, his coat was damp and his head drooped a bit. She situated her gear, tying her worn rifle scabbard off the side of her saddle, then her fishing rod over that. Gage looked edgy. She held her questions and mounted without further discussion. Blink followed her guidance as sedately as an old lap dog.

"What did you do to him, Gage?"

"He and I came to an agreement about the proper way to escort a lady from town."

"I liked his fire."

"But I didn't. And since I don't know what we're

riding into, I thought we'd be better off with you in control of him rather than lettin' him run you."

They rode in silence for a couple of miles, moving at a gentle trot into the wide open range. There was no cover to be had, other than a few scrappy sage bushes and the gentle swell of a hill, here and there. Gage slouched comfortably in his saddle, but his posture didn't fool her.

"Why have I brought my gear? What's going on, Gage?"

"I have to meet someone up at Meeker's Pass. If I don't come back, you get yourself up to the mountain and stay hid. I'll find you. Or McCaid and Sager will. One of us will come for you."

Leah looked away. They were approaching the river. A short distance to the west would bring them to a small lake that pooled in the rising contours of the land. Further west were the rich forests of the Medicine Bow mountain range. A shiver rippled through her as her soul heard the call of the freedom it craved. She could run while he was gone, but she knew she wouldn't. She had to stay and fight for Defiance.

She looked at her temporary husband, who watched her with a steady, emotionless regard. She had the uncanny feeling he could read her thoughts. She turned away, severing their connection. "The lake is this way."

When they reached the lake in the foothills, she settled her gear in her favorite spot, then led Blink over to a patch of grass and ground and tethered him. Gage did not dismount. He wasn't staying.

"Load the rifle and keep it near you, Leah," he ordered her.

Anger began to simmer along the edges of her nerves.

She slipped the gun from its scabbard and loaded several cartridges in it, then slung the strap over her head so that it rested across her shoulders.

"This, Jace Gage, is why my mother warned me to never, ever marry a gunfighter." Jace had been scanning the surrounding woods. She felt his gaze settle on her, saw a muscle working in his jaw.

"Don't worry. We won't be married for much longer. I'm going to check the area out, and then I have a rendezvous with the marshal's man at the pass. Take this." He handed her a covered basket. "Maddie packed us a lunch."

She took the basket and set it aside. She didn't look back as Gage rode away. Glancing across the shimmering surface of the lake, she watched the bugs busy at the surface and the ripples caused by the fish stalking them. She regretted the day could not simply be about fish and sun and the warm summer breeze.

She wondered if she would ever again have such a day.

Jace rode east for a distance before cresting a hill and approaching the pass. He was fairly confident Kemp would have no more than one or two sentries posted. After the men Jace had shot or run off last time he was up here, and then the attack on

Leah, Kemp couldn't spare much of a crew to man the pass.

He passed the protected alcove carved by wind where Kemp's men kept their mounts. Only one horse was tethered there by the half full trough, which confirmed Jace's suspicions. He tied his horse a little further down, then shouldered his rifle and climbed upwards, making his way slowly over the boulders toward the front of the pass. One ledge stood the highest, offering the greatest vantage point. It was there he expected to find the sentry, and he wasn't disappointed.

The man stood with his rifle leaning across his arm, watching to the southeast—a safe choice, given that Defiance was behind him. The air that had been a breeze below became a wind up on the high ground. It whined as it wound around the boulders and scrub pines, loud enough to camouflage Jace's approach. He moved up behind the rock the guard leaned on, drew his pistol, and cocked it a frightening few inches behind the man's head.

"Put the rifle down and drop your gunbelt," Jace ordered. The man turned around, his rifle still in hand. Jace tensed.

"Mr. Gage?"

"Eddie?"

The boy shut his eyes and released a long breath. "Here, take these." He held out his rifle with one hand and started to unbuckle his holster with the other.

"Set 'em down, then move over this way. Who else is here?"

"No one. Just me." Eddie set the rifle down and put his gunbelt next to it. Jace kept his pistol on him until he moved away from the weapons. "The sheriff will kill me if he learns I didn't shoot you."

"I gave you the chance to leave, Eddie. Why are you still here?"

"The sheriff was killing any man who said he was done, anyone who tried to leave. I couldn't go. He needed a sentry at the pass, so I volunteered. Thought I'd be safe here, outta the way."

"No one's stopping you now. Get on your horse and go."

The boy shook his head. Fear was carved into his features. "I can't. He's got men in Cheyenne, men everywhere. He'll find me and kill me—or worse, he'll send someone after my parents and my sister."

"I'm meeting one of the marshal's deputies. How about I send you to Cheyenne with him? They could hold you until this mess is over, then I'll come for you."

"What about my folks? Someone's got to warn them." He shook his head and shoved his hands in his pockets. "I sure let them down. I didn't mean to get caught up in all of this. I got tired of the ranch work. I just wanted a beer at Sam's, and now I'm in it up to my neck."

Dust rose from the road over to the south. A rider was moving in at a fast clip toward the pass, only a few miles away. Didn't look as if anyone was on his trail. "Well, you got two choices, I guess. You can go with the marshal's man to Cheyenne, or you can go home and protect your folks. It's up to you."

"I'll go home. If my dad doesn't kill me, I'll stay put and guard them."

Jace smiled and put a hand on the boy's shoulder. "I've got a friend who owns a ranch north of town. You and your folks could go up there to wait this out."

"They won't go. They won't leave the spread. They settled that land before my sister and I were born. It means more to them than we do, I think. And we got livestock to care for. No, we'll stay and fight if we have to."

Jace buckled Eddie's gunbelt and slipped it across his shoulder, then picked up his rifle. "Stay up here—keep out of sight. I've got to talk to the marshal's man. I left Leah at the lake. When I'm done here, we'll fetch her and see you home."

The boy held out his hand. "Thanks, Mr. Gage. I won't mess this up."

Jace moved down through the levels of boulders to stand at the entrance to the pass. The wind brought the rider's dust in ahead of him. He pulled up a few feet from Jace, but did not dismount.

"Gage."

Jace nodded, returning the greeting. "Lambert."

"Good to see you're still standing. They've got bets on you in Cheyenne."

"That so? Where's your money settin'?"

Lambert grinned, but didn't answer. "The shipment's on. You got about a week to get things under control here."

"They will be," Jace assured him.

He looked beyond Jace, down the long chute of

the pass, lit now by the midday sun. Jace followed his gaze. The road was barely wide enough for a wagon or carriage to move through. The walls were twenty feet high in places. Not a comfortable place for a wary man to have to ride—or stand.

A shadow spilled over the side of the canyon wall. Both men looked up. "Mr. Gage! That ain't—" Eddie started, but never finished his sentence, for a gunshot shattered the quiet. The sound exploded through the pass, bouncing and magnifying as it hit the rock walls. Eddie clutched his chest and fell forward, into the pass. Jace tried to break his fall. "Ah, Christ! Eddie?"

The boy grabbed the edge of one of Jace's bandoliers. His jaw moved, but only a hiss of breath came out. Jace leaned forward to hear him.

"You lied," Eddie rasped with his last breath.

Jace looked up at the marshal's man, who was holstering his gun. "What the hell did you shoot him for?"

"I thought he was gonna draw. Ain't it you who's always saying better a dead enemy?"

Jace took one stride over to Lambert's horse and yanked the man from his saddle. A sharp cross to the temple left him dazed enough for Jace to push him up against the nearest boulder. "Who are you workin' for? I gotta wonder, 'cause that ain't behavior the marshal would condone."

Lambert raised his hands, indicating his now-peaceful intentions. "Just giving you a hand, friend. Thought you'd appreciate having one less bastard to deal with."

"That's not the kind of help I need." Jace clenched

his teeth and spoke with his face shoved close to Lambert's. "Nor is it the way I handle things. He wasn't armed. I have his weapons." He released the man, but still gave him a hard glare. "I'll tell you what. You head back to Cheyenne, gather up your things, and hightail it outta town. If you're still there when I get back, I'll have you arrested for this boy's cold-blooded murder."

"That's not going to happen, Cage. This is war. Like when you killed your wife. You say anything about this, and I'll make it real clear how that all went down three years ago." Lambert moved around Jace and went back to his horse. "You better get your thinking clear, otherwise the marshal's gonna think you threw in with the sheriff, that you've developed a taste for killing. Which you have. Wouldn't take much to convince him you're a liability.

"I made a call here. It was the wrong one. So what? I couldn't tell he didn't have his gun on him." He mounted up, touched the brim of his hat, and rode out, leaving Jace with the wind and the dead kid in the hot redstone canyon.

Jace slid to his haunches against the rock wall, trying to breathe, struggling to make sense out of what had just happened. How had Lambert known about Jenny?

There was only one way. Rupert Hardin. Jace cursed. The bastard had been one of the few Rebels to survive the skirmish that day, when Jenny had died. He'd been taken to Elmira Prison Camp. When he'd killed one of the guards, he'd been moved to a different prison, and Jace had lost track of him. But he had to be out now. And the man was clearly gunning for him.

Jace watched the crisp, blue shadow creep toward him from the base of the opposite canyon wall. His mind was numb. After a while, he lifted Eddie's body over his shoulder and climbed up the rocks to their horses. He tied Eddie to his horse, then made his way back to Leah, moving slowly through the woods of the ridge.

"You lied." Eddie's accusation haunted Jace. His word was all he had left.

And it wasn't enough anymore.

He followed the winding line of cottonwoods up river to the pool where Leah liked to fish, wondering if she'd heard the gunshot, wondering how the hell he was going to explain all the blood on him. Eddie was well-known and liked in town. Jace didn't need to guess whether she would mourn his loss. She mourned all the losses in town, even the deaths of Kemp's thugs.

Dismounting, he led his horse and the one carrying Eddie's body into the thin woods that shaded the lake, tying them away from her horse. He'd take Leah home, then come back for the boy and bring him out to his family. They deserved to know what had happened to him. No sense causing her more pain by letting her see Eddie's body, he thought as he pulled Eddie off the horse and laid him on the ground nearby.

Jace walked toward the lake, needing to see Leah with an urgency he was helpless to explain, a need as elemental as breathing. The running water and the breeze in the trees should have muffled the gunshot. Hopefully she wouldn't have been spooked. Hopefully she was still here.

He cleared the woods and saw her, standing in the cold lake, bootless, her pants turned up at the calf. She'd discarded her rifle, leaving it next to the picnic basket, whose items were scattered across a corner of a blanket.

Sun glinted off the crown of her head, sparking red highlights that glowed like embers in the slim shaft of sunlight cutting through the trees. Briefly, his mind fixed on the discovery that she was the only person he'd met who might be able to show him the way back to a life worth living. He sure as hell didn't know the way. That thought was elusive, imperfectly formed, and lost when she turned to face him.

Her eyes held such joy at seeing him that he sucked in a breath. He knew he was at a decision point. A precipice. Live or die. His fate was in her hands. She'd become his anchor, his tether, tying him to a world he was more than ready to let go of, but had never quit wanting to thrive in. He pulled the knife out of his boot. Kicking off his boots, he never took his eyes from hers. He moved forward, into the circle of sunlight that swam around her.

Her gaze lowered, slipping over the blood staining his bandoliers and clothes. He watched the warmth in her eyes drain away, chased by the revulsion that twisted her features. She stepped back. He reached for her. She drew back further, a hand covering her mouth.

No. It's me, he silently urged, words he was too

much a coward to speak aloud. *See me, the man behind these guns, behind this blood. Please.*

She stumbled away from him, her movements ripping apart the hope he'd begun to feel. He turned back, seeing the picnic basket through waves of moisture he could not blink from his eyes. He looked down at the stains he wore, the blood of her friend. *"You lied."* Eddie's voice condemned him.

In a fury, Jace trudged to the shore, jerking the buckle of his gunbelt free and releasing the thongs tying his guns to his legs. He dropped his gunbelt, then yanked the bandoliers over his head. He stumbled into the shallow water, ripping off his gore-encrusted vest. Dropping to his knees, he lifted a fistful of sand and pebbles to scrub against the leather. Over and over, he rubbed at the stains on his vest and in his soul, but could not wash them away.

Leah swiped a tear from her face with the back of her hand. The relief she'd experienced when she'd first seen him now warred with the horror of what he was. It made no sense, what she was feeling. It hurt. When she looked back at him, she saw him stumble into the water, dropping to his knees to scrub his vest. As she watched, he lifted fistfuls of pebbles to scour his thighs, his chest, his face.

Something in her broke.

She went to him and knelt before him. "Jace, stop." He didn't hear her. He switched his feverish attentions back to his vest. "Jace." She touched his forearms. He didn't stop. She pulled at his vest, trying to take it from him. He did look up at her then, his pale blue eyes black with madness. Twin wrinkles were drawn between his dark eyebrows. His cheeks were red and scraped. He yanked the vest from her and tossed it to shore, never once taking his eyes from her.

Her breath came in fast gasps. She reached her hands to cup his scraped cheeks. He grabbed her by her waist and pulled her up against himself. She gripped his upper arms, feeling the tension knotted in the tight cabling of his muscles. He buried his face into the crook of her neck. His breathing was irregular, coming in gasps as if he sobbed. Silently.

"Jace." She wrapped her arms around him, feeling his pain wash through her. "Jace, please. Don't."

His hands pressed her into his face, his fingers splayed wide against her shoulder blades. He moved one hand up to cup the back of her head, threading his fingers into her hair, immobilizing her. Possessing her. He rubbed his face against her throat, back and again. She was aware of the scrape of his moustache, then his teeth, then his tongue. A heat took root between their bodies, cocooning them from the effects of the cold water around them.

Leah let her hands move over his back, his wide shoulders. She dug her fingers into his thick, sun-kissed brown hair. His body, so much larger than her own, felt foreign in its size and hardness. He pulled her head back, arching her neck, baring her for his explorations. His mouth opened over the center of her throat, his tongue licking its peaks and curves, as if he would feast on her. He sat back, dragging her with him, spreading her astride his lap.

He possessed her body completely, one hand at the small of her back, pressing her against his lap, the other gripping the back of her head, directing her movements. His mouth was at the soft underside of her chin. She pressed her face against his temple, breathing his scent, feeling the ridge of his brow with the corner of her mouth. She kissed him there.

He began pumping her hips against his, lifting her, then pushing her down, slowly, against the hard shaft of his erection. A pressure swelled low in her belly. His mouth took the edge of her jaw, like a soldier claims a ridge in battle. Triumphantly. Her lips parted. She brushed her lips against the hollow of his cheek, hungering for him to match his mouth to hers. Her arms tightened over his shoulders. She watched his face, wishing he would look at her, but his eyes were closed.

And then he took her mouth, tilting his head at an angle to hers. His jaw opened, forcing hers to do the same. His tongue entered her mouth in a slow, sweet arc. She surrendered herself to him, in all ways, body and soul. She ceased being aware of where her body ended and his began. She caught the rhythm he gave her, hips to hips, mouth to mouth, tongue to tongue. Her bones were like half-baked bread, soft, pliable, expanding. Becoming something else, something the man in her arms was the key to. She was in a place where only feeling existed, no thoughts, no fear, just heat melting her body, spanning outward from the area between her hips. She rubbed herself against him, meeting his thrusts. Their feverish motions made waves in the shallow water. She broke her mouth from his to kiss his cheek, the corner of his jaw.

"Leah," Jace rasped. "Ah, Christ, Leah."

Leah opened her eyes, looking unseeingly at the bank behind Jace, grasping for a hold on reality. A spasm ripped through her from the place where her hips met his. She was helpless to stop it. Her gaze came to rest on the blanket and his bloodied bandoliers. She pushed away from him, but he held her hips against his.

"Jace. No."

"Please. Please, Leah."

And then nothing mattered, for the thing that was happening to her exploded within her. She bucked and rocked and slammed against him, her entire body owned by the spasms that rode her. When she came back to herself, little tremors still slipped through her. She grasped fistfuls of his wet shirt, pushing against his shoulders, her elbows locked straight.

He was looking at her mouth, his eyes unfocused. Slowly his gaze lifted, meeting her eyes. Some emotion she couldn't recognize washed over him. He shoved her from him as he scooted back away from her. He rose from the water, stumbling backward. At the bank he turned and went to the blanket. He jammed his feet into his boots, even as water still drained from him. He yanked his bandoliers over his head, settling them across his wet, half opened shirt. He picked up his gunbelt and buckled it around his hips, bending to tie the thongs about his thighs. He shoved his knife back into the sheath in his boot, checked that the derringer was still in one of his bandoliers, grabbed his vest, then strode with swift angry steps through the towering cottonwoods to the place where he'd tied his horse.

Leah lifted a shaky hand up to brush her hair from her face. She still sat on her rump where she'd landed when he pushed her from him. The cold temperature of the river eased the heat radiating from inside her body. She folded her knees and dropped her forehead on them, her mind a whirl.

Never before had she been so out of control of her own body. The feeling was frightening. And thrilling. Her heart was racing.

Eventually, she moved out of the river. Kneeling on the blanket, she put Maddie's dishes back into her basket. Jace had left a sock behind. She folded it into the blanket. Putting her own socks and boots back on, she pushed the cuffs of her pants back down, then fetched her horse and went about securing her gear, the picnic basket, and basket of fish to her saddle. She mounted up and turned toward town.

Clearing the woods, she saw Jace atop his horse, standing at the ridge, facing Defiance. She was in no hurry to catch up with him. Her heart still beat with an unnatural speed. She did not pause as she drew even with him, did not look at him.

He started down the hill as he fell into pace beside her. Neither looked at the other. "Do you know where Eddie's family lives?" he asked before they had gone far. The wind might have stolen his words, but for the steely determination in them.

She did look at him then. He looked raw, heathen, with his soiled white shirt opened beneath his bandoliers. His vest, perhaps ruined now, was crumpled across his lap. "Why?" What business did he have with the Perkins? She was glad he'd run Eddie off the first morning he was in town. It was one less person she had to worry about. But perhaps Eddie hadn't left. Maybe Jace had seen him in town again.

"There's something I gotta do after I get you back to town."

It was hours later that Jace returned to town. He got his horse settled for the evening, then shouldered his saddlebags and took up his bedroll. Maddie and Leah were in Maddie's kitchen—he could hear them as he passed by the open door. Their chatter was light. Ordinary. So different from the conversation he'd just had with Mr. and Mrs. Perkins when he'd brought their dead son home to them. Leah was setting the table, her back to him. But Maddie saw him and came hurrying outside. He shouldn't have paused, but he did.

"You clean up and come on back now, Jace."

"Not tonight, Maddie."

Her lips thinned and she clutched her apron, then stormed down the steps and confronted him, every bit an angry hen. "I didn't spend all day cooking for my own delight."

"Maddie—I'm not fit company."

She set her hands on her ample hips and looked him in the eye. "Jace Gage, you married my best friend's daughter. Now her mama's not here to give you what for, but I am." She studied him, as she searched for the right words from the many clustered in her mouth. "You do look like you've had a hell of a day, but you need to know that there's no burden that's too heavy for a group of friends to help you carry."

"This one is."

"Clean up and come back. You don't have to talk. You don't have to be entertaining. We just want you with us."

Jace moved around her and headed to Leah's house. He stripped and scrubbed himself, then ducked his head in the bucket of cold water Leah had left for him. Even holding his breath as long as he could, he couldn't purge Mrs. Perkins's keening wails from his mind. Or the image of Mr. Perkins punching the porch support, again and again, until his knuckles bled. It was no comfort at all to them to learn their boy had decided to come home when the marshal's man mistakenly thought he was armed and shot him.

But it had been no mistake. Eddie was warning Jace about something—something Lambert didn't want him to hear.

He ducked his head into the water again, his arms encircling the bucket, his fingers digging into the wooden ridges of the bucket's side. His lungs began to burn. He wondered if a person could will himself to die. But he couldn't even do that right.

He broke free, gasping for breath before he'd fully cleared the line of water, choking and coughing.

Leah had set his folded, clean clothes on the bed. He dressed, then shoved the rest of the clothes back into his bag. The memories came flooding back, overlapping with his disgrace from today as his mind replayed his pleading with Leah to stay, to be with him. He had begged his wife, too. Not to let him live, but to kill him by her own hand. Instead, her real husband had placed the noose about his neck. He'd yanked the rope to draw it tight. But Jenny did step forward then, holding the rope taut while her husband pummeled his stomach.

Jace had stared at her, seeking a clue as to how the devil could hide in the guise of an angel. His angel. The woman he'd pledged his heart and life to, the woman he'd hoped to make a home with when the goddamned war ended. She drew harder on the rope, stretching his neck by inches. Her brother, Rupert, stood behind her, drawing the slack tight, taking Jace's weight, helping her kill him. He could barely breathe for the beating he was receiving. Blood thundered in his ears. His heart fought to live though his soul was already dead.

Jenny had used him to spy on his unit, which skirmished daily with the raiders of her real husband's unit. She'd lain beneath him, gasping with passion, hating him the whole while when he could sneak away to meet with her. Until that last, fateful time when his enemies had been all around her, and they'd strung him up.

And then Sager and Julian were there, but he couldn't hear the gunfire, couldn't see what was

happening for the black shadows darkening his
vision. Sager cut him free and put a Colt in his
hands. He was on all fours, coughing and gagging,
sucking sweet air into his lungs, the metal of the
gun barrel digging into his palm. When he looked
up, Jenny had a rifle in her hands and a bead on
McCaid. He remembered lifting his hand, thumb-
ing the hammer—and nothing else.

Dinner that night at Maddie's was exceedingly
uncomfortable, Leah thought. Maddie had invited
the Kesslers to join them. Malcolm would be along
once he'd closed up the store. These people had
been a part of her world most of her life, and yet
tonight she was out of step with them. Her mind
kept revisiting what had happened at the river,
making it impossible for her to concentrate on the
conversation around the table.

Jace stepped through Maddie's side door, silenc-
ing the friendly chatter in the room. He wore a
clean shirt and pants. And though he had left off
his bandoliers and vest, his gunbelt was strapped
around his hips. The air of a remorseless killer was
about him tonight. His movements were edgy. He
hung his hat on a peg by the door and, taking a seat
next to Jim, nodded at the Kesslers and Maddie. He
ignored her. It was just as well. She couldn't have
formed a coherent sentence around the tightness
choking her throat. She tore her gaze away from
him, deciding to pretend he wasn't there.

It didn't help that he was wrapped in the same
silence that held her. He didn't look at anyone and

barely touched his food. His cheeks were scraped where he'd scrubbed at them in the river. Whose blood had he had on him earlier? And why, why had he held her the way he did in the lake?

She was relieved when Malcolm blew in through the kitchen door, full of noise and energy. "It sure smells good in here, Maddie! I could eat a horse!"

Maddie retrieved his plate from where it had been warming on the stove. He broke a roll in half and stuffed it into his mouth before he'd even settled at the table.

"Sorry I'm so late. Some of Kemp's boys came in as I was locking up. We got to talking, and I lost track of the time."

Sally reached over and patted his arm. "There's no rush to talk and eat, dear. Go slowly—with both—else you'll choke!" She and Maddie exchanged a smile. Leah swallowed against the tightness in her throat. Since her own mother's death last winter, these two women had become her mothers, as they were to Audrey and Malcolm and grandmothers to Audrey's orphans.

Malcolm chewed and swallowed, then took a long drink of water. "The sheriff lost his sentry out at Meeker's Pass." Leah's heart started a wretched beating that left her breathless. Jace stared at Malcolm. "Said there was blood everywhere, but no sign of the guard. He and his horse were both gone!" Sally pressed her hand to her throat.

"Now, Malcolm," Jim warned. "That isn't a fitting story for the women—"

"The sentry was Eddie," Malcolm interrupted him. Like a wave of water rushing down a drain, all eyes turned to Jace. She could read his guilt in the dark flush that colored his face.

"No! Oh, no! Why, Mr. Gage? Why did you shoot him? He was only a boy!" Sally asked, unable to hide the catch in her voice.

Jace dropped his gaze to his plate for the space of a breath, then pushed away from the table, grabbed his hat from a hook by the door and stalked out of the kitchen into the day's fading light.

Leah was stunned. The room fell silent. Malcolm looked from person to person, understanding dawning in his face. "Oh! No! I didn't know Gage was out that way. I thought Kemp's boys were turning on each other. Leah, you know Gage wouldn't shoot unless someone drew on him."

Leah swallowed hard. Her hands were shaking. "Do I know that?" She glanced around the table at the faces of the people she loved and trusted. "How can I know that? What do we really know about him?"

Jim folded his napkin and set it on the table. "You learn to judge a man when you live where we do. You have to. Gage is a good man."

Leah shook her head. "I fear I'm no judge of character."

"It isn't an easy thing. Your mother was no judge either." Sally fidgeted with her silverware.

Leah caught the look that flew between Maddie and Jim. She looked at Malcolm, but he only gave a slight lift of his shoulders, as much at a loss as she was. "What do you mean, Sally?" she asked.

Maddie stood and started pulling dishes together from around the table. "There's no need to open painful topics. Your mother, God rest her soul, did the best that she could."

Sally nodded. "You're right, of course. I meant no harm, Leah. Your mother was a passionate woman. She made the only choices she could make, I suppose."

Leah lay awake late into the night, wondering if Jace would come back, now that everything between them had changed. She remembered the blood that had dried on him, the mark of his trade, and wondered if she even wanted him to return when he was everything her mother had warned her against.

Remembering Sally's comments earlier, she thought about what her mother's life had been like. She'd seen it from the eyes of a child, but not the perspective of an adult. What was it that the others knew about her mother that she didn't? Her mother had been devoted to her father. She fussed about him at mealtime, mended his clothes, kept the house just so for him. But was that love? And what of the terrible things the sheriff had done to her the two times she and her mother had tried to leave town? Or all the times she had come home from hunting to find her mother bruised and sore from one mishap or another. Had the sheriff been responsible for that as well? Had her mother once held a flame for Kemp?

That thought was incomprehensible. The man was a beast, and her mother was far too much a lady to succumb to the likes of him. No, she doubted

Sally's comment about her mother's passionate nature. She'd never remarried after Leah's father died. *"Promise me, Leah, promise you will never love a gunfighter."* There had been plenty of men interested in her mother, though none of them stayed around very long. The sheriff had some strange claim on her. He kept anyone who might have been interested in courting her at bay. It would have been a blessing had her mother found another husband to take them away from Defiance. But none of the men in town had been strong enough to face the sheriff.

Leah shoved the sheet from her, rolling over to find a cooler section of the bed. There was no breeze, and the day's heat was trapped in the little house.

Would Jace come home? Would he stay at Maddie's? What was it he'd done to her at the river today? He had taken over her body, turned her bones to molten liquid that burned for his touch. His touch alone. No other man had ever caused her to feel that wild abandon. Was this why her mother had warned her away from gunfighters? Or could all men do what he'd done to her today?

Leah tossed and turned for a long while, until exhaustion overwhelmed her. When she woke in the morning, she patted Jace's side of the bed, her eyes still heavy with sleep. He wasn't there. Bitter disappointment washed through her. She sat up abruptly, leaning over the bed to see if he slept on the floor. He did! He had come home! He lay on his bedroll, his hat on his head.

Quietly, she slipped out of bed, feeling unaccountably relieved to see him. It made no sense. He was a killer. He'd offered no excuses, no apologies for killing Eddie yesterday. But she'd seen how it had affected him.

If only he weren't a gunfighter, they might have found a way of making a life together.

That thought brought her up short. She stepped away from him, fearing he might sense her presence and wake up. She wanted to wash and dress while he still slept. She'd laid her clothes out the night before so that she could dress quickly in the morning. She filled the bowl with water from the pitcher for her morning ablutions. After assuring herself that he still slept, she slipped out of her nightgown, camisole, and drawers. With the summer's heat having finally come in, she regretted not being able to sleep only in her camisole and drawers. But with Jace in the house, she'd wanted the extra layer her nightgown afforded her.

She dipped the sponge in the bowl and lathered it with soap, then touched it to her neck, drawing a sharp breath at the water's chill temperature. She drew the wet sponge down, over her breasts, and paused, shocked at the feeling her own touch gave her. It hinted at the heat that Jace had flamed within her yesterday. She cupped her breast with her other hand, feeling her nipple pebble, wishing it was Jace's hand on her, not her own.

A small sound behind her brought her head up quickly. She looked into the mirror to where Jace lay, relieved he still slept. She remembered everything about their embrace in the frigid river water. The feel of his mouth on her throat, the way his hand at the back of her hips had set the motion that brought her such an extraordinary feeling.

Yanking her mind from its salacious thoughts, she quickly finished washing, then dressed, ignoring the yearning that, now awakened, longed to be sated.

Jace was damned, he thought as he watched his wife. He'd hung out at Sam's until that establishment had closed, then made his way here, in no hurry to be locked in such tight confines with his wife. Leah had slept fitfully. Unable to stop himself, he'd touched her hair, wishing things were different between them. He was careful not to wake her—he wanted to avoid more of her condemnation. He'd unfurled his bedroll and positioned it strategically, having learned days ago his wife had an affinity for early morning sponge baths. The perspective he had this morning gave him an unusual advantage: he could also see her mirror image. *Christ.* There were two naked women, stroking themselves, watching their hands move over their nude bodies.

His dick had turned to stone and rested at an uncomfortable angle, but there was nothing he could do to rearrange himself. He couldn't help the strangled breath he drew when she cupped her breasts, testing her own nipples. She'd heard his gasp and quickly looked in his direction. He'd forced himself to regulate his breathing. If she ever discovered he watched her morning ritual, he would never again get to see it.

And watching was all he could hope to get out of this marriage.

Chapter 16

Leah heard someone come through her little picket gate the next evening. It was too early for Jace to come home—he usually stayed at Sam's until the saloon closed. Picking up a hand towel, she hurried to the front window as the front door opened.

Jace. He stepped inside and closed the door, facing her. Neither of them spoke. Leah's hands clenched on the towel she held as waves of conflicting emotions battered her mind. He was a killer. She could not refute the truth of that. Whatever his justification, he'd shot Eddie yesterday. Dead was dead.

Yet she was helpless to explain why she reacted to him as she did. It was not out of fear. She'd never before felt this way with any man. Her fingers tingled as if she yearned to touch him. Her breasts were swollen and achy. Her stomach was fluttery. She was hot and feverish. Breathing was hard. He hung his hat on the peg, pausing a long moment before facing her.

He turned to her, watching her, his jaw tensing

and releasing and tensing again. Her vision narrowed to him and only him. She shook her head, resisting surrendering though she didn't even know what she was resisting. She stepped back. He stepped forward. Slowly, step by step, he gained the ground she lost. She backed into the wall. He stopped an arm's length from her. Her body was on fire, the ache low in her hips painful.

"I-I'm sick, Jace." She didn't look at him as she admitted this weakness.

"What hurts?" His voice, rough and raw, played against her sensitized nerves. She wrapped her arms about her waist.

"Everything. I have a fever."

He palmed her forehead, her temple. "No fever." He lowered his hand to the curve between her neck and shoulder and shook his head. She knew her breathing was dangerously shallow, but she could not take a deep breath.

"I've never felt this way before. I don't know what is wrong with me." She ventured a look at his face. His blue eyes had gone black, his pupils dilated. "I can't explain it. I ache for you. I need you to touch me. I think you are the only one who can ease it." He stepped closer. His thumb caressed her throat. His heat circled her neck, her body. "It hurts, Jace."

"I know." His head lowered to hers. His breath brushed her lips. "It does." Her lips parted as tension coiled low in her belly. "We are not keeping this marriage."

She nodded her agreement. She did not want to

stay married to a gunfighter; she just wanted this agony inside her to stop.

"But I can give you release," he offered.

"Please—" She'd barely gotten that word out before he took her wrist and drew her from the wall. He slipped behind her, pulling her back against himself, a hand at her waist.

"Do you trust me?" His question rasped against her nerves.

Did she trust him? A gunfighter—a murderer?

She couldn't live a minute longer if he didn't put his hands on her body, touch her, possess her. There was only one answer she could give. "Yes."

"Lean against me." He released her wrist and tossed aside the hand towel she gripped, then began to draw her shirt from the waist of her pants. The slow drag of the cotton between her underclothes and pants sent a shiver through her. His lips were at her ear. His teeth raked her earlobe. She drew in a sharp breath and slanted her head to expose her neck to him. He smoothed his hand over the exposed end of her shirt, pressing against her abdomen, then moved slowly up over the buttons, over her ribs, between her breasts, up her chest to her throat, turning her face toward him.

His mouth took hers, his lips closed, his nose against hers. His other hand lowered across her hips, to cup her pubic bone. He ground the heel of his palm against that place Leah had only recently become aware of. Her lips parted on a sharp intake of breath. His jaw opened then as well. He thrust his tongue into her mouth, in and out, against her tongue, over her tongue, under her tongue.

Leah couldn't help the throaty groan that slipped from her. She reached up and wrapped her arm around Jace's neck. With her other hand, she gripped his muscular thigh. And then his hand moved down her body to slip beneath her shirt, beneath her camisole. His palm was hot. Its calloused length dragged along her skin, up, up, so slowly, until he cupped a breast. And then he repeated the gesture, capturing her other breast with his other hand.

This, God, this was what she'd craved this morning when she'd touched herself. He held the twin mounds, easing his thumb and forefingers up to her nipples, rolling the tensed peaks back and forth. Leah wrapped both hands around his neck, her fingers digging into his hair.

"Was this what you wanted, Leah?"

She nodded.

"Say it," he ordered.

Say what? What were the words? "I want this, Jace. I want you."

"Unbutton your shirt and camisole. Let me see you." She reached down to the end of her shirt, which was wrinkled and twisted where his hands reached beneath it. She released the bottom button.

"Start at the top."

She moved to the top buttons, unfastening the line of them before pulling the sides apart to let her shirt hang free. His hands tightened on her breasts, his fists doubled the size of them and showed as dark shadows through the thin cotton material. Swallowing hard, she set to work on the tiny buttons of her camisole until it, too, hung open. And then he moved his hands, massaging her breasts, watching over her shoulder as he moved the mounds in his hands, manipulated her nipples.

"God, you're beautiful," he growled. He took her hands and brought them up to cup herself, then he opened the top of her pants and slipped a hand down inside her drawers. She closed her legs, embarrassed by moisture collecting at the juncture of her legs. "No. Open for me."

"Jace—"

"I've got you, Leah." He held her with an arm about her waist. Even if she'd wanted to, she couldn't have broken free. He began to press against her from behind. She realized his penis was ridged, engorged. He bent his knees and lifted her, fitting himself against her buttocks. "Stand on my feet, Leah."

She spread her legs and stepped atop his boots. He pushed against her, beginning that rhythm he'd used in the river. His fingers moved over her hidden curls into the secret folds beneath.

"Ah! Oh, Jace!" Leah gasped as he stroked her swollen skin. His fingers spread her flesh, moved back and forth, exploring all of her before dipping inside her, deep into the place that craved him, even as his thumb worked that sensitive spot. Leah began matching his movements, pressing against his hips, bucking against his hands. A curious languor stole her will, melted her bones, and made her cling to his steady forearm. Closer and closer, she neared that sensory explosion she'd experienced in the river. Even knowing—this time—that it was coming, she was unprepared for the joy that washed through her when it happened. She threw back her head and cried out his name. She heard him make a low, guttural groan as he held her hips to his, rubbing fast and hard against her buttocks.

Slowly, the world began to right itself. She was panting, still clasped in his arms. She leaned against him, and he leaned against the wall. He took his hand out of her pants, bringing it up to cup a breast as he turned her face for his kiss. It was a gentle kiss, a soft pull of his lips against hers.

"Feel better now?" He smiled a slow, sated smile. The first smile she'd ever seen to touch his eyes.

"Yes. No. I fear the fever will come back." She stroked his arm, worried she might have dug her nails into him. "Did you"—she hesitated, embarrassed to talk about such things—"did you find your release, too?"

She looked up at him in time to catch the flush that darkened his face. He gave a single nod. She pulled away from him, wondering what to do now. She wanted, more than anything, to have him stay with her, hold her.

She looked at the bed, at her own disheveled clothes. "Have you eaten supper? Are you hungry?" He shook his head. She crossed her arms in front of herself. "Jace, will you stay with me tonight, hold me?"

"That ain't a good idea, Leah."

"I don't want to be alone. Not tonight." She looked at him and finally admitted the truth. "Not any night until you leave."

He crossed the room to her. Lifting a hand, he touched the tips of his fingers to her cheeks, stroking. She couldn't begin to understand the bleak look in his eyes. His jaw tensed when he met her eyes. He drew her braid forward over her shoulder and released the tie. Spreading his fingers through the lower folds, he unraveled it, inch by inch. He reached his hands to the base of her skull, dragging her hair through his fingers, pulling it forward over her shoulders. Holding her chin with the pads of his thumbs, he tilted her face up. Stepping nearer, he stared down into her eyes. He breathed her scent as his eyes swept shut, and he brushed his mouth against hers in the lightest of touches.

"I'll stay. Tonight."

Leah drew her shirt and pants off, then folded them and set them on a trunk near the foot of the bed. It was foolish to be shy now, but nonetheless, she fastened the top couple of buttons of her camisole, then climbed into bed and moved to her side.

Jace poured water into the basin, then took his shirt off. Leah quickly looked up at the ceiling to give him privacy as he washed. She listened to him splash about, then a quiet rustling as he drew on fresh drawers.

The bed dipped as he settled on the opposite side. Leah could feel her heart hammering in her chest and almost wondered if he could hear it. For several long moments, neither of them moved. When she turned and looked at him, he did the same, then lifted his arm. She smiled and moved nearer to lie on her side against him. He wore only his drawers. The sheet was drawn across his lap.

She loved the way her body fit against his, she thought as she draped her thigh. She folded one arm over his chest and rested her head on his shoulder, listening to his heart, surprised to hear it beating as fast as her own. She ran her palm over his chest, exploring the feel of his chest hair, the layers of muscles of his lean torso.

Without warning, he lifted her to straddle his hips. The ridge of his erect penis was shockingly stimulating between her legs. She moved her hips, sliding against him. He lifted his hands up her chest, spreading the open sides of her camisole. He unfastened the two buttons, exposing her breasts. He sucked in a sharp breath at the sight of her. He traced the twin mounds with his forefingers, drawing invisible circles around them. Leah's breathing grew unsteady.

He took hold of her ribs, drawing her closer to his face. "Put your tits on my face."

The rough timbre of his voice rumbled through her. She cupped her breasts. "These aren't 'tits', Jace Gage. They're breasts."

"Mm-hmm. Put them on my face."

She leaned forward, settling herself over him. He pressed her to the sides of his face. Turning one way, he kissed the soft side of her breast, his whiskers rasping against her flesh. He turned the other way, kissing his way down to her nipple. Leah sucked in a sharp breath. He took the puckered nub into his mouth and rubbed his tongue against the sensitive peak.

Leah couldn't help the strangled "Oh!" that slipped from her.

He grinned up at her. "I could drown in your tits."

"Breasts."

His grin widened, his teeth compressed one peak as his tongue flicked her nipple. "You call them what you want to call them," he said, speaking around the nipple in his teeth, "and I'll call them what I want."

Releasing her, he slipped her camisole off her shoulders and threw it aside. Holding her now with his arms wrapped around her, he kissed his way up her collarbone to her neck, her jaw, finally capturing her mouth. His mouth slanted against hers, open, hungry, his tongue searching out her tongue. Her hair slipped over his face, curtaining them. His hips rocked between her legs.

Jace groaned and leaned back. "Leah, do you remember I said I could make love to you every night without consummating our vows?"

She nodded.

"I lied." She studied his face. "I want you something god-awful, but I'm not staying here when I finish with the sheriff, and I can't risk leaving you pregnant. We have to stop."

"Jace—" she began to argue.

"Please, Leah."

She touched his cheek. Her body was on fire. She could feel the answering heat in his. If it weren't for the look in his eyes, she would abandon all rational thought and surrender to the sensations ravaging her body.

Slowly, painfully, she straightened. "Will you stay with me tonight?"

He nodded. "I'll stay."

Leah moved over to lie next to him. The night was hot and still, with no breeze. She stared at the ceiling, wishing she knew how one went about calming a body as enflamed as hers.

She wondered if she was flawed. What was it Sally had said at Maddie's? *"Your mother was a passionate woman. She made the only choices she could make."* Passion. That was exactly what she'd felt for Jace. But she hadn't made bad choices—there had been no choices to make. She was forced into this marriage. And they weren't keeping it. She would never hand over her life to a gunfighter.

She turned and looked at Jace. He was staring at the ceiling. "Jace? What happens after you leave Defiance?"

"You get your life back."

"But to you. What do you do?"

He drew a deep breath. "Find a new town to clear, I guess."

"Do you like being a gunfighter?"

"It's what I am."

"Is it? Must it be?"

He turned to look at her. "What are you asking?"

"You could change."

"Into what? A shopkeeper? No," he scoffed.

"You could buy a ranch. You could settle down."

"A man like me doesn't settle down, Leah. My past made my future."

"You could change."

"Can you change? Give up your hunting and

your business and come help me out at a ranch?
Put on a dress and act like a woman?"

She rolled over, contemplating his question.

After a long moment, he sighed. "We are what
we are, Leah."

Chapter 17

Jace watched the shadowy shape of Leah's house as he walked home. It was late—late enough for her to be asleep, though not so late that he wasted time sitting at the saloon that he could have spent holding her in his arms.

Home. It was a strange thought, foreign even. He'd hoped for a home once, with Jenny. But that dream had been ripped from him these many years, wiped from his mind, gone so completely that he hadn't given it another thought. Until now.

Leah had asked if he would change. And change he must if he was ever to settle down. Perhaps he could become a sheriff here once he ousted Kemp. But the town was dying and likely would not need a sheriff for long. No. If he made any change at all, it would have to be to hang up his guns completely.

A movement to his left arrested his wandering thoughts and abruptly yanked him back to the here and now. A shadow moved—a man. Jace reacted instinctively, drawing his knife and pressing the man against the back wall of the abandoned hotel. Blood thundered through his ears. Had Kemp's man come gunning for him, he wouldn't have had a chance, distracted as he was. The man held his hands out, palms up, clearly showing he had no malicious intent.

"Please—I ain't lookin' for trouble," he pleaded.

Jace drew a breath, then pulled back from the man. "Then you're in the wrong town, friend."

"You've been asking the boys about Kemp's gold."

"That's right. You know where it's hid?"

"No. But I do know he never leaves town, and he don't trust no one enough to take it and hide it for him. It's here, in town somewhere. That's all I got to say to you."

"Why are you telling me this?"

The man took his hat off, letting Jace get a good look at his face. He'd seen him around the saloon often enough. He went by the name of Hugh McDonald. "I don't like what them boys did to Miss Morgan—er, yer wife now. And I reckon the way you're going, Kemp ain't gonna win this battle. I wanted you to remember when the lead starts flying that I'm on your side."

"That's not good enough, mister. If you're on the opposite side of my gun, you're gonna die. I suggest you get outta town."

"I can't. Kemp's killing anyone who tries to leave. We're holed up here till the damn payroll comes through for the loggers. I haven't seen my wife in weeks."

"Then you better stand next to me when the firing begins."

The gunman nodded, and Jace knew he was looking at a dead man. Sometimes—a lot of times—Jace hated this job. Kemp's man looked both ways down the alley, then tipped his hat to Jace and started down the long, narrow passage, heading away from the street.

Jace stayed where he was for a while, collecting himself. He cursed. Walking around daydreaming about a woman and a way of life that would never be his was a sure way to get a person's head blown off.

Sweat trickled into Jace's face in the hot morning sun. He had dozed while Leah's bread rose, and when Maddie stopped by to escort Leah for her delivery rounds, he'd gotten up. He'd been avoiding her for days, coming home after she slept, rising after she left for her deliveries. But every night when he joined her in bed, she rolled toward him and held him in her arms, her sleep unbroken. And every night, he spent hours unable to sleep, his body noting all of Leah's soft curves, all the things he could be doing with his hands and mouth.

Today, he had a disquieting feeling that something had changed in town. It was too early yet to stroll over to Sam's to figure out what was different. The shipment was due in only two days now. The shift he sensed was probably only the arrival of more men who had been trickling into town, hoping for a cut of the gold shipment.

Jace was relieved when the woodcutter delivered a load of firewood, glad to have something to do. He set about splintering several days' worth of kindling for Leah's stove, then began splitting the rest of the logs so they could be stacked. The work was physical but mindless, giving him a chance to think.

The waiting was the worst of a job like his. But it would be over shortly. And when it was done, he could go down to Cheyenne and file for a divorce, and then, finally move on. *But to what?* a persistent, nagging little voice at the back of his mind kept asking him. And he knew the answer. To more of the same. It was what he was, what he had become. He could no more change himself than Leah could change herself. He paused, leaning on the axe handle. He hoped she never changed. He never wanted to think of her in any way other than exactly as she was now, wearing boy's clothes, tossing a knife with deadly accuracy up in the woods.

Unbidden, the ugly image of her folded up under the kitchen table, shaking, her clothes in shreds, rose to his mind. When he left, she would be alone once again, to fend for herself in a dying town, a town he knew she would never leave. She would be its last damned resident and still she would stay. He swung the axe with such ferocity that its blade cut deeply into the chopping block. Sweat trickled into his eyes.

He swiped an arm across his forehead, and

when he looked up, she was there, offering him a tin of water. "You look hot."

He took the water and swallowed it in two swigs. "Thanks for bringing water up to the house," she said and nodded at the work he was doing. "And for the firewood. The woodcutter said you paid him. I'll pay you back."

Jace handed her back the cup. "No need. I think I can afford my wife's wood while I'm here." She settled herself on a large stump that had been rough-carved into a seat. He wished she would go away, wished he hadn't noticed how the sun caught the red highlights in her hair, wished her voice didn't turn his insides to fire. He set another log on the block and swung the axe.

"Will you eat supper with me tonight?"

He didn't answer her. He focused on his next swing.

"I usually eat with Maddie. Sometimes Malcolm joins us, when he's not eating with Sally and Jim. It's easier to cook for a couple of people than it is for just one. So several days a week, we all come together for a meal and contribute to it in some way, either with a food item or with the preparation or the clean up."

Christ. Her voice wound around him a satin ribbon, cool and smooth. And so goddamned sweet. If she didn't quit talking, he would drag her inside her house, pin her to the wall, and fuck her like a mindless, rutting animal. That was all he really was, a murdering, killing beast. Jenny had said it was so. He clenched his teeth.

"Yes!" he nearly shouted. "I will join you tonight." He drew a breath. "Go tell Maddie I will see to her wood when I'm finished here, as my contribution to the meal."

Leah clapped her hands and jumped to her feet. She took hold of his arm and pulled him down to place a quick kiss on his cheek. Jace sucked in a sharp gasp of air when she touched him, but she was gone before it even filled his lungs. He turned to look after her.

Two days. How the hell was he going to survive two more days?

When he finished chopping both Leah's and Maddie's wood, he headed down to the livery. Gart knew who came in hours before Jace could see for himself at Sam's, since he handled their horses. As he stepped inside the shadowy interior, Jace's senses were on full alert. Something was gnawing at him. Maybe it was nerves about the coming show-down at Meeker's Pass. He eyed the horses in the stalls, but didn't find any new ones.

He made his way outside to the corrals out back, where Gart was filling the water troughs. Jace braced a boot on the bottom rung of the fence and folded his arms on the top slat as he counted horses and looked for new mounts.

The hostler greeted him and jogged over to his side. "Need a horse, Gage?"

"No. Looking to see if anyone new came in."

"One new one, that sorrel over there. You figure more are coming in?"

"I am. Kemp's gearing up for that payroll wagon."

Gart pulled out a rag and mopped the back of his neck. "When's it gonna end, Gage?"

"I guess a couple of days now. It'll be all over then."

Bill Kemp stepped into Sam's. Dinner was soon to be served, a meal none of his men missed. Fewer than a third of the seats were filled tonight. That damned Jace Gage had culled his gang down to a skeleton crew. There was a new face in the mix tonight, a large man who wasn't afraid to look the sheriff in the eyes. Men like him could do the work of several. Bill could use him for the work he had planned tonight.

"You." Bill pointed to him. "Come talk to me," he ordered as he took his customary seat. Sam's waiter brought out a beer and a plate with a grilled T-bone steak and a baked potato. Bill cut into the steak and took a bite, taking his time chewing as he considered the man who had joined him at the table. He had short brown hair and several days' growth of beard. The look in his brown eyes told volumes. The man had a chip on his shoulder. Bill liked men with a score to settle; they were always easy to manipulate.

"You look familiar. Do I know you?"

"No. Name's Rupert Hardin. I'm guessing you're Kemp?" Bill nodded. "Heard you were hiring guns. That still the case?"

"I am."

"Good. 'Cause I've come to kill Jace Gage."

Bill grinned. "That so? How do you intend to do that? These bumbling idiots have been trying for two weeks to do that very thing. What makes you think you can?"

"Failure ain't an option. He killed my sister. I'm gonna put an end to him."

Chapter 18

Leah startled at Jace's abrupt entry. Had he been only minutes earlier, he would have caught her still in the tub. The small interior of her home was humid from boiling water for the bath and grew several degrees hotter with his return.

He took one look at the tub, then began disarming himself. When he kicked his boots off and dropped his suspenders, Leah forced her gaze away. She rearranged his shaving gear, fidgeting, wishing he didn't stand between her and the door.

"You hangin' around to wash my back?"

Leah glanced at him in the mirror, thinking it was somehow safer to look at his reflection than to see him in the flesh. He drew his shirt off, pulling it over his head. Leah's mouth went dry.

"No." She faced him. "I'm sticking around to see that you get a proper shave."

One corner of his hard mouth slowly tipped upward. "You ever shave a man before?"

Leah drew her bottom lip between her teeth to moisten it, but even that small action caught his attention. "I've cleared the fur off of a deer skin. Can't be much different."

Jace's brows lowered. "It sure as hell is!" He sent a quick glance over to the tub. "You didn't put lime in that water, did you?"

"Of course not." She collected her loose hair and tied it with an old ribbon. "Jace, when I dug your shaving gear out of your pack, I saw the photograph you carry around." She ventured a look at him, and was thrown by the tension in his face. "She was your wife, wasn't she? She was beautiful."

He started toward her. The corners of his jaw tightened, his blue eyes cold as winter ice. His lips were pressed into a thin line. He set a hand on either side of her, pinning her against the dresser, trapping her in place.

"I've only ever hated one person in my life. Through the war, through my work clearing towns. One person. And that was my wife."

Leah's eyes dipped to the scar on his neck. Her breathing was coming in fits and starts. "What happened to her?"

"She died."

She couldn't get enough air with him standing so near her. Yet she wished he were closer. "Why do you keep her picture if her memory pains you?"

"To remind me that women are never what they seem."

"That isn't always true. I am what I seem to be."

He dipped his head toward her. Leah's lips parted as she anticipated his kiss. "You hide what you are. Lace beneath the rough clothes of a boy. Tracking skills of an expert hunter. The aim of a seasoned marksman. You are not what you seem, Leah," he whispered gruffly before pulling away. He unfastened the buttons of his fly and dropped his pants along with his drawers to pool at his feet. She did not blink and did not look down. He stepped away from her and into the water.

Leah spun on her heel and headed outside. Crossing her front yard, she leaned against the low fence by her vegetable garden and watched the chickens peck at their feed. She plucked a tall grass flower and began pulling off pieces of its fuzzy end. Her heart was beating unusually fast. She was exactly what she seemed, a woman who liked hunting. A woman who wanted to be a wife.

A woman who was in a very bad fix.

How did a woman go about keeping a man who didn't want to be kept? And when had she decided she wanted to keep Gage? Doing so went against everything her mother had taught her. And what was there for a retired gunfighter to do in Defiance? Nothing.

Leah pushed off the fence, snagging a splinter in her palm. She winced as she drew it out of her skin. The wood was rotting, and there wasn't more to be had now that the lumber mill was closed. Jace had been right. The town was dying.

She turned around and looked up toward the general store, pressing her aching palm against her thigh to ease the sting. She didn't want the town to die. Surely the fate of Defiance didn't have to be a foregone conclusion. Once the sheriff and his gang were gone, commerce could return. And when it did, families would come back.

Defiance would need men like Gage, strong, just men. She looked at her palm. The pain had lessened. A thought took root in her mind. Jace could buy up the old mill and make it run again. He could be the start of the town's revival. *They* could be the hope the town needed.

Jace stepped out on her porch. He wore a clean white shirt and his homespun pants. He'd left his bandoliers off and only wore his gunbelt. His brown hair, streaked with blond, was overlong and still damp. He'd combed it away from his face. He'd shaved and trimmed his moustache. Leah had never seen a face so full of angles and secrets. How was she going to convince him that she'd made a decision for them and that it was the right one?

As he moved down the stairs and came toward her, his eyes never left hers. He stopped barely a foot from her. She couldn't help the small grin as she reached up to touch his smooth cheek. "You clean up rather nicely, Gage."

"You keep lookin' at me like that, I may rethink our situation."

Leah studied him, wondering if he was being flippant, or if he could be swayed. It had to be possible. She leaned closer. Her thumb stroked the ridge of his jaw. "Would that be so bad?"

Emotions chased each other across his blue eyes. Hope and fear. "It can't be."

"Of course it can be." Leah pulled away, retreating because it was hard to think when he was so near her. She stepped around him and started for the gate, shooting him a smile over her shoulder. "In fact, I have a plan."

His whole body went still. "What kind of plan?"

Leah stopped at the gate and turned to look at him. "One that lets us keep this marriage. One that doesn't require you to be a rancher or shopkeeper or a sheriff or a gambler."

He crossed his arms and glared at her. "All I know is killing."

"But you could learn something new." She smiled at him. "You could buy the old lumber mill outside of town and become a business owner. You could make Defiance your home." She didn't wait for his response, but reached for the gate latch.

"Stop right there, Leah Allison Gage," he ordered brusquely. Warily, she turned around. He arched a brow at her. "Did you just propose to me?"

Leah bit her lip, then surrendered to the smile that broke free. "I believe I did, Jace Holden Gage."

His eyes held hers. She wondered if he would refuse her out of hand or if he would at least consider what she was suggesting. "Then I'm gonna need the kiss that goes with that proposal."

At a leisurely pace Leah moved back to where he stood, loving the way his heated gaze made her feel. She stopped in front of him and placed her hands on his chest. Looking at his lips, she anticipated the feel of them against her own as she stroked her hands up to his shoulders, then locked them about his neck. She pulled her body fully against his, pressing her breasts against his ribs as she drew him down for the kiss. Looking into his eyes, she whispered, "Make me your wife, Jace Gage."

Jace's mouth slanted across hers as his arms wrapped around her. Leah tightened her arms around his neck, pressing her mouth to his, lifting herself against him. He thrust his tongue into her mouth. She sucked on it and felt his groan against her lips. He straightened, lifting her slightly. She was only vaguely aware of the world moving. It wasn't until they reached the stairs that she realized he was taking her back inside. When she pushed away, he set her down on her feet again.

"Jace, what are you doing?"

"I'm gonna make you mine. Right now."

"In every way that matters, I already am yours." She took his hand and held the back of it against her heart. "I don't want to rush this first time. And Maddie's waiting on us for supper."

The look he gave her blew fire through her veins. He lifted his free hand and slowly brushed a lock of hair from her face; his eyes followed the path his fingers took across her skin. "So, it's an old lumber mill for us, is it?"

"It sits right outside of town, by the river. And you'll be able to cut all the wood you need to build a big, white church here in town."

His brows lowered. "A church? Defiance doesn't need a church. It ain't a respectable little town."

Leah took his hand and led him toward her front gate. "Of course it isn't now, but it will be when it has a church." She moved through the gate and crossed the road, thinking he was following.

When she didn't hear him behind her, she turned and caught the dark way he watched her.

"I'm never gonna make it through this meal," he growled.

She grinned, lifting her eyebrows. "Then you better eat fast, cowboy." She laughed and stepped onto Maddie's drive, putting a little more motion into her stride than was strictly necessary. He caught up to her in three long steps. Startled, she spun around, a squeal of shock breaking from her as he bent over and pressed his shoulder against her middle. He straightened, hoisting her over his shoulder, then turned toward her house.

"Jace Gage! What are you doing? We're late for supper."

"Supper can wait."

Leah laughed, then felt the tension that sound caused in his body. She tried to push herself upright, but he only lifted her farther over his shoulder, dangling her in a precarious position. "Jace, put me down."

"No."

They were at her gate. "Jace Holden Gage! I sacrificed my fattest chicken for this supper. We can't waste that hen. Besides, Maddie will know what we're doing."

"Honey, I'm gonna have you screaming so loud the whole town will know what we're doing."

A frisson slipped through her at his bold statement, bringing with it memories of things she didn't want to recall. Her mother had screamed, more than once. Leah hadn't known at the time what was happening. By the time the sheriff unlocked the door and walked out, her mother's eyes had gone flat, and her beautiful face had been marred with his handiwork. That couldn't be what Jace meant, was it? "I don't want to scream, Jace. I don't want it to hurt."

"Leah—" Jace was kept from answering when Maddie called out behind them.

"Will you two quit horsing around and come to supper? It's getting cold."

"Please, Jace." His shoulder dipped when he sighed, but he turned around.

"We'll be right there, Maddie," Jace answered.

At the steps to her porch, he lifted her down, lowering her against his body, slowly, slowly, down to the first step. Seeing the tension in his face, Leah could barely breathe. She pressed her hands flat against his chest.

"Have I ever hurt you?" he asked, his voice a raw whisper.

"You tied me to you once."

Jace grinned. "And then you slept like a baby, late into the morning." He brushed a lock of hair behind her ear. "You said you trusted me. We can't have a marriage without that. We got nothing without that, honey."

"I do trust you, Jace. I'm just a little afraid of the physical side of marriage."

He bent forward and pressed a kiss to the corner of her mouth. Leah felt the draw of air he sucked into his lungs and knew he struggled for control. A part of her wished he would carry her back home and introduce her to the intimate aspects of being a wife, despite their waiting supper. Maddie clattered and banged dishes around, making an unnecessary amount of noise inside her kitchen. A muscle bunched in the corner of Jace's jaw. "You better eat fast, woman."

Leah moved up the steps, but Jace's hand captured hers, stopping her before she reached the last step. He took hold of her waist and leaned forward to press his smoothly shaven cheek against her jaw.

"Do me a favor in there tonight," he rasped. "Don't look at me." He nuzzled her face. "Don't smile. Don't laugh. And please, God, don't lick your lips." He caught her earlobe between his teeth and razed its length. She could hear his rough breathing. "I'm still renting a room here and would be happy to make use of it."

Leah's heart skipped a beat, rendering speech impossible. Before she could collect herself to respond, he ushered her inside. Maddie was at the stove, her back to them. Leah was enormously grateful the older woman didn't see the awkward way she moved into the room, though she knew her reprieve was short lived. Her neighbor was far too observant not to notice that Leah's relationship with Jace had changed suddenly, especially after catching them out front horsing around the way they were.

Jace held her chair for her, then held Maddie's for her before taking his own seat across from Leah. Maddie said a quick and heartfelt grace. Leah fumbled with her napkin, trying to focus on something, anything, other than Jace.

Unfortunately, he was less than cooperative. He

asked her to pass the mashed potatoes and the beans and the rolls. Each of these she handed him without making eye contact. The act of avoiding him was oddly intimate, and that thought made her cheeks warm. She ventured a look at him, only to catch his intense regard. She swallowed reflexively, not for a minute doubting he'd make good on his threat to carry her off to his rented room upstairs.

She wondered how far she could push him before he broke.

"So, Jace, I understand the loggers' payroll will be coming through in a couple of days. Are you ready for it?"

"Ready and then some." He broke a roll in half. "I'll have to head out to Meeker's Pass tomorrow. I want to watch the sheriff get his men settled. I'd like Leah to stay here while I'm gone. I don't want a repeat of what happened the last time I left town."

Leah started to argue that she didn't need a keeper, but stopped. It was a futile argument—she knew Maddie would agree with him. It didn't matter that the boardinghouse was as indefensible as her home. Perhaps she and Maddie together would be better able to fight off invaders—two women sporting guns were more formidable than a lone woman caught unaware.

Leah frowned down at her plate as she listened to Jace and Maddie discuss his plans. She thought of the future she would share with Jace at the mill, of the church he would build her. Defiance would soon have a preacher, and when it did, this daily violence would be a distant memory.

"Maddie—can you remember the sheriff ever

taking a trip out of town?" The strangeness of Jace's question broke into Leah's thoughts.

Maddie was reflective for a minute. "No, now that you mention it, I can't."

Leah swallowed hard, fighting back memories. "He not only never left, he never let my mother and me leave either." She didn't look at Jace, didn't want him to read in her eyes what she wasn't saying.

"So where would he have stashed his gold if he never left town?"

"Could be anywhere," Maddie said. "His apartment, the jail."

"My house." Jace and Maddie looked at her in surprise. "He was always there, before Mama died."

"You would have seen him with it, as many times as he hit the stages coming through town," Maddie argued. "No, it's more likely that he hid it up in the mountains somewhere."

"He didn't go to the mountains, and he wouldn't have let it out of his sight," Leah countered. "It has to be somewhere he is, somewhere within his control."

"I wonder if Paul or Hammer knew?" Maddie asked. "They were his men for a long while. Maybe they shared his secret with some of the other men?"

"Not that I've been able to discover," Jace said. "Those two together didn't have the intelligence of a fence post. Kemp wouldn't have risked exposing his stash to them." He took another bite of his roll, chewing it as he gave the hidden gold some thought. Leah knew he'd take a closer look at her house. It made sense, given Kemp's unbalanced interest in Leah and her mother.

"One way or another, this ends at Meeker's Pass in a couple of days." Jace looked at Maddie. "If I don't come back, Jim knows the name of my lawyer in Denver. He'll see that Leah is taken care of."

Maddie reached over and took hold of Jace's hand in a brief, maternal touch. "Do you have family, Jace?"

Jace stared at her. "My parents died before the war."

"I'm sorry."

His gaze shifted to Leah. "I've only Leah." The lazy grin he gave her made her wish they had skipped supper. "My wife."

A bolt of excitement slashed through her. "Jace is going to buy the lumber mill when this is over, Maddie."

Maddie looked from Leah to Jace, then back again. "I'm glad. Real glad. Defiance needs a man like you, Jace. And I would have been very sad to see you take our Leah away."

Leah fell silent. In a few short minutes, Jace would take her home and make her his wife in truth. Her breath caught. She glanced at his hands, wondering how it would happen, how it would feel when he first reached for her. She studied his mouth, edged in lines. He so rarely smiled, but today he'd laughed and teased her. She looked into his pale blue eyes and her heart stopped. He was staring at her, watching her watch him. She didn't smile—her control was too tenuous.

Maddie cleared her throat and came to her feet.

"Well! A smart hostess knows when a meal is over."
She began gathering dishes. "Can I offer you two a
cup of coffee?"

"Coffee?" Leah jumped to her feet, inordinately
nervous. "Ah, no thank you. Jace did you want
some?" He leaned back and lifted an eyebrow; a
slow grin warmed his mouth as he watched her
squirm. "No, Maddie, we'll both pass," Leah answered for him. She took his plate and hers over to
the sink. "I'll give you a hand with these."

"I think not. You two run along and enjoy your
evening."

"Maddie—"

Maddie took hold of her shoulders. Her face was
full of humor, her eyes laughing. Leah felt a blush
burn her cheeks. It was as if Maddie *knew* what was
going to happen. "Go. These won't take me a
minute. It's not a two-person job."

"That was a fine chicken this evening, Maddie.
Don't think I've ever had better," Jace said as he
took the final few dishes to the sink. He took hold
of Leah's arm and started leading her toward the
door. Leah felt warm and quivery inside, stiff and
fearful outside. Would it hurt? Maybe she wasn't
ready for this. She definitely wasn't ready for this.

They left Maddie's and walked in silence down
the drive. "Leah, you've gotten quiet."

Leah nodded, unable to find her voice. Her
mouth had gone dry, as if stuffed with cotton.

He took hold of her hand and stopped walking,
turning her to him. "Are you afraid?"

She nodded again, looking up at him.

He smiled. "How about we each make a promise?

I won't touch you in any way that hurts. And you promise to tell me if something feels uncomfortable. Deal?"

"Yes."

White teeth flashed in his brief grin. "Good." He turned toward her house, and she saw the exact moment the humor left his expression. She followed his gaze and discovered a man descending the steps of her porch. Jace took hold of her arm and pulled her close.

"Go back inside Maddie's. And lock the door."

"Jace—"

"Go now, Leah. Tell Maddie to get her gun and to use it if she needs to—without second guessing."

Leah looked over her shoulder at the man who was now by her gate. "Do you know him?" A quick nod was her answer. "Who is he?"

"He's my brother-in-law . . . I guess." Jace pushed her toward Maddie's. "Inside, now. Lock the doors." Leah hurried away.

"That the new missus?" Rupert asked as he stepped in front of Jace.

"You're in the wrong town, Rupert," Jace warned.

The man grinned. "That's an interesting voice you got there. Looks like a helluva scar, too. Bet that hurt."

"It hurt, but not like a couple of years in prison would. I'm surprised they let you out."

"There was a wave of amnesty for those of us unfortunate enough to get caught up in the war." He crossed the street, prowling closer to Jace. "I immediately set out to find you when I heard you'd survived the war."

Jace flashed his hands, palm-out, by his guns. "You found me. Let's take care of this right here, right now."

His opponent laughed. "I ain't as stupid as you think, Yankee. I heard the stories about you in every damned town where you'd been. You're a plague, an abomination, like you were in the war, changing things to suit yourself and everyone else be damned, claiming the law's on your side."

"Then what do you want?"

"I want you to know your days are at an end." He stepped closer. "But I'm not going to shoot you. No. That would be too quick. I'm going to finish the hanging."

Jace shook his head. "Seeing as you came after me, you must be hankering for an early death, Rupert. I'll be happy to oblige you. Why don't you do what you have to, and I'll see that justice is served?"

Rupert lurched forward. "You killed my sister! You aren't the hand of the justice."

"I loved your sister."

"But she didn't love you, did she?" Rupert grinned. "She played you. She loved her *husband*."

"Did you put her up to it? Did you tell her bigamy was forgivable in a time of war?"

"It was her idea."

That statement hit Jace like a fist in the gut. And he knew Rupert didn't lie, for Jace remembered his wife confessing her hatred of him as if it had been an obvious thing.

Jace watched his old enemy turn and head down the street to the saloon. Maddie's kitchen door opened. Someone ran down the steps and came toward him, Leah most likely. He didn't look behind him. She rushed all the way down the drive, stopping behind him. He didn't want her there, didn't want her to see him. Not now that Rupert was here. Not knowing what he was going to do to his brother-in-law, in cold blood or not. He stood still. If he didn't move, didn't breathe, she might walk on past him.

She slowly closed the distance between them. Jace clamped his jaw shut, waiting for the vitriol that would spill from her mouth to indict him. They had come so far this afternoon. She'd seen him as something other than the killer he was, shown him a new image of himself. She was why he hadn't put an end to Rupert already, but the urge to kill the bastard still writhed beneath his skin, like a second being dwelling within him. He was a plague. Leah touched his arm. He tensed, waiting. Then his gaze sliced in her direction.

"Are you hurt?" Her voice was barely a whisper.

He blinked. Her calmness was disorienting. "No."

She nodded, her mouth tilted slightly in a smile of relief as she searched his face. He met her look, showing himself to her, letting her see the ugly beast within him that wanted Rupert—and all the bastards of the world—dead.

She rubbed his arm. "Maddie's put some coffee on. She wanted us to come back inside for a slice of rhubarb pie. Will you join us?"

He shook his head. Couldn't she see what he

was? "I wanted to kill him." She dropped her hand and drew back. Smart girl. She did see him now—the real him. "It ain't gonna work, Leah, this dream of yours. I can't hang up my guns. I've killed too many. There's always sons and brothers to hunt me down. And you, too, if you're with me."

"Jace—" Leah started to speak, but he took out a pistol and checked the chamber. It was a reflexive action; he knew the gun was loaded. He repeated the action with his other pistol.

"Go have your pie, Leah. I got work to do."

"Jace, no!"

He glared at her, pretending indifference to the moisture pooling in her eyes. "This is what I am."

"They'll kill you."

"Yep. But I'll take a few more of them with me before that happens."

Chapter 19

Leah paced inside the small confines of her house late into the night, waiting for Jace, worrying. How could she lose him when she'd only just found him? What was the man they had seen this evening to Jace? Why had he sent her to hide from him? She and Maddie had watched from the kitchcn window, but they hadn't been able to make out any of the men's conversation. And when she'd tried to talk him in to returning to Maddie's for dessert, he'd been a different man. Hard again. Empty.

She'd been a fool to think she could change him, that he would care for her enough to choose a different path. Her mother's warning about never loving a gunfighter reared its head. She crossed her arms and held herself as she leaned against the rough wood planking of the living room wall. Logic did little to help her through this situation. She wanted Jace as a wife wants her husband. In her life, in her bed, in her heart. Yet she knew a normal life would never be theirs—neither of them was willing to change. Jace could no more hang up his guns than she could pack up her life in her saddlebags and follow him from town to town, facing this agony every night for the rest of their lives.

Tonight would be their last night together, and it was the only one she would ever have as a wife. She took another pass about the room, wondering how she could make the night last, for she knew, whether he divorced her or not, she would never marry again.

She blew out the lamp, then stood nervously beside the bed, awed by the enormity of what she was about to do tonight. She unbuttoned her camisole and slipped it from her shoulders, then loosened the drawstring on her drawers and dragged them off her hips. She set both garments aside, then slipped beneath the cool sheet on her bed. The cotton, cold against her skin, caused her to be acutely aware of her nudity.

She lay unmoving, letting her body acclimate to the feel of the linens. She didn't have long to wait. She heard Jace's now familiar stride come up her front steps. She rolled to her side facing the wall and drew the sheet up to her neck, ignoring the heat that began to build within her. Jace entered the room silently. He removed his boots, unbuckled his gunbelt and hung it over the short post of her bed. She heard a rustle of clothes, then a splash of water in the basin. He washed himself, then opened the back door and tossed out the old water.

Leah's heart began a loud thumping in her head.

There was nothing left now but for him to join her in bed. He lifted the sheet. The mattress dipped as he stretched out beside her. He lay still for a long while. Too long. Leah wondered what she would do if he didn't reach for her. And soon.

Jace rolled to his side, away from her. Leah squeezed her eyes shut, trying to shore up her courage to go to him. But before she could move, Jace rolled all the way over. He set his hand at her waist and drew her against his chest. Burying his face in her hair, he took a deep breath. Her nipples peaked, and she knew the exact instant when he realized she wasn't wearing her nightgown. Or anything else.

His fingers tested her skin. He drew his hand upward, capturing a breast.

"Aw, Christ, Leah," he groaned against the nape of her neck. He let his hand move up to the skin of her chest, up her neck to her chin, then reversed direction, moving down over her ribs, her belly, to the curls at the juncture of her legs.

He explored the curve of her hip, moved down her thigh. The rough texture of his calloused hand gently stroking her skin set her nerves to tingling as she anticipated where he would touch her next. He moved against her as he scooted down the bed a bit. And then his mouth was against her skin, hot and wet. He kissed her shoulder blade, kissed a line down the valley of her back as his hand massaged a breast.

A low moan broke from her lips. "Jace—" She tried to roll over.

He pressed a hand against her back, keeping

her immobile. "No. No words. No talking, Leah."
He trailed his mouth against each rib, then to the
soft indentation of her waist. He drew off the sheet,
then stroked his hand over her buttocks to her
thigh, an advance assault.

He slid further down the mattress. His face
moved against the upward curve of her bottom, his
touch releasing liquid heat within her. He raked
his teeth against one flank, then kissed his way
down to her upper thigh.

His tongue touched her skin. "God, I love the
way you taste," he murmured against her. Holding
a hand against her hip, he forced her legs apart.
The bed shifted as he knelt between them. He
grazed a straight line down her inner thigh to her
ankle, then up again before he moved over to the
next leg and repeated the torture. The feel of a
man between her legs, touching her with his hands
and mouth, set Leah's flesh on fire. He wouldn't
let her turn over or pull away. It was both decadent
and delightful.

He reached between her legs and found her
cleft. She was wet there. She tried to close her legs,
but couldn't while he was kneeling between them.
"Jace, stop."

"Why?"

She looked over her shoulder at him. She tried
to push herself up, but he held her in place. "This
isn't proper!"

"Does it feel good?"

"Yes—"

"Then it's proper enough. Lift your hips up.
Like this." He took hold of her hips and hoisted

her up until she knelt with her bottom in the air, her legs spread, her cheek on the bed. Again she tried to push herself up to all fours, but he forced her shoulders down.

"Jace—"

He leaned over her. She could feel his erection against her inner thigh. "Do you remember when I said I would make you scream?"

She could only nod.

"It wasn't out of pain. If what I do hurts you, stop me. If not, then leave me to it." He kissed her shoulder. "Agreed?"

Again she nodded.

He spread her thighs open further, then settled beneath her on his back, his head between her knees. Slowly, slowly, he drew her down on his mouth. Leah gasped at the first contact, her body jerking reflexively against his mouth, seeking more of his shocking assault. She groaned a low, inarticulate moan. The touch of his tongue, warm and wet, sucking, stroking over her hidden core sent violent shivers through her. He mouthed the bud at the top of her opening until her very bones began to melt. A fire took hold of her, flaming all conscious thought. She pressed her face into the pillow, muting her cries of passion as she bucked helplessly against his face.

The waves had barely subsided when his hands stroked over her hips, her waist, her ribs to capture her breasts. "Jace, please—" she whispered, though she had no idea what exactly she was begging for. His rough hands circled her breasts, slipping down to her nipples. He squeezed the taut peaks, rhythmically tightening and releasing them as his tongue found her sensitive nub again.

This time, her orgasm had barely begun before he pulled away. "No—" she protested. But he was already kneeling between her thighs, positioning himself at her opening. He slipped inside of her, just a little, stretching, stroking her. Leah couldn't take the torment. She bucked against his hips, hard, taking him deep inside of her. The pain was like a quick pinch, gone as fast as it started, but Jace heard her gasp.

"Jesus, Leah. Don't move." Jace had a firm grip of her hips, holding her still for a long, brutal moment, his body shaking where it joined hers. Then he began to withdraw, slowly, the whole movement an intimate caress. He pressed forward again, repeating that motion. A warm flush spread heat across her body. Involuntarily, she began to meet his thrusts, pumping against him. Her movements grew faster and faster. The wave was coming, drawing strength, building in intensity. He reached beneath her and pressed against her sensitive flesh. Leah cried out as her inner muscles contracted, tightening around his iron erection. He pumped against her pulsing muscles, pulling at her, sending her over the edge. With one final thrust, his own release came. He grunted as he drained himself into her with hot sluicing jets of his seed.

He pulled free and collapsed next to her. Leah pushed herself up on her elbows to look at him, not at all certain what to expect from him as he lay with an arm hooked over his eyes.

Sensing her stillness, he looked at her. He lifted

his arm further. "Come here." Leah didn't wait to be asked twice. He pulled her in close against his side and kissed her forehead. Turning on his side, he folded his arm beneath his head and reached to smooth a lock of hair from her face.

"When you leave tomorrow, will you be back?"

He gave her a half smile, sad perhaps, though it was too dark to make out the emotion in his eyes. "I'll be back. A thousand gunmen couldn't keep me from you."

Leah drew a shaky breath. He had only to face a dozen, but they could well be the end of him. She started to roll over, but he pulled her into his arms.

"Jace—" His name broke from her lips with a sob.

"No. No tears, Leah. I will be back. And when I return, I'll hang up the guns. I'll build my world around you." He kissed her temple, her cheek, then nuzzled his way down to her neck. He held her so tightly that it was hard to breathe, but the tears still came, silently washing down her cheeks. He kissed her chin and moved up to her cheek, tasting the salt of her tears.

He pressed his face against hers. His hand cupped the back of her head. His mouth hovered over hers. "Be here with me now, Leah. Feel me." *This may be all that we have.* The words were never spoken, but they hung between them with the same frightening finality as if they had been uttered aloud. Her lips trembled against a sob she could not stop, but his kisses were relentless, pressing and releasing, forcing her attention away from her fears. His tongue sought hers. He moved over her, both hands now holding her face to his. His body began a gentle rocking motion that sent shivers up her spine.

He hardened against the opening of her legs. She held on to his back, returning his kisses, rocking up against him. He kissed his way down her neck, over her chest, to a breast. Cupping the mound, he took her nipple into his mouth and sucked. Her womb clenched. He pushed himself against her entrance as he reached down and lifted her knees. "Let me in, Leah."

She opened her arms, pulling him up to her as he slipped into her slick warmth. The sorrow welled up within her again, but she fought it back as he lay over her, watching her, letting her feel him with every stroke of his body. Gradually his tender, slow movements built speed. The muscles in his face tightened. Her body responded to the changes in him. He reached between their bodies and massaged that sensitive spot, sending her over the edge. She cried out and bucked up against him, feeling her body grasp at his erection. He pounded against her as if fighting the cresting wave, but it took him too, and his hot seed pumped into her again.

Briefly, he relaxed against her, then he lifted his head and looked at her. Neither of them had the right words to speak at that moment, so they just looked into each other's eyes.

"Leah—" Jace started to break the silence, but a rapid pounding at the front door stopped his words. He frowned, looking across the room, then back to Leah.

Rolling off of her, he picked up his denims and stepped into them, buttoning them enough to keep them on his hips. He threw his gunbelt over a shoulder, then went to the front window. Seeing who it was, he yanked the portal open. "Malcolm! What's wrong?"

"You gotta come, Jace. They've ridden for Hell's Gulch. Audrey's out there. And the kids. I thought I could talk them out of going. They took torches, wore hoods. Jesus, Jace. You gotta come fast!"

Hearing the panic in Malcolm's voice, Leah knew her friend was in danger. She looked at Jace and he at her. He shoved a hand through his hair, then faced Malcolm. "Go get our horses saddled," he ordered Malcolm. "I'll gear up."

He dressed quickly, draping his bandoliers across his shoulders, buckling his gunbelt and taking up his rifle. He sheathed his knife and grabbed his hat. Leah had dressed as well and now handed him his saddlebags.

"Come." He slapped the saddlebags over his shoulder, and taking hold of her hand, he led her to Maddie's. He pounded on the kitchen door as Malcolm brought the horses down from the stable.

Light brightened the kitchen window. Maddie opened the door. Looking at him, at Malcolm, her face hardened as she nodded at them. Jace drew Leah up into a tight embrace. He kissed her cheek, then let go of her and started down the steps. Astride his horse, he glanced her way once more.

"Come back to me, Jace Gage." In the faint light of Maddie's kitchen lamp, she saw a muscle bunch in his jaw. He nodded once, then touched his heels to his mount and set off down the drive.

"Come on inside, darlin'," Maddie urged. "I'll put you in his room."

"Maddie—" Leah's voice broke.

The older woman wrapped an arm around Leah. "I know, child. I've sent a man off to war myself. It ain't something I ever want to do again." She pulled back, frowning at Leah. "Why was Malcolm with him?"

"The sheriff sent men out to raid Hell's Gulch."

Maddie shook her head and started toward the stove. "Best start some coffee. I can see that neither of us will get any sleep tonight. Sheriff Kemp is due for a bad ending. I'll bet that man of yours gives it to him."

Leah slumped into a chair at the table. "I hope he comes back. It hurts, Maddie." She sniffled and drew her knees up in front of herself, as if tucking herself into a tight ball would lessen the pain of Jace's leaving, or the danger he faced, or the trouble Audrey and the kids were in out at Hell's Gulch.

Maddie gave her a sad smile as she looked up from grinding the coffee beans. "That's because you're in love with him."

Leah jerked her gaze toward Maddie. "No, I'm not. I got used to him, that's all."

Leah finished her baking much later than usual the next morning. Both she and Maddie didn't feel it was safe for her to be alone in the wee hours of the morning, given what had happened the last time Jace was gone. As she took the last of the bread pans from her oven, she heard a commotion across town. Men's voices—lots of them. She stepped outside as Maddie hurried up the drive.

"What's happening?"

Maddie gripped Leah's hands and stared into her eyes. Leah felt the blood drain from her face as she returned the older woman's intense regard.

"There's a wagon full of men from Hell's Gulch."

A dim buzzing began in Leah's head, a hum that threatened to mute the shouts and noise coming from up the street. The raid was over, but Jace hadn't come home or he would have come to see her. Maybe there was a perfectly good reason he wasn't back yet. Maybe he'd stayed at Hell's Gulch to clean up. Or maybe he'd gone ahead to Meeker's Pass to get ready for the gold shipment.

"Wait a minute. I want to bring my rifle." Leah retrieved her rifle from Maddie's kitchen, slinging it over her shoulder as she followed her friend up the street. Around the corner, bodies were being lifted out of the wagon and laid in a row in front of the sheriff's office, at least a half dozen of them. Leah pushed her way into the front of the onlookers. Tears wet her cheeks and caught the dust the morning's hot wind stirred up. She searched each face of the dead and injured men, terrified she would find the face of the man she loved among them.

At that realization, she nearly broke. She did love him. She loved her husband. A gunfighter, a man whose trade was death like this. She turned and spied the driver standing by the lead horses. "Where's Gage?"

"I dunno, girl."

"Was he hurt?" she persisted, taking hold of his lapel as she forced him to focus on her.

"Damned if I know. I never saw him. Saw his work all right. He just opened fire and men started dropping. Middle of the goddamned night. No one but a devil could see anything as dark as it was last night."

Leah went to two more men who had ridden in with the wagon. Neither of them knew anything about Jace. One of them was tying several riderless horses to the hitching post. Standing among them was Blink.

Leah's world tilted. Had Malcolm been wounded? Had he fought with the sheriff's men—or against them? She asked about both Jace and Malcolm now, but no one knew anything. A small kernel of hope settled in the pit of her stomach. If no one knew about Jace and Malcolm, then perhaps they were fine. Maybe they were still out at Hell's Gulch with McCaid and Audrey.

Leah ducked beneath the hitching post and freed Blink. Backing him up, she was nearly clear of the mayhem before a man stopped her. Thinking she would have to fight for the horse, her hand strayed to the hilt of her knife.

"Jace gave me a message for you," the man hurriedly whispered. "Said to tell you he was fine and would come here directly after Meeker's Pass."

Leah drew a breath of relief. "And Malcolm?"

The man shook his head. "It was the worst thing

I ever saw out there. Dead sheep everywhere. Men dropping like flies. Buildings burning. It was a god-damned battlefield. Malcolm's dead."

Leah's knees shook. Not Malcolm. God, what would Audrey do without her brother? "What of Audrey and the children? What news do you have of them? And Mr. McCaid?"

"The rest of the family wasn't hurt, not that I heard of anyways." With that pronouncement, the man melted away. Those of the sheriff's men who were ambulatory were being assisted into Sam's. A few too gravely injured to walk were carried inside the saloon. Maddie offered her assistance with the wounded.

Leah led Blink away from the noise, into the blinding morning sun. She tied him up inside Maddie's stable, then fetched two pails of water for him. On her return from the pump, she found the sheriff standing by the stable doors. In a flash, her terror, confusion, and worry fused into anger. She knew he was fast with his fists, but she didn't care. He was why Malcolm was dead and why Jace was still in danger.

"When is it going to end, Sheriff? How many more people have to die before enough's enough?"

"It ends when my town is my own again. It ends at Meeker's Pass."

Leah poured the water into the trough in Blink's stall. "Why don't you ride out of here? You and the rest of your men, like Jace told you. Let it go."

The sheriff lurched over to her side and yanked her arm, spinning her around. "Let it go?" He leaned down, shoving his face near hers. His mouth was drawn back over bared teeth. "Everything I've done, all of it, I did for your mother and you, you little whelp."

Something shifted within Leah, clicked—though the words he spoke made no sense. She forced herself to focus on what the sheriff was saying. "What are you talking about?"

"Your mother. She was my wife. She ran away from me. Took you and ran. She latched on to the first gambler she could find who would exchange her services for helping the two of you out of the States."

Leah yanked her arm free of his bruising grip. "No."

"Took me years to find you. Years."

"You killed my father."

"I am your father!" he bellowed, bending low to shout into her face. "Leastwise, she said I was. Maybe that was a lie, too." His face twisted with anger. He nodded as he glared down at her, hearing his own words for the first time. "Yeah, likely it was a lie. You're nothing like me and very little like her."

Leah heard only every few words after that. ". . . everything . . . your mother." A cold sweat blanketed her body in the hot, dry stable. The sheriff left, but still she didn't move.

So many mysteries were now brutally clear. It explained why the sheriff was always interested in her and her mother. It explained why he kept the men from them, why he'd forced her to marry. And why no one had stopped him. They knew. They knew the horrible, awful truth that he was her father.

Layer after layer of untruths peeled away, revealing naked understanding. Her mother was an adulteress. She remembered Sally's comment about her mother being a passionate woman who'd made the best choices she could given the temperament she had.

Leah walked across the street, trying to reassemble the shards of her life. She'd reached her front door when she heard her gate swing shut behind her. The man Jace had fought with the previous day stood there, in her yard. She shouldered her rifle and aimed it at him. "State your business, then move on, mister."

"You the one married to Jace Gage?"

"I'm Mrs. Gage."

"You know you weren't the first Mrs. Gage, don't you?"

"Mister, I got a finger sitting on a touchy trigger. I don't recommend you take the long way to saying your piece."

"I'd heard he married again, and I came to warn you."

"Warn me about what?"

"He tell you he's a widower?"

"I'm not concerned with his past."

Anger flared across the stranger's features. "Well I am, wouldn't want the same thing to happen to you that happened to my sister. He killed Jenny— killed his wife." His brows lifted at her shock. "No, I see he didn't tell you. And no doubt he warned you to stay clear of me. He didn't want me carrying tales to you."

"She hanged him."

"The hell she did. I was there when that happened.

I saw it all! She told him all along that she was already married, that she wasn't free to marry him. Her husband was away with his unit, you see."

"He was a *bigamist?*" Leah struggled to process that bit of information. Given the way everything else about her life had been a lie, she couldn't find the energy to doubt this stranger's tale.

"He forced her to marry him, told her that her husband was already dead. But he weren't dead. I was with him. When we got a furlough to come home and see family, we found out what Gage had done to her." He looked at Leah, his jaw set. "She didn't hang him—we did, her husband and me. He violated my sister. We should have been there to protect her." His eyes grew unfocused as his mind dipped into the past.

"His friends rode in to town before we could finish. They started shooting at everyone, everything. They killed my friend. I was shot. My sister was crying. I saw Gage grab a gun and shoot Jenny. She was pleading for her life, begging him to spare her, begging until he blew her head off."

"No." The word was barely a whisper. Leah lowered her rifle from her shoulder to her hip, but still kept it trained on the man. She was sickened. The logic of this man's story didn't mesh with the Jace she knew, but the violence did. The man glared up at her. There was something in his eyes that set her nerves on edge. "You've said what you came to say. Now you'd best clear out."

He held up a hand. "I'm going. Just wanted you to know that I'll take care of Gage out at Meeker's Pass. He won't be a worry of yours for long."

Leah kept the gun trained on him as he left her yard and headed back toward the mayhem at the sheriff's office. *"My past made my present,"* Jace had said. Was this what he meant? How many bereaved relatives had he left behind in the battles he'd fought during the war or the towns he'd cleared since it ended? What other brothers would come forward to avenge their wronged sisters?

What was the truth of his marriage? He'd said he loved his wife. And he said he hated her. Which was it? She leaned against the wall, her mind in turmoil. She understood at last—and too late—why her mother was forever warning her never to love a gunfighter.

She went inside her home and retrieved her saddlebags and gear, then went back to Maddie's stable and saddled Blink. She had to get out, had to leave town so that she could think. She didn't want to talk to Maddie or the Kesslers, or anyone who had known the lie her mother lived and helped perpetuate it. She didn't want to see Jace and hear more lies or the half-truths that she longed to believe.

She wanted to go and never look back.

Chapter 20

Jace lay on his stomach overlooking the ledge where the sheriff's men were positioned—among them, Hugh McDonald. Rupert had separated from them earlier in the day, heading south toward the entrance to the canyon. If he didn't turn up before this confrontation ended, Jace would have to track him down. He'd opted instead to keep with his mission and stay focused on the payroll shipment.

The visibility from his vantage point to the pass below was limited—the large rock cliff on his right blocked his view. The ledge below Jace was the most strategic position from which to waylay a wagon in the narrow pass. The men on that ledge had good cover from the road and could see three hundred yards down the last two bends in the road that cut through the pass below.

Around noon, a cloud of dust rose at the mouth of the canyon. A big cloud, according to the excited shout of one of the men below him. The loggers' payroll coach and guard had started into the pass. He watched the sheriff's men get into position. The coach below was coming fast. Dust floated above the horses, marking their progress.

One of the sheriff's men took out his pistol. Hugh lifted his revolver and smashed it down on his head, knocking him out. Jace shot at the rock in front of the man sighting down his rifle toward the teamsters driving the payroll coach. The man lurched to his feet and was shot from below. The three other men turned and looked at Hugh and at Jace above them. Hugh leveled his pistol on them, ordering them to drop their gunbelts and surrender.

Jace rose to his feet, pleased with how easily the ambush had been brought under control. Then pain exploded in his shoulder blade. He fell and rolled, fast enough to avoid the next hit from the butt of a rifle. Rupert Hardin. Jace grinned up at the man who still gave him nightmares. He should have died that day he'd tried to hang Jace.

No matter. He would die today.

Jace swept his foot out, knocking Rupert's legs out from beneath him. Rupert's rifle went scattering over the ledge to drop to the level below. Jace rolled over and sat on his opponent, gripping his neck, squeezing him, tighter and tighter as the rope had squeezed Jace's neck all those years ago.

Rupert pressed his thumbs into Jace's eyes, forcing him to release his hold to push Rupert's hands away. Jace got a clean jab at the man's jaw. They rolled across the curving surface of the boulder, each throwing punches.

The marshal's men had climbed to the ledge below and had taken charge of the situation. Two of them climbed up to where Jace fought Rupert. Riggins and Lambert. Out of the corner of his eye, Jace saw Lambert draw. He knew he'd claim he was trying to help. He'd kill Jace and get away with it. Jace's momentary distraction worked to Rupert's benefit. They rolled closer to the edge. He pushed Jace's head down, holding him with both hands fisted around his neck. Jace shoved his elbows between Rupert's arms, breaking his hold. He yanked Rupert's head forward for a head butt that stunned him enough for Jace to leverage a boot under his crotch and hoist him up, over the edge. He landed on his back on the crumbling, rocky edge of the ledge below. The rocks gave way, slipping beneath Rupert as he tumbled the rest of the way down to the road below.

Jace didn't turn to watch his fall. He eyed Lambert and Riggins, who came forward to give him a hand up.

"What are you doing here, Lambert? I told you I'd see you hang for shooting Eddie."

"Who's Eddie?" Marshal Riggins asked as he glanced between the two of them.

"He's one of the sheriff's men I shot when I came out here a few days ago. I met Jace at the pass, down below. Thought the kid was armed."

"He wasn't armed. He'd already surrendered to me."

Riggins came over and took hold of Jace's shoulder. "It's over now, son. The payroll's on its way through Defiance. Your job's done here, Jace. It's done."

Jace frowned. "I didn't find the gold."

"We've got the sheriff." The marshal gestured down the ledge toward two of his men who had brought the sheriff up from town. "We can work on that while we wait for his trial back in Cheyenne."

Jace followed them down to the level below. Hugh was tied up next to the sheriff. "Marshal!" Jace nodded to Hugh. "He's not one of them. He's working for me."

"Thought you worked alone."

"Usually I do. But it would be foolish to turn down help now and then." One of the marshal's men untied Hugh. He rubbed at his wrists, then came over and shook hands with Jace.

"Thank you, Mr. Gage."

Jace nodded. "Go home to your family."

The man smiled. "You don't have to tell me twice!"

Jace confronted the sheriff. "Well, Kemp. I can't say it's been a good run for you, but I am glad to see the last of you."

"I ain't gonna hang anytime soon, boy. Don't you worry, 'cause I got something the marshal here wants."

Jace smiled. "Maybe. But maybe there are just some secrets we take to our graves, Kemp."

Chapter 21

Jace knew he was grinning like a fool. It was over, all of it. His nightmare of a first marriage. The sheriff and his gang were dead, gone or arrested. Defiance was freed. He was freed. He crested a hill and saw the town in the distance.

His wife wanted a church. He pictured where he'd place it—on her street, its whitewash so bright it would shine even at night, its steeple so high, everyone would know long before they reached the town that Defiance was a God-fearing community. It would be his gift to Leah, and her gift to the town.

He settled his horse in Maddie's stable, curious to find that Blink wasn't in his stall. He didn't have a chance to give that much thought as Maddie rushed into the stable. "Jace! You're back!"

He held her briefly in a hug, a little surprised at her welcome. Where was Leah? Why wasn't she here to greet him? "It's over."

"The sheriff?"

"Is headed to Cheyenne with the marshal."

"Then it is over. Jace—"

Tension ripped through him at her halting comment. Something wasn't right. "What's the matter, Maddie? Where's Leah?"

"She's gone. She took Blink and rode for the hills."

Jace took hold of Maddie's arms. "Why? Was someone after her?"

"Not that I know. She was with me when the wagon came in from the Hell's Gulch raid. We got the news about Malcolm. It was a shock to her." Jace cursed and headed back toward the stable. "She'll be back—give her time."

Jace wasn't listening. He cut across Maddie's yard and made for the livery. His horse had been ridden hard for three days. He needed a fresh mount. If she'd left the day the wagon came in from McCaid's, then she'd had two days to lose herself in the mountain. Hell and damnation. Why had she run?

Five days later, Jace jolted awake. He lay atop his bedroll in the clearing Leah had first taken him to all those weeks ago. For a minute, he kept still, taking stock of the world around him. It was dark. And cold. What had roused him? He heard his horse whicker . . . and an answering snuffle from another horse. His fingers slipped into the grip of his Colt, the steel cold around his fingers. He cocked the revolver as he swung up, pointing to a shadow that loomed over him, instinctively sighting in on his target.

"Morning, Jace." Leah's sweet voice moved over him like a summer breeze, but didn't ease his tension. She stood over him, holding the reins to her horse.

He blinked the last vestiges of sleep from his eyes and uncocked his gun. "Leah? Christ, I could have shot you." He had been searching for her for nearly a week, had followed all the paths he could find. Two days ago, he'd decided to come back to this spot and see if she would show up.

And here she was, standing next to Blink, too quiet for his peace of mind. The sun had begun to rise, softening the pre-dawn sky to lavender. He rubbed his face, playing for time.

"What are you doing up here, Jace?"

"What am I doing? I came to retrieve my wife, who was supposed to be safely at Maddie's. What are you doing up here? Why did you run? Didn't you get my message?"

"I want a divorce."

The words were like knives in his ears, slicing all the way into his soul. It hurt. Christ almighty, he'd known better than to let a woman in again.

Jace slowly stood up. "No divorce. We consummated the marriage. That was the deal." Her silence was deafening—he sensed her withdrawal. He lurched forward and grabbed her arms, pulling her against him. "Come back to Defiance with me. We'll figure this out. We'll work through this. I know this marriage didn't happen the way you would have wanted . . . I'll court you. We'll start over." God, he was begging, just as he'd done before, with Jenny.

She shook her head. The morning's light, growing brighter every second, lit the glitter of moisture in her eyes. "It can't be fixed, Jace. It was a lie. My whole life has been a lie."

Jace sucked in a breath of bitter morning air. "Did you lie to me, Leah? Did you never mean to be with me when I finished with Defiance?"

Her chin trembled. Her nostrils flared. At least she did him the honor of meeting his eyes as she tossed him out of her life. "Do us both a favor. Leave these woods. Leave Defiance. Leave the Territory. Do whatever it is that you want to do, just leave me alone."

Time folded in on itself in Jace's mind. He'd been in this spot before, grasping another unwilling wife. Her eyes had been liquid with tears, too, like Leah's. He saw her sneer at him. *I never loved you, you fool. I used you. You were so easy.* He had stared at her face, knowing he was seeing it for the last time. Curly brown hair, big hazel eyes. Freckles. Innocence so thick you could cut it with a knife.

Jace looked over his wife's head to her husband, the man his unit had been hunting, the man his wife loved. The truth hit him like a sledgehammer. "You're a spy."

"Of course, I'm a spy. Did you think I would willingly lie with you, a filthy Yankee?" She spit on his shirt. Her husband stepped forward and tore her out of his arms, then shoved Jace over to stand beneath an ancient oak tree. Men swarmed around him. Tying his ankles, his wrists behind him, fashioning a noose that they dropped over his head. He hadn't fought them. He'd merely stood still, watching the woman he loved, willing her to do this with her own hands.

The rope was tossed over the branch. Her husband brought the rope's end to her and told her to string him up. Her eyes had narrowed as she took the rope. She drew it tight. And smiled.

Jace let Leah go. She, too, had lied to him. She stepped to the side of her horse and mounted up. He turned and began dismantling his campsite, refusing to watch her ride away. The scar about his neck burned like a fresh wound. He rolled up his bedding, kicked dirt into the fire, saddled up, then rode out.

The day's heat thickened as he cleared the woods and moved down to the Plains below. At the rise outside of town, he paused. Grasshoppers snapped and leapt across the summer-browned grass. The mid-day sun beat down on him as the calm breeze sucked him dry. Heat radiated back from the baked earth. He could smell his horse's sweat. Everything was the same. And everything was different. He sat there, in the burning sun, contemplating what was next.

What did a man do when he had no job, no woman, no family, no purpose?

He looked at Defiance. Then he looked at the low hills that shimmered out to the east, pink and brown, wavering in the summer heat. His horse started toward Defiance, and he didn't stop it.

Leah sat on a boulder overhanging a steep ravine that led to a narrow valley far below. For the last twenty-four hours, she'd been aware of Jace's friend, Sager, trailing her. She could have dodged him, but knew he was not one to be put off so easily. A man like him would dog her all the way to California if he'd set his mind to it. She'd picked this clearing to face him.

She didn't turn when she heard rocks crunch beneath his mount's hooves. The leather of his saddle creaked as he dismounted. He walked to the edge of the ravine and stood silently next to her. Wind blew up the side of the cliff, crisp with the altitude, tangy with the scent of pine.

"There's folks in town worried about you." Sager broke the silence.

Leah stared determinedly westward. Her chest tightened at his words. He crouched next to her. Neither spoke for a minute. He picked up a twig and broke it into pieces, letting it fall into the shadows below them. "How long you gonna run, Leah?"

Leah folded her knees and wrapped her arms about her legs. "I don't like my life, Sager. I want a new one. I want to walk until I'm not me anymore, until I can't feel anything." Tears started a trail down her cheeks, but she made no move to brush them away. It hurt. Everything hurt. "It was a lie. Everything. It was a lie."

"What was a lie?"

"My whole life. My parents. My mother. Her lover. The sheriff. Me. All of it. And now Audrey's gone and Malcolm's dead and Wolf's dead. And I can't change any of it. Not one single thing." She fixed her gaze on the distant horizon, absorbing the freedom it promised. "Have you ever wanted to run, Sager? Run and run and run until you outrun yourself?"

Sager sat on the ledge next to her. "Most of my life."

Leah sniffled and ventured a look at him. The wind agitated his jagged black hair. "What did you do?"

"I ran. I tried to be someone I wasn't. And then the war came and I killed." He blew out a long breath. "And then I met Rachel and she put the pieces back together."

"Jace can't fix me."

"I reckon that's true. You can't be fixed if you aren't ready to mend."

Leah's chin trembled. She waited a second, searching for composure. "He killed his wife."

"No." Sager's amber gaze sliced toward her. "I killed his wife."

Straightening, Leah looked at Sager, waiting for him to elaborate.

"Near the end of the war, he fell like a lead weight for a local girl. There was something not right about her. McCaid and I, well, we didn't trust her, but Jace doesn't do things by half measures. He adored that woman. He would sneak out of camp to meet with her. Then one day, he said he'd married her. We were fighting a band of Rebel guerillas who called that town home. They were getting the upper hand. McCaid saw what was happening before either Jace or I. She was spying on us for her man."

Sager looked at her. "She was already married when she married Jace. McCaid told Jace what he'd discovered. Jace went to confront her, found her with her husband. That band of dogs strung him up. They were hanging him slowly, hoisting him right off the ground when McCaid and I arrived. I cut him down. They opened fire. McCaid was holding them off. I gave my revolver to Jace, and when I looked up, his wife had a bead on McCaid. Two guns fired. Mine and Jace's."

The plaintive wind filled the space around them with its sad wail for a long moment. "I gotta tell you, I don't know what's worse, Leah. Killing the woman you loved, or having your best friend do it." He looked at her. "It was war. And she was a spy. We both did what we had to do."

Leah buried her face in her knees, willing the wind to be the only thing she heard.

Sager rose. "When you figure out that you can't outrun yourself, you might also realize Jace is a man worth fighting for. I hope, for your sake and his, that you do it soon because you left a good man hurting back there. I've seen him break before. It ain't something a soul gets over too fast." He walked over to his horse. Leah didn't move. She heard him mount up and ride away.

Jace sat at the back table where the sheriff used to sit, nursing a bottle of whiskey. He'd been there for two days. Maybe three. Sam didn't chase him out at night. He just set a fresh bottle in front of him and locked the door as he left each night. Jace's bleary gaze swept the room. There was a chance that one or two of the men who remained were still loyal to Kemp, but Jace didn't care. A bullet in the back would fix a whole lot of problems.

A man came to stand next to him. Jace shifted to glare up at him and was surprised to see his friend, Sager, standing there.

"Who the hell sent for you?"

Sager grinned, a flash of white teeth in his tanned face. "Good to see you, too! Rumor had it you got rid of the sheriff. Came to see for myself." Sager motioned to Sam for another glass, then reached for Jace's bottle and filled it. "Maddie told us about Leah."

"Us?"

"Rachel and me." He sipped the whiskey.

Jace leaned both elbows on the table and took a long draw from his glass. "Leave it alone, Sager."

"You know, Jace, if you had a bullet festering in a wound, I'd dig it out for you. This ain't that different. What happened?"

"The sheriff was going to force Leah to marry one of his thugs. I had to marry her to stop it. And now that the sheriff's gone, she's got no use for me." He shrugged. "That's it. Ain't nothing to fix."

"That why you been here at Sam's for days?" Sager set his whiskey down and put a hand on Jace's shoulder. "Let's go. Maddie's got a pot of coffee and a soft bed waiting for you."

Jace shrugged him off.

"The answer ain't in that bottle, Jace."

Jace tossed the contents of his glass back in a single swallow. "No? Then where is it? Where the hell is it?"

Sager sighed. "I don't know. Time, maybe."

"As if time helped before." He looked at Sager. "You shoulda let me hang."

"We couldn't have done that, no more than you could have kept yourself from loving your wives— either of them." He put a hand on the back of Jace's neck, intending to forcefully take him from the saloon. "C'mon. Things will be clearer in the morning."

Jace pulled free of Sager's hold and lurched to his feet. "Leave me the fuck alone, Sager!" His hands reflexively dropped to his guns.

Silence blanketed the room. Sager looked from his friend's crazed eyes, to his hands and back again. "You gonna shoot me, Jace?"

Thunder sounded in the room as everyone scrambled to clear the space around them, backing to the walls, slipping out of the front and back exits, ducking beneath tables. The panicked noise forced a thread of rational thought through Jace's mind. Seeing the change in him, Sager released a long breath. Jace shoved past him and out into the night.

Purely from habit, he found himself heading toward Leah's. Maddie had been seeing to her chickens and garden. All stood as if it only awaited her return from a brief absence, not as if she was gone forever. He stumbled up the steps, remembering every interaction with her. Challenging her to a camping trip. Kissing her. Rescuing her from Kemp's men. Consummating their marriage. Inside her home, everything was as she'd left it. Loaves of bread still in their pans, baskets at the ready for her deliveries. What had happened the morning she took off?

He shoved the pans aside and set his rifle down next to them. He shucked his gunbelt and bandoliers and piled them on the table. He fished the knife out of his boot, divesting himself of his last weapon. What would Leah think, seeing him without his guns? A harsh laugh broke from him. She would never see him again. It didn't fucking matter. He laughed all the way outside, across her yard, to the street where he turned and looked back at her house.

It was an abomination—the entire row of houses was ramshackle. Rage settled over him, like a shroud, smothering him. He couldn't believe he'd ever seen her house as homey. He started up the street. Why the hell was he still here? He should leave. What point was there in staying?

He kicked a gatepost at the house nearest Jim's store. The entire fence collapsed. He ripped one of the slats off and threw it at the house, pleased at the crash it made as it hit a broken window. He took up another slat and climbed closer to the house, throwing it at a different window. A long piece of siding jutted at an odd angle to the house, warped by weather and neglect. Jace pried it free. Then found another and ripped it off. Soon wood was flying everywhere.

He had one thought and one thought only: to tear the whole goddamned town apart and wipe Leah's memory from this entire corner of Hell.

Chapter 22

By the next morning when Sager walked up to Jim's, one shanty was destroyed, and Jace had made good progress on a second one. Sager hadn't slept but a couple of hours in the last three days. He'd tried again this morning to talk some sense into Jace, but the man had gone somewhere in his head that kept him from rational thought or behavior.

Stepping inside the general store, Sager tried to think of a way to help Jace. Rachel was there in the back room, holding their son, chatting with Sally. She met his eyes. He shook his head. A commotion out front kept him from saying more. In quick order, the store filled with a passel of kids, followed by Julian McCaid and his bride-to-be Audrey. Hugs were exchanged and brief small talk.

"What are you doing in town?"

McCaid looked at Audrey and smiled. "Audrey's agreed to marry me. We've come to have Jim perform the ceremony." Audrey smiled up at him, but Sager could see the shadows in her eyes. Losing Malcolm had taken its toll.

"That's great news!" The men shook hands and the women hugged Audrey. And then the room settled back into silence.

McCaid noticed something wasn't quite right.

"What's wrong?"

Sager made a face. "It's Jace."

"What's wrong with Jace?" He looked from Sager to Jim.

"I had to send for Sager, Julian," Jim explained. "We thought you'd left. No one could stop him. He's gone berserk."

"What do you mean?" Julian asked. The room grew silent.

"Leah left him," Jim started.

Sager gave Julian a dark look. "She's not coming back."

Jace cursed as his fingers slipped yet again. They were bleeding from hundreds of cuts and splinters. He tightened his grip on the old siding strip, feeling the pain that sliced at his hands. He braced a foot against the side of the house and pulled. It loosened a little bit.

Two shadows fell across his. He didn't turn to see who was there. He didn't care.

"Hi, Jace. What are you doing?" He heard Julian's question, but it was as if he'd asked someone else, someone who could answer. Jace ignored him.

"Jace, what's goin' on? What are you doing?" Sager asked, coming up and touching Jace's shoulder. Jace shrugged him off. Sager put a hand on Jace's shoulder and another on his arm and pulled him away from the house. "Come on, it's enough now."

Jace wasn't done and didn't want to be interrupted. He planted a fist in Sager's jaw. "Leave me the fuck alone." He turned back to the piece of siding, which he now had half off. "She did," he muttered. Leah and the whole town had left him alone. Why the hell couldn't they do the same? Julian came up behind him and pulled him away from the house. Jace landed an elbow in Julian's ribs and turned to face his friends, fists clenched. Julian and Sager jumped him, slamming him back against the splintering siding, restraining his legs with theirs, pinning his fists above his head.

"What the hell's wrong with you?" Julian asked.

"Get off me," Jace growled.

"Not yet. Not till you're calmer," Julian declared.

"Jesus, look at his hands."

Jace shut his eyes. He knew what they were seeing. The remnants of his leather gloves hung in shredded tatters from his fingers and palms. Bright red blood flowed freely from his torn skin, splinters spiking through the swelling flesh.

"That's it. You've done enough. Let's get you cleaned up." Julian pulled him from the wall but did not release him. He and Sager walked on either side of Jace, holding his arms folded behind him as they headed for the public water pump a little ways down the street.

Jace didn't resist. There was no point. They pushed him to sit down at the low wall surrounding the pump. Rachel and Audrey sat on either side of him and began to fuss over his hands. He looked up the street, seeing the house he'd demolished and the one he was working on. Yesterday, he'd thought only of erasing Leah's existence from the town.

Now he wanted anything but that.

He wanted her home, here with him. He wanted the life she'd offered, the life that was a lie. Audrey dampened a cloth and washed his face. She held his chin and studied his eyes as she made another pass over his cheek. The cloth was cool against his hot skin. Audrey knew Leah. They'd grown up together. If anyone could explain her to him, Audrey could. "She wanted a church," he told her.

Audrey smiled.

"I'm tearing down those shacks. Gonna build her a big white church." A muscle at the corner of his jaw flexed. "Then maybe she'll come home."

Audrey and Rachel exchanged a look. "With a bell," Rachel added. "It needs a bell so that we can ring it and call her back."

He looked at Rachel and nodded. "A bell." The women poked and prodded at his hands, pulling splinters free. It didn't hurt as much as ripping down the houses, but he welcomed the pain all the same. Anything was better than the ache in his chest.

Thunder rolled overhead. Maddie said they should go inside, but he didn't move. Julian yanked him to his feet and the girls wrapped his arms around their shoulders and led him inside. Julian said something that made Sager laugh, but Jace didn't hear it. These women loved his friends. He wondered if Julian and Sager knew how lucky they were? Inside Maddie's foyer, he pulled them into a hug, pressing a kiss to their foreheads, each in turn.

"Thank you."

"Jace—we aren't done fixing you up yet," Rachel warned.

"No. Thank you for loving those two bastards outside."

Audrey laughed and pulled him toward the kitchen. Maddie was pouring hot water over the cold already in the tub. The privacy screen was half drawn. Rachel started on Jace's shirt buttons.

"Oh, no. I can wash myself, thank you." He pulled free and started unraveling the bandages they'd wrapped around his hands. Behind the privacy screen, he fished in his pants pocket for his cigar butt, then stripped and got into the tub. The hot water settled about him, easing his physical pains, driving others deeper inside. He closed his eyes and tried to force his mind to be quiet.

"Jace, I've brought your clothes and shaving gear from Leah's," Audrey said as she stepped around the screen to set his things on a chair. She put her hands on her hips and frowned down at him. Jace bit the cigar and slipped deeper into the water.

"I don't understand it," Audrey fretted. "Did you see how she left the house? Her full day's baking sitting out, some loaves still in the pans. It's as if she just stepped outside and vanished. She left before she'd even made her deliveries."

He took up the soap and made foam in the water, hoping the milky wash would offer him some cover. "She didn't vanish. I saw her up the mountain. She said it was a lie, everything was a lie. I don't know what that meant. She wouldn't tell me."

A noisy clatter of dishes drew Audrey back into the kitchen. "She'll be back," Maddie said. "She always comes back."

Jace dropped the soap bar back in its dish and rinsed his hands, which burned from the soap in his cuts. He leaned back and thought about what Maddie had said. *She always comes back?* Did she run away often? Why? And now he was one more thing for her to run from. He shut his eyes and thought about the church. He'd build that for her, then leave. No point staying where he wasn't wanted.

He washed himself from head to foot, then soaked till the soapy water began to make him itch. A fierce rainstorm raged outside. Lightning and thunder shook the windows. The women chattered as they moved about the kitchen, preparing a big supper to celebrate Audrey and Julian's wedding.

Christ. He wished he were anywhere but here.

When he'd run out of time to stall, he pulled himself from the tub and dressed in the clothes Audrey had left him. He emptied the tub and set the wash corner to rights. He'd no sooner stepped around the screen than the women drew him over to a seat so that they could work on his hands a bit more while Maddie gave him a shave. They worked in silence, until heavy boots sounded in the hallway outside the kitchen. Julian burst into the room. Taking a look at the women gathered around Jace, he bellowed, "What the hell's going on in here?"

Audrey sent him a glare. "Julian McCaid, please lower your voice. You'll wake baby Jacob."

Julian's brows furrowed. "What's the delay? We're ready for a wedding up front."

Jace looked at the women clustered about him and offered a cocky grin. "I guess they weren't finished with me yet."

Audrey laughed and stepped between Julian and the rest of the room. Setting a hand on his chest, she backed him to the door. "Out. We have work to do."

At the threshold, Julian came to a hard stop. "How much longer?"

Audrey stood on tippy-toes to kiss his cheek. "An hour. No more."

Maddie shook her head when Audrey rejoined them. "That man's at the end of his patience. Why don't you slip upstairs and get yourself ready? I'll finish with Jace."

Rachel jumped up and put an arm around Audrey. "Come along, Miss Sheridan. Time to make a bride out of you!"

Watching them, Jace swallowed hard. Neither of his wives had been happy about marrying him. He made the mistake of looking at Maddie, who read in his eyes every secret he wanted to hide. She wiped foam from the razor and stared down at it while they listened to the girls' receding voices. Then the only sound in the room was the rain outside.

"I know about the lie." Her words were barely a whisper, as if she fought with herself to speak them.

A dull throbbing started in Jace's head. A warning. He didn't want to hear what she meant—but couldn't live another second without knowing. "What lie?" he prompted.

"What Leah said, about everything being a lie." She looked at Jace, visibly bracing herself for his reaction. "The sheriff is her father."

Jace shook his head. "The sheriff killed her father."

"The sheriff killed the man who ran away with his wife. Mary, Leah's mother, was married to Bill Kemp—all along. We knew, all of us, and we swore each other to secrecy." Maddie's eyes filled with moisture. Or maybe it was his eyes that made her image waver. He ripped his gaze away to stare at a far wall.

"Leah was so young when Mary's lover was killed. We thought it was for the best to keep her in ignorance, especially since the sheriff didn't appear to want Mary back. Not entirely, anyway. I don't really know what happened between them. But Leah's life has been a lie, one that we forced on her."

Jace couldn't draw a full breath. Was that why she'd left? Was that all of it—was he not part of why she'd run? Could he stay and wait for her return? He looked at Maddie. "Finish the shave. I'll go wait with the men out front."

Jace paused in the hallway outside the kitchen. McCaid, Sager, and Jim were talking in boisterous voices. Sally was trying to keep the children in order. He forced a smile as he entered the room, feeling out of sorts with his bandaged hands and broken heart.

When Rachel brought Audrey into the room, a look came over McCaid. A look of awe. Joy. A certainty that the best years of his life were only beginning. Jace looked at his feet, unable to watch the couple as they said their vows. He would never have what they had, what Sager and Rachel, Jim and Sally had.

Not without Leah.

Jace stood in Maddie's kitchen early the next morning, cutting off the bandages.

"Good Heavens! What are you doing, Jace?" Maddie exclaimed as she hurried to his side. "You leave those bandages where they are." She grabbed his wrists, arresting his progress.

"Can't do it, Maddie. I got work to do."

"You can't very well work with your hands in shreds. Give yourself a few days."

"I have gloves. Put some of that salve on my hands and be done. I got a church to build."

A few minutes later, Jace crossed the street to Leah's house. He'd been there only once since his return. His guns were on her kitchen table. He remembered dropping his gear here after nearly shooting Sager. He needed to clean his guns. Jesus. He'd just shucked everything that day.

He moved her stale loaves of bread and cleared the table so that he could see to his guns. When that was finished, he thought about strapping his gunbelt on, but chose not to. He felt naked without his weapons . . . and somehow *new*. He went outside and walked up the street to the second, half-demolished shack. Sager came to stand next to him and handed him a cup of coffee. Jace looked at him. "You're up early."

Sager shrugged. "The church ain't gonna build itself."

"No, it's not," Julian said, coming up to stand next to them. He looked at Jace. "Tell me you have a plan for turning these shacks into a church."

Jace nodded. "I have a plan. And when we're done, we'll fix up Leah's house for the preacher."

"Can we help, too?" Jace looked around to see Audrey's four foster boys standing by, eager to work.

"You may—once you put shoes on," Julian answered. "Then go up to Jim's and have him get gloves for you." He looked at Jace. "They can start sorting the lumber. We'll have to reuse what we can."

A week later, only Leah's shack was still standing. Piles of lumber were grouped according to size and condition. Windows, doors, and odd pieces of furniture were stacked in the road. Orders had been telegraphed to vendors in Denver for six arched church windows, two extra large doors, and a church bell. Wires had also been sent to Cheyenne, Denver, and Santa Fe, appealing for a clergyman to come serve the town—a call that had not yet been answered.

Audrey, Rachel, and Maddie began serving lunch. Jace accepted a plate from Maddie, then perched himself on a saw-horse as he started to eat. Audrey's older boys were acting strangely, looking at him, then looking away, exchanging nudges and whispers.

"Something on your mind, boys?"

"No," Kurt and Luc both answered.

"They think you look funny without your guns," one of their sisters answered. Julian looked at him, his features wary.

"Well, you'd best get used to it. I'm not a gun-fighter anymore."

"What are you going to do now, if you're not the Avenger anymore?" another of Audrey's foster daughters, asked.

Jace looked around at the children, his friends, their wives, and Maddie. He'd avoided giving the topic much thought, but what he really didn't want was a whole lot of discussion about the topic— mostly because he didn't know himself.

"I don't know. Figured I'd get this church built for Leah, then maybe move on."

That pronouncement brought a heavy silence from the adults. Audrey and Maddie exchanged a look, but quickly busied themselves with lunch dishes. Sager held Jacob, and gave Jace a long look. Jace stabbed his potato salad with a fork and shoved it in his mouth. He was spared further discussion on the topic by the arrival of several freight wagons.

Julian greeted his construction foreman and introduced him to the men. "What's this?" Jace asked.

"It's my construction crew and the lumber I was going to use to build a school house at Hell's Gulch. I decided that can wait until next summer.

Figured you could use the men and supplies for the church."

Jace met Julian's eyes. "I can. Thank you."

The next days passed in a blur. Between the construction crew and men showing up to work who had once been the sheriff's men or who were from outlying ranches, progress on the church began to happen rapidly.

"Jace!" Hugh McDonald said one morning when he arrived at work. "Looks like you got enough help here. How about if I go down to Denver and rustle up a preacher?"

Jace wiped his left sleeve across his forehead, clearing away the sweat from the hot July day. He looked back at the church, which was nearly finished, but still lacked a minister. He nodded. "Yeah. Do that. Kidnap one if you have to. If you don't have any luck in Denver, head down to Santa Fe." Jace fished some money out of his pocket and handed it to Hugh. "Here's for your expenses. If you need more, wire me."

Hugh shook his head and held up a hand. "You saved my life. This is the least I can do."

Jace met his eyes, feeling humbled. "I don't care if you find a priest, reverend or minister. Hell, I'd even take a rabbi. Just bring back a man of God."

Hugh tapped his heels to his horse's sides.

Jace called after him, "A *sober* man of God!"

Two weeks later, the church was finished. The construction debris had been cleared away as had the surplus lumber and supplies. Leah's house had a new roof and a new coat of paint. He was done here. It was time to move on, Jace thought as he stood in the nave of the new church. The tall glass windows they had installed that morning made the space feel sacred. He looked at the afternoon light filtering in from the western side, illuminating beams of dust left from the construction. The wind no longer blew through the building, but it was still empty. There were no pews. No altar. No crosses.

He shoved a hand through his hair, staring at the crisp whitewashed walls. What the hell had he been thinking, a gunfighter building a church? He was a killer. What did he know about building a sacred space? It was as empty and useless as his marriage. He crossed the room, in a hurry to leave, wishing above all that he had not stayed, that he had left Leah and Defiance and his broken dreams far, far behind.

It was time to strap his guns back on and hightail it out of there.

He yanked open the door, but his way was blocked by a woman holding a kitchen chair. He leveled his best glare on her, but she didn't back down.

"Mr. Gage," the woman greeted him. "We've come to thank you for what you've built for us here." Jace lifted his gaze to the two teenaged boys standing beside her, also holding chairs—and beyond them to a long line of women. And chairs.

"Chasing the sheriff out was enough, sir. It really was. My husband and I feared we would have to leave our homestead and move somewhere else, somewhere less attractive to ruffians and thieves. We would have lost everything, sir. You not only saved our home, but you built this church." Jace frowned down at the woman, wishing she wasn't blocking his escape. "Sager sent out word you needed chairs until pews could be obtained. So we brought you ours. You use them as long as you need to."

She pushed past him before he could answer. Jace stood back and let the long line of women and children enter. In short order, twelve rows of eight chairs were lined up like a motley bunch of soldiers standing at attention. The women walked around the small interior, exclaiming over the windows.

The church filled with a discordant banging as the team hanging the bell worked to get the heavy piece in place. The noise clashed with the excited laughter of the women. He wanted to leave, but the women had begun filing out, and every one of them paused to introduce herself to him.

Audrey and Rachel were the last to leave. "You've done a good thing here, Jace." Rachel kissed his cheek.

Audrey gave him a smile as she put her hand on the center of his chest, right where it hurt. "I'm not at all surprised that Leah ran for the hills, with all that has happened recently. Give her time. She will be back. I know it."

Before they could turn to leave, the bell went silent. The girls sent each other a look, and then the silence was broken with a beautiful sound as the bell made its first full ring. Back and forth, the peals took on life, growing in depth, filling the church and the town with its rich tones.

He wondered if Leah could hear the bells.

As the last echoes died away, Jace followed

Audrey and Rachel outside, where dozens of people were milling about in the street in front of the church, greeting each other, setting up tables, unloading wagons. Women snapped bright colored tablecloths over rough wooden trestles. Pies and casseroles and foods of all sorts soon covered the tables. Two men rolled barrels of beer down from Sam's and set them up in the shade of Maddie's drive.

The noise and motion and sun broadsided him. For a moment, he simply stood there. He'd never seen so many people in Defiance. Judging from the number of wagons parked in the flattened area where the old shacks had been, they were area ranchers who had driven in for the day.

A group of men approached him. "I'd like to shake your hand, Mr. Gage." One of the men introduced each of the others with him, but Jace knew he would not remember their names.

"What you've done here is a miracle."

Jace looked back at the church. "Not a miracle. It's just a church."

"It isn't just the church. You saved this town. We would have had to leave to spare our boys being drawn into Kemp's gang, like the poor Perkins boy," a man with bushy sideburns said.

"You freed good men who were stuck in the sheriff's mess and didn't know how to get out."

Jace was uncomfortable with their praise. He looked around at the gathering, realizing he'd never stayed in a town once he'd cleared it. He'd heard some of the towns had thrown some mighty celebrations, but he'd never been there for them.

One of the men clapped a hand on Jace's back

and led their small group toward the prairie side of the church yard, where barbeques were fired up, roasting beef and pork haunches. "Pete here brought the pork, and I brought the beef." He pointed back to the other side of the church. "The women folk have been cooking up a storm so that we could have a feast here today."

Jace looked around the noisy, busy area, wishing Leah were there. How she would have enjoyed the festivities. Not a single person moved furtively or showed fear or apprehension. It was as if all of the town's joy had been corked in a bottle and had suddenly broken free.

"What are your plans now, Mr. Gage?" one of the men asked.

Jace froze, coming face-to-face with the one question he wasn't ready to answer. He shrugged. "I dunno. Move on, I guess."

"Defiance could use a man like you. We're in need of a sheriff, you know." The words fell from the speaker's mouth as easily as if they were discussing new boots. Jace looked at him, really looked at him, wondering if he had any idea what he was asking. Stay here, where Leah had abandoned him. Stay and face, every day, the life he could have had, had she not lied to him.

He wasn't man enough to do it.

"No." There must have been something in his expression that set the others on edge. They swapped glances and grew silent, fidgety. Jace excused himself and walked over to where Julian and Sager were standing with their wives and Maddie.

Audrey hooked her arm in his and smiled up at

him. "This is a sight to see, Jace. You've done an amazing thing for Defiance. I never thought to see it like this again. Leah would have loved to be here."

Jace clamped his jaw shut and looked unseeingly at the activity around them as he forced his mind to stay blank.

"Do you think Defiance has a chance?" Rachel asked.

"It does now," Maddie answered. "This area has rich pastures and plenty of water. I can't see the cattle"—she looked at Julian—"and sheep operations pulling up stakes if they don't have to. All of these ranchers need the support of a town."

Their conversation was interrupted by the arrival of another wagon. Hugh McDonald had returned—with a man who was singing "Amazing Grace" at the top of his voice, waving his arms energetically, his movements out of step with the song.

"I found us a preacher!" Hugh called.

Anger shot up Jace's back. He made a beeline for the wagon. "I told you to bring back a *sober* man of God."

"Yes, well, I can explain that. He was right as rain when we left Denver, but when we got off the train in Cheyenne, he began with a stomach complaint that gripped him harder the closer we came to Defiance. I figured he could benefit from a sip or two of my stomach cure." He held up a bottle whose label was worn around the edges. "But it had the odd side effect of making him sing. Damnedest thing I ever saw."

Jace took the medicine bottle from him. The cure's name was long gone, but the label proudly announced the contents as the world's best stomach adjuster, guaranteed to cure all digestive and bowel ailments. Jace removed the cork and sniffed it. "This is pure whiskey."

Hugh sighed. "Well, now, did you think a man of God would voluntarily sip whiskey? Of course not, but it's what he needed to settle his nerves. I reckon we got ourselves a verifiable teetotaler here in the person of the Reverend Adamson, 'cause he only had a few sips of the stuff before he got himself up like this."

Julian and Sager helped the preacher out of the wagon and into the care of the women. "A few cups of coffee will have him regretting that stomach cure," Maddie said as she helped the man toward her home.

Jace didn't have time to sort the matter out further. When news that a preacher had arrived made its way through the ranchers, the celebration became even more festive. The women dragged him into judging their pie tasting competition. Every pie he sampled was better than the last, and each was the best pie he'd ever tasted. In the end, he chose a creation baked by a timid and pale young war widow who wouldn't look him in the eye. She won a quilt that Sally had funded which had been crafted by several of the other women in the competition.

"I started the women on that quilt when we heard you were coming to town, Mr. Gage." Sally offered him a brief smile. "I had faith in you—I knew we'd be having this celebration."

"Mr. Gage—" Agnes Brooks, the creator of the

winning pie stopped him. She handed him the quilt. "I'd like you to keep this as a token of our gratitude and a gift for when Leah comes home. And she will be home. I have no doubt of that." The woman wouldn't look above his shoulders. He had to work hard to hear her soft voice. "Many of us owe her a debt we can never repay. There were two very harsh winters during the war while our husbands were away. She took care of us, bringing us fresh meat as often as she could."

"She brought me and the boys an entire elk late November of '64," one woman said. "We were able to eat off it, all seven of us, until February."

Jace listened in stunned silence as woman after woman mentioned some kind deed Leah had done for them. His Leah. Who had been but a child herself at the time.

No. Not a child. She had probably never been a child. Jace held the quilt. "Thank you." He looked at the women. "I'll keep it for Leah."

Jace sat alone on Maddie's front steps well after midnight that night. The ranchers had long ago cleared out and headed for home. He wandered over to Leah's place and stepped inside. He'd piled her things by the door to make room for the Reverend Adamson, who was spending his first night at Maddie's boardinghouse.

Jace frowned at the small stack of crates and linens, the sum total of Leah's life. He'd given her a church, but he'd taken her home. He could bring her things over to Maddie's, but that wasn't a permanent solution. He'd left her nowhere to live when she came back. If she came back. He supposed she could take one of the abandoned houses in town, but he didn't like the idea of leaving her here alone.

He was no closer to a decision the next morning when he saw his friends off outside the Kesslers' store. It was a noisy leave-taking, full of jokes and hugs and tears as everyone bid each other farewell. Rachel and Sager told Jace they'd be expecting him up for a visit before he left the area. Julian and Audrey promised they would be back next summer and would have everyone out to Hell's Gulch for a weekend. Audrey and Julian's foster children lined up to say good-bye.

One of the older ones shook his hand. "This has been one summer I ain't never gonna forget, Jace. I'm real glad we got to meet you." That sentiment was echoed by six more children.

And then Jace faced one of the little girls—the one who rarely talked. She took hold of his hands and drew him down to her level as the other children noisily piled into the back of Audrey and Julian's wagon. The hairs lifted on his skin as he felt her petite face next to his ear. "You wait for Leah. She needs you."

He straightened and looked down at her. He didn't have the strength to expose his broken heart, so he didn't answer her.

And then Audrey was there. She took hold of his shoulders and kissed his cheek. "We'll write. And we'll be back next summer. We love you, Jace."

McCaid came and took his hand. He looked at a

loss for words. "Yeah, I guess we do," he finally bit out.

Jace smiled. "I'm glad you married her, McCaid. She was the right one for you."

Maddie and the Kesslers stood next to him as the wagons pulled out. It was odd to stand there on the empty street, left behind. He was usually the one to leave.

"Won't you come inside, Mr. Gage? I've got a pot of coffee on," Sally invited as the others filed back inside the store. Having nothing else to do, he joined them.

Jim took up his place behind the counter. "Well, Jace, what are your plans now?"

Sally brought out the coffee. Jace sipped his, wincing at the heat. "Guess it's time for me to head out. Maybe Leah's trying to outwait me—maybe she'll come back when I leave."

Maddie set her cup down with enough force that some of the coffee sloshed out. "After all that you've done here, all that you've done for her, you're just going to leave?"

"She's never been gone this long before, from what I can tell. She ain't coming back, Maddie, leastwise, not while I'm still here."

"She always has. She will this time, too."

"And why is it that she's always running off, anyway?" Jace asked, casting a look around the room at Maddie, then Jim and Sally. Anger made the scar on his neck burn. They'd been letting a girl run off to the woods since she was eight years old. They had lied to her her whole life. Did they think she would never discover the truth? Lies never stayed hidden in a little town like this.

"We loved her," Sally offered in a small voice.

"You loved her, but you lied to her. Why do you think she ran this time—because of the lies."

Maddie's eyes raged even as her face paled. She came to stand in front of Jace. "Yes, I lied." She waved a hand at the others in the room. "We all lied. We did the wrong thing for the right reason, and I would do it all again if I had to. It helped keep the sheriff from Mary. He used Leah to control her. He did the same thing to all of us. The lies were all we had to protect ourselves and each other."

Jace looked at Jim. "He forced you to feed him the wires, that makes you an accessory to every stage hold up Kemp was responsible for. Why did you do it?"

"Because by the time I realized what the wires were, I'd already passed him several of them. He threatened Sally if I were to go to the law. I saw what he did to Mary. I couldn't risk it happening to Sally. Or Maddie. Or Audrey and the orphans."

Sally silently wept. Jace turned his burning gaze on Maddie. "And you? What did he have on you?"

Maddie swallowed hard and had the grace to look miserable. "My independence. I had a contract to provide food and lodging to the stage passengers. That contract was with him."

Jace shut his eyes. "And Mary? What did he need from her?"

"I don't know. He was never a sane man. He seemed to only want to abuse her. We all knew Leah was his daughter, but he never claimed her—

or his wife. Mary thought Leah would be safer that way. But it didn't matter, didn't keep either of them safe. The sheriff used Leah to control Mary."

Jace wondered which of them had sent her into the woods to fend for herself from the time that she was eight. Did no one ever stand up for Leah? He cursed. No wonder running was her first instinct. "Is that all of it? Are there more secrets that will hurt Leah when she learns of them?"

The three old friends exchanged a look. "One more." Maddie's voice was flat. Jace's gut tightened. "Mary knew the sheriff was getting worse, more violent. She wanted to try to get Leah out of town. She sent Leah up to snare some rabbits late last February so that she could confront Kemp. He beat her up so badly, she didn't recover. Leah came home right when she was dying." She looked at the counter where her hand rested on the wood. "We told her her mother was dying of a lung infection." She looked at Jace.

The anger he'd felt earlier was gone now, chased away by an aching sense of bitterness. He wished he'd come to this town sooner. He wished he'd had the chance to lay into the sheriff and do to him what he'd done to Leah's mother. "How do I fix it? How do I help her?" He heard the words break from his mouth and realized he intended to stay and see this thing through.

"Truth, honesty, and compassion," Reverend Adamson said from the doorway. Jace looked at the newcomer. "Forgive me for eavesdropping. I walked through town, but couldn't find anyone to talk to." He smiled at the small gathering. "You have no idea how glad I am to find you in here. I was beginning to think I was going a little mad."

Jace wiped the back of his hand against his eyes. It must have been the grit that blew in from the open door that had irritated them. "Truth and honesty. Those are the same things, Reverend."

"No. They are different. Truth is never lying. Honesty is full disclosure. You must handle all your interactions with her now through those three filters." Sally fixed another cup of coffee and handed it to the reverend. He nodded his thanks. "I understand Leah was the catalyst for bringing me here. I look forward to meeting her."

The room fell silent as they considered the preacher's advice. "Jim, that old lumber mill out by the river—do you happen to have the deed to it?" Jace asked.

Jim flashed him a big smile. "I don't, but I know how to reach the owner, if you wanted to talk a deal. I do have the keys."

Jace shoved his fingers through his hair and sighed. "I guess it's time I made a more permanent change. Leah mentioned the old mill. It's as good a place as any to wait for her return."

Chapter 23

Jace arrived at the church as the last peal of the bell sounded. He settled his horse near the others at the hitching post and went up the steps to greet Reverend Adamson, wondering if the preacher was as nervous as he was for this first sermon.

"Mr. Gage." The reverend shook his hand. "Glad you could make it."

"Reverend. Glad to see you didn't need any more stomach cure for your first sermon in Defiance."

"Indeed. Hugh McDonald will be chopping my firewood an entire winter for that little trick." The reverend laughed and followed him inside, drawing the door shut behind them.

The church was packed. Men stood at the back and along the window aisles. Jace moved to stand with them, but Hugh told him there was a seat reserved for him up front. The congregation stood and the room grew uncomfortably quiet as he moved to the front row, where two empty seats sat next to each other. He took the aisle seat and looked across the empty one to Maddie. Never had he felt the void of Leah's absence as he did just then.

Reverend Adamson began the service by welcoming the townspeople and introducing himself. He made a quick apology for the state he was in when he arrived, and asked that everyone stand up and join him in his favorite hymn, "Amazing Grace." Jace stood with the others. He closed his eyes and tried to recall the words to the hymn.

Gradually, he became aware of a disturbance at the back of the room, by the door. He turned to see a white-faced Leah standing there, wearing her rough hunting clothes, her hair in a messy braid. The congregation's singing ground to a halt.

Jace's heart began to thunder. She was *here.* She'd come back. He stepped into the aisle. She looked stricken, fear and guilt and hope coalescing in her eyes. He gestured for her to join him. She shook her head and hurried out of the church.

All eyes turned to him. It took him a heartbeat to get his breath. He hurried after her, catching up to her by Maddie's fence where she was untying Blink. She mounted fast and would have ridden away, had he not pulled her from the saddle.

She pushed free of him and backed away. "What are you doing? You can't keep me here. You can't stop me!"

Jace held up his hands. "I'm only stopping you from getting on a horse that's too tired to carry you further. If you want to go, we'll move your gear to my horse." He kept his voice low and even. It was the hardest thing he'd ever done not to close the three feet separating them and pull her into his arms.

She drew a shaky breath. "I heard the bells. I've heard them every day for a week." She looked at him. "You built the church."

"Sager and McCaid helped, as did many men from town."

Leah wiped a tear from her cheek. "It's the most beautiful thing I've ever seen."

"Won't you join us? It's the first service."

She shook her head and looked down at her clothes. "I can't go in there like this." She tugged at her shirt. "And I can't change because I don't live here anymore it s-seems. I-I don't know where my home is." She drew a shaky breath.

Jace took a step closer to her. "Your home is with me."

Leah folded her arms and looked at the ground. "Is it over? The sheriff?"

"It's over. The sheriff is in jail in Cheyenne. We'll talk about that later. There's a church service waiting for us."

"No. I'm filthy."

"I don't want you to miss this."

"I can't, Jace."

"You can, by God." He moved another step closer. "It's because of you there's a church here at all. Most of those people owe you a debt of gratitude for all that you've done for them. If you show up to church in your work clothes, who are they to condemn you, when it was you who kept them alive over several dark winters?" He took the last step to her side, though he still did not reach for her. He leaned forward and spoke in a voice that urged her to look at him. "You can go in there.

And you will hold your head high, because you are brave. And strong. And because I have waited a very long time for your return."

Leah did look up at him then, her midnight blue eyes searching his, looking for answers that he could not give her. What had this town done to her to make her so feral, so wild and afraid, this beautiful girl whom he loved beyond life itself?

He secured Blink to the fence once again, then dug through her packs to find a towel or shirt. "Let's go to the pump, wash your hands and face. Then we'll go to church."

The sun warmed Leah's back as she held her hands beneath the spout. The water came out in a gush as Jace worked the lever. She rinsed her hands and splashed water on her face. When she straightened, Jace handed her a towel. As she pulled the linen over her face, she noticed several things had changed about him. He'd exchanged his rough homespun and denims for a spiffy suit of black wool, complete with matching waistcoat and trousers. His white shirt was capped with a high crisp collar and a black bow tie. His hard jaw was clean shaven. Even his moustache was gone. The only things she recognized about him were his crystalline blue eyes and his old cowboy hat.

"Ready?"

No. "I'll soil your clothes if I sit next to you. I better stand at the back."

He tossed the cloth over by Maddie's drive, then

took hold of Leah's arm. "No wife of mine is standing at the back of a church I built."

As they neared the church entrance, Leah could hear the congregation singing a hymn. The harmonious sound of so many voices raised in song—men, women, and children—washed over her, welcoming her. It was a sound she hadn't heard for many long years, not since the traveling parson stopped making his occasional visits to Defiance. She paused in front of the steps and looked up at Jace. She shouldn't be here. Not like this. It was disgraceful. She wanted to run. She should have hidden until the service was over.

He must have read the panic in her face. He drew a long breath, then cupped her cheeks and forced her eyes to meet his. "There is no place I would rather you be at this moment than by my side. Please. Come in and sit with me. No one will harm you. No one will speak against you. No one would dare."

Leah squared her shoulders and started for the steps. She closed her eyes as she perched at the threshold. And then she stepped inside. The space was filled with families she saw only rarely, sometimes not for years. The preacher smiled a greeting and kept the hymn progressing. Jace led her through the whole church, right up to the front where two vacant seats were.

Maddie was there, sitting next to her. She reached for Leah's hand and gave it a tight squeeze. When the hymn was finished, the preacher began his sermon. Leah tried to listen, but her mind was swirling with all the changes that had happened in town. The houses, from Audrey's house up to Jim's store, were gone. The dirt had been leveled, the debris removed. It was as if they had never existed.

Her home had a fresh coat of whitewash. She had gone there first, hoping to clean up before coming to the church. But while her furniture was there, her things were missing. There had been men's clothing in the dresser drawers belonging, she supposed, to the preacher.

And the church. It was finer than any she had dared ever dream would grace Defiance—large enough for the whole town to sit in once pews were brought in. Its high ceiling and tall windows made it bright and airy and cool in the hot summer sun.

She looked up at Jace, thinking he was the most wondrous of all the surprises that day. He wore no guns. And he'd listened to her, heard her when she said she wanted him to build her a church. Her gaze lowered to his hands. She saw the discoloration of dozens of marks that indicated recently healed cuts.

Unable to stop herself, she reached over and turned his hand over, palm up. The tips of his fingers were scarred the worst. Smoothing her fingers over his, she could almost feel the pain he'd endured. She glanced up and caught him watching her. His expression was hard, closed to her searching gaze. She released his hand and faced forward, trying to ignore the frisson of fear that cut through her.

Something had happened to him while she was away. She'd thought he would have left by now, but he'd stayed. She had no doubt he would punish her for her absence, as the sheriff had time and again punished her mother when anything had been disagreeable to him.

She didn't doubt her reckoning was near.

When the service was over, they were among the last to leave. Jace introduced her to the reverend. Leah started to apologize for her appearance, but he stopped her mid-sentence.

"Nonsense, my dear. You joined us from a long journey. And I wish to offer my deepest gratitude for what you and your husband have done. You've built a fine church and given me what I hope will be a long and satisfying career here." He took her hand and patted the top of it. "And if you hear tall tales of how I arrived, rest assured they are much exaggerated." He leaned forward. "It was only a few, wee drams of Hugh McDonald's stomach cure."

Laughter broke from Jace in a way that made her glance at him as the reverend left the church. "He was drunk off his ass, scared to death of coming here," he whispered.

"Jace Gage, we're in a church. And you're talking about Reverend Adamson."

Jace gave her an odd glance but did manage to look contrite. "In all fairness, though, I think Hugh may have kidnapped him." Humor wrinkled the corners of his eyes, but Leah doubted his joy went very deep. Men laughed as easily as they hit.

They went outside. Women whom she had seen only a few times in the last several years came forward to greet her, to thank her for having Jace build the church, to offer belated condolences on her mother's passing, and to catch up on all of their news. And then Maddie was there, folding her in an enormous hug.

"I am so glad to see you." Maddie held her at arm's length and looked her over. "You're reed thin, child. You and Jace should come for Sunday dinner. Jim and Sally will be there, as will the reverend."

"Thank you, Maddie, but I think I'd like to take Leah home," Jace said, declining for them.

Leah's gaze dropped to her boots. She had no idea where home was, and was not looking forward to facing Jace when they got there.

Chapter 24

Leah followed Jace down the long drive to the mill. She hadn't been here in years. She had expected it to be as run-down as the town, but it buzzed with activity. Hammers pounded a staccato beat in the hazy afternoon sun. Men were on ladders repairing siding on the old mill. Others were on its roof. Some of the men she recognized as ones who had formerly worked for the sheriff.

They pulled up by a hitching post in front of the old Winston home. Leah had come here a few times in the past. The former owners had relocated late last year to a town on the west coast that was booming and had a plentiful supply of trees for lumber. Perhaps they had seen where Defiance was headed.

One of Jace's men jogged over to greet them. He came to a full stop when he realized who she was, yanking off his hat to greet her. "You found her, boss!"

"No. She heard the bells and came to the church."

"Bet that was a sight to see." He grinned at Jace. "Welcome home, missus."

"Put the horses up, and see that Blink has a good rub-down."

The man led the horses away, leaving Leah alone with Gage. She looked at him, expecting to see a change come over him. Now that they had no witnesses, he could let loose his temper. "Have you been out here before?" he asked her.

"Not in a few years. My mother sometimes baked special orders for Mrs. Winston, and I would deliver them. Have you bought the mill?"

Jace nodded. "We finalized the transaction a couple of days ago. We used Julian's construction crew on the church. Then I put them to work here. I've had them focusing on the mill. I don't know yet how sound the roof is on the house or what other repairs might be needed."

Leah folded her arms and waited, unsure of herself or her place in all of this.

"Shall we go inside?" He took off his hat and looked at it in his hands. "I haven't spent a lot of time here. I apologize in advance for the state the house is in. I haven't done more than shake out the dust on the bed I'm using."

He opened the door and stood back for her to enter. After the heat of the August day, the interior was cool. There was a wide entrance hall with stairs on one side and common rooms on the other. A thick layer of dust covered most surfaces. What furniture remained was draped, as if the Winstons had only left for a season but would soon return.

Tracks in the dust on the floor showed a path from the front door up the stairs.

"Your things are in the parlor. I didn't know if you would be back for them. Or if you did come back, whether you'd be staying."

Leah looked at the small pile of crates and trunks, everything that she owned. It didn't amount to much, certainly not enough for her to be locked into staying if she needed to leave quickly. For good.

"Do you want to see the rest of the house?"

Leah nodded. The parlor opened into a large dining room. Beyond that was a kitchen every bit as big as Maddie's. The stove was nearly double the size of Leah's mother's. On the table sat a crate of pots, pans, and implements from her own kitchen. The Winstons had installed a pump at the sink—a luxury beyond imagining, and one that made her itch to get busy in the kitchen. She knew Jace watched her. She was careful to keep her face neutral.

"I don't know what the Winstons left and what you might need. If I didn't bring something from your house that you want, I'm sure we can make arrangements with the reverend." He looked around at the mess of the abandoned kitchen. "Make a list of what you need. We'll get it from Jim or order it up from Cheyenne or Denver."

The last room on the lower floor was a study, tucked into the back corner of the house. She was pleased with how spacious the rooms were—each of them as big or bigger than her entire house. The Winstons had a large family, and the house was built to accommodate them. Leah followed the path in the dust up the stairs to the second floor. There were five bedrooms upstairs. Jace had taken one of the larger ones. The dust in his room was lighter, but only because he'd occupied the space and stirred it up. It was still caked on the dresser and coated the wardrobe and any other flat surface in the room.

She moved down the hall, inspecting the other rooms. Each had a full complement of furniture, and each was as filthy as the next. The Winstons had left quickly and had taken very little with them. Leah sighed. It would take a week to get the house habitable. A week. And in that time, she would decide if she was staying or going.

"I could bring your things up here, if you'd like?"

"Please."

Jace carried a stack of her crates upstairs, telling himself it was a step in the right direction that she wanted to get her things settled. Still, her silence made him nervous. They'd slept together for a fortnight, yet they were as good as strangers now, neither understanding nor trusting the other.

"Where do you want these?" he asked, but as soon as she pointed to the room next to his, he wished he hadn't given her an option. He set the crates down and went back for a second load. When he delivered the last trunk, he straightened and dusted his hands, facing her in the confines of her room. Something about her always reminded him of a wild animal. Cornering a frightened animal could be a bloody experience. He stepped away from the door, giving her an exit.

She thanked him for carrying her things up.

"Why"—she looked at him, then looked away—"why aren't you angry?"

He wondered how to answer that question. The reverend's advice filtered through his mind. *Truth, honesty, and compassion.* He was angry. Angry to the bone. He'd hated her, feared for her, and mourned her. And then, he'd simply lived without her. Now here she was, standing in front of him, within arm's reach, yet still he could not touch her. Oh, he was plenty angry, and he tried like hell to rein it in.

"What makes you think I'm not angry?" His voice was rough. She paled at its tone. He ripped his bow tie free and loosened his collar as he left the room. "I'll change, then show you the rest of the property."

They toured the stables, barn, lumber yard, and mill. By the time they reached the bunkhouse and dining room, Cookie was preparing to call the men in for supper. Jace introduced Leah to Cookie.

"How do, ma'am," he greeted her, pulling on the forelock of his hair. Jace said something about getting seated at the table and Cookie halted him mid-sentence.

"Oh, no, you don't. You waited near to five weeks for the missus to come home. You ain't taking her homecoming supper here with the boys. I'll make a tray and send it up to the house."

Jace looked at Leah, worried how she would feel about being alone with him. "That'll work. Thanks, Cookie." He led her outside before she could argue. "Why don't you go up to the house? I need to visit with the foreman about work assignments for the week; then I'll bring the tray."

Leah made her way back to the house. The grounds were badly in need of a cutting—or a hungry goat. The Winstons had been gone not quite a year, but Mother Nature had already made great strides in reclaiming the property. It would be nice to see it brought back to its former condition.

In the kitchen, she found a bucket and filled it with water from the pump. She would love to take a long bath, but there wasn't time before Jace would return and she didn't want to be caught nude for the storm that would be breaking soon. She knew his anger was barely banked—she could see it in his eyes.

She wiped out the basin in her room, then filled it with the fresh water and gave herself a quick wash. She found a change of clothes in the trunk that Jace had packed for her. She brushed her hair and braided it again, then fished out her tooth powder from her packs and brushed her teeth. Feeling like a new person, she was glad Jace had given her a bit of time to freshen up.

When Jace still hadn't returned yet, she found extra sheets still folded in the linen closet. She shook them out outside, then made up her bed. Tomorrow she would see to all the laundry and get clean linens on their beds. Tonight, something dust-free to sleep on was the best she could do.

She went down to the kitchen and swept the room, then cleared the crates from the table and wiped it down. She found linens they could use for napkins and set them on the table. A breeze entered through the opened back door, warm and sweet smelling. Leah went to stand in the doorway, looking at the brilliant colors that the setting sun threw across the sky. It was perfect.

Too perfect.

The church, this home, the mill, the fact that Jace had hung up his guns. And worse, he had done all this without even knowing if she would come back—she hadn't even known herself if she would return. He'd done everything she'd asked of him. But still she was afraid to let her guard down. She'd begun remembering things, bits of interactions between her mother and the sheriff. The sheriff had never done anyone a kindness freely. There was always a price. She feared once she relaxed and accepted her new circumstances, she would learn exactly what Jace's price was.

The sun was low in the horizon when Jace made his way back to the house. He entered by the front door and walked through the dining room into the kitchen. She was there, standing in the open doorway, arms folded in front of her as she stared westward to the mountains. He'd always found the Medicine Bows beautiful. But at that moment, watching her stare at them, he hated the mountains.

She heard him enter, he knew, for she stiffened. She did not turn to greet him. He set the tray on the table, then went to lean against the opposite door jamb, next to her. He had watched a mustang being broken a time or two. They'd all had that look in their eyes, the haunting haze of a dream dying. He thought again how like a wild creature she was, poised for flight. There was a simple reason animals ran when they did, and it always had to do with instinct or fear. Which was driving her? he wondered.

"Are you hungry?" She shook her head. Ignoring that answer, Jace picked up the tray and headed for the back door. "Will you join me?"

She looked at him warily. He warned himself to go slowly. "When did you last eat?"

"I don't remember. This morning. Yesterday."

He wasn't convinced. He stepped outside and sat on the top step, putting the tray between him and the spot where she stood. He didn't ask her to sit, but she did. He dished out a generous serving of roast beef, mashed potatoes, and green beans, then handed the plate to her with some silverware. She took the plate, but did not take a bite.

"Please eat. It ain't like you to cave so easily when the battle between us has barely begun."

"Are we at war, Gage?"

He met her look, holding her gaze longer than he should. "Yes." Oh, yes indeed. And it was a war he did not intend to lose.

He turned his attention to his own plate. They ate in silence for a stretch. He couldn't light on a safe topic. He knew the one question he wanted answered—why she'd left Defiance—would send her running for sure.

When he'd cleared his plate, he set it aside. He was glad to see she'd eaten most of the helping he'd given her. He looked at the sky. The sun had dipped below the ridge of the mountains, and the brilliant colors were slowly fading to gray.

"When Wolf followed you home, how did you tame him?" Jace asked, without looking at her.

"I don't suppose I ever did tame him. You can't really tame wild animals—you never take the wild out of them."

"He stayed with you. He could have left, but he didn't. Why?"

"He chose to stay. I think he knew his old life was over, and he needed somewhere to belong. Besides, I fed him."

Jace swallowed hard. Leah looked down at her plate. She set a half-eaten biscuit down, then looked up at him. *She knew.* They weren't talking about Wolf, but about her. She set her plate back on the tray with a clang and hurried down the steps, moving in the direction of the stable.

He lurched off the steps after her. "Leah—wait." She didn't turn around and she didn't slow down. "Leah! Stop!" He was going to catch up to her, to touch her, make her hear him, see him. Blood throbbed hot and thick through his body. Another step, then he grabbed her arm, spinning her about. Her cheeks were wet, her long lashes dampened and darkened with moisture. He wasn't moved. His first wife had been fluent in the use of tears. He knew they meant nothing coming from a woman.

But this was Leah. His Leah. She didn't use such tricks. He pulled her up against his body. Angry though he was, he instantly recognized her soft curves, the lemony scent of her he'd yearned for. Before he could check the motion, he lifted her into a kiss. His arms wrapped around her, cupping her head. She could gouge at his face for all he cared. He had to taste her. *Now.* His mouth slanted across hers, harsh, possessive. Her lips parted with the rhythm of her sobs, and he took advantage of the opening to thrust his tongue into her mouth.

Her arms tightened about his neck even as her tears wet his nose. He pulled back, dragging his eyes over her face, hungry for a path to her soul, a way to reach her, fearing all the while that he never would. He shoved her away and wiped the back of his hand against his mouth.

Goddamn. Why did he always bind himself to women who hated him?

"Why did you run? Why do you always run?" His voice was raw. Plaintive. He hated the sound of it, had hated the sound of it for three long years. "You left me. You goddamned left me." Leah cupped her hands over her mouth and nose as her tears poured freely. She said nothing.

Perhaps there was nothing to say.

Jace stayed away until late in the night. He didn't want to crowd Leah. It was close to midnight before he made his way up the stairs. The house was dark. No lamps were left dimly burning to light his way. What had he expected? Just because she was back didn't mean the house was home—for either of them. He lit a lamp and made his way upstairs, afraid that she had left. A cool breeze ruffled the curtains through an open window in her room. Her empty room. She *was* gone. Just like that. One stupid move on his part and she ran. His head started a nasty thrumming, a warning to find her fast, before he lost her forever. He vaulted down the stairs, searching the rest of the house for her. When he didn't find her inside, he crossed the yard to the stable. Blink was still there, dozing in his stall. All the other horses were accounted for as well.

Where was she? Had she taken off on foot? In the dark? He turned and would have headed over to the bunkhouse to rouse his men, but something snagged his attention out of the corner of his eye. Leah. She was asleep curled up on a hay bale.

He sucked in a long breath and held it until his heart stopped pounding. He doused his lamp, then set it on a shelf. Still deeply asleep, she gave no resistance when he lifted her. He pulled her soft body against his, breathing her scent into his lungs. At the house, he hesitated outside her room, wishing he could put her to rest in his bed.

He entered her room and set her on her bed, then removed her boots and pulled the covers over her. He wanted to sit in the chair and simply be near her, but he figured he'd transgressed enough for one day.

Somehow, he would have to get through her defenses. Slowly. Easily. Without any more stupid moves like forcing a kiss on her.

Chapter 25

Leah stood in the middle of the kitchen the next morning, feeling as if she were at a fork in the road, deep in uncharted territory and not knowing which way to turn. Everything had changed. She'd told Sager that she wanted to run until she wasn't herself anymore, and she'd come back to find that very thing had happened. Only now, she didn't know who she was. She was used to doing for herself—keeping her own timetable, making her own goals.

But she was married now. She was part of Jace's life and he of hers. Where did she fit? Must she follow Jace's rules as Sally did Jim's? She'd seen too clearly what happened when her mother had broken some rule of the sheriff's. She didn't want Jace to be the boss of her—she was too used to making her own rules.

Jace entered the kitchen. Leah looked up at him, catching the change in his demeanor from cheerful to wary when he saw her standing there. "Morning," he greeted her. She didn't answer. "What's wrong?"

Leah sighed. If they were ever going to have a future, if they were ever to have any hope of enjoying their life together, she had to find a way to trust him. "I don't know what to do."

"About what?"

"About me."

Jace had stopped at the door when he'd first seen her, but now he moved to lean against the table. He folded his arms and watched her. "Are you saying I get to choose? Then I choose that you move your things into my room and we make love twice a day."

"Jace! I'm being serious." He bit his bottom lip as he listened to her. "Defiance is too far for me to continue my bakery business."

"But you could bake for the men at the bunkhouse. And for me." He grinned at her. "And maybe some folks in town could still place special orders."

"And will I be allowed to go hunting and fishing?"

He arched a brow at her. "Allowed?" He straightened and came toward her, his blue eyes dark like a mountain lake in a thunderstorm. "Honey, if you want to go hunting, I'll clean your guns when you get back. If you want to go fishing, I'll take the day off and go with you. If you want to head for the hills for some time alone, just promise me you'll be back—and know that I'll be here waiting for you." She slowly backed up as he advanced, until her shoulders hit the wall. "You got all your options open to you. All I want is to have you in my life."

"Why? Why are you being so nice?"

He braced his arms on either side of her shoulders

and studied her face. "Why." The word broke from his mouth as if it were the only syllable he could speak. He stared unseeingly at the wall behind her. "Why." He drew a long breath. He looked down at her, his pale blue eyes full of emotion. "Because you gave me a chance to make a living without guns. Because of you I live in a town that needs me. Because of you I got a future that I never thought to see. There's one problem though."

Leah sniffled and swiped a tear from her cheek. "What's that?"

"I don't know how to tell my wife that I love her. I don't know how to help her trust me." He lifted a hand and slowly, carefully touched his thumb to the edge of her jaw. The look of reverence in his eyes stole her breath.

"You love me?"

"Beyond life itself. Everything that I am, everything that I have, everything that I will become is yours." He straightened and looked down at her. "Tell me what you want in life, and I will make it happen."

She wiped her cheeks again, realizing what he said was the truth. "You've already given me everything. I don't know what to say."

A smile slowly warmed his face. "How about if we start with breakfast? We'll have to eat with the boys. But after breakfast, we'll send to town for some supplies. Then we'll see the house put to rights. When that's done, maybe you'll let me take you to Cheyenne."

A tremor of fear leapt through her. The sheriff had never let her and her mother leave Defiance.

But he was gone, she reminded herself. He couldn't stop her from leaving this time. "Why Cheyenne?"

"Because this marriage didn't start quite the way it should have. I thought maybe you'd let me spoil you, give ourselves a new beginning."

That day was one of hard physical labor. Jace never left her side. He and his men carried the rugs outside and beat them until they were dust free. They moved the furniture so that she could mop the floors. He strung up new laundry lines and organized the men to wash every window in the house, inside and out.

Cookie wouldn't let them eat with the men. He sent up meal trays for breakfast, lunch, and dinner. Leah had an enormous appetite—she realized how little she'd eaten in the weeks she'd been gone.

After dinner, Leah went outside to collect the last round of laundry. When she returned, the kitchen was hot and steamy. Two huge pots of water were boiling on the stove and a screen had been drawn around a corner of the room. "You found the tub!"

Jace grinned at her. "And got the bird's nest out of the stove pipe. Why don't you get in while the water's hot?"

"I'll get a towel and my nightclothes."

"I already did. Hand me that laundry. I'll go put it away."

Leah stepped behind the screen. A pair of

drawers and a camisole were folded on a chair, and a bath towel was draped over the back. A candle flickered next to a steaming cup of tea that sat on a small side table. The tub was already filled and simply awaited her. He'd found her special soap made from her supply of lemon verbena and set it in the soap dish. Having her bath made for her was sheer bliss. She stripped and stepped into the water. It closed over her shoulders and aching back like a warm embrace. She washed quickly, while the water was warm, then leaned back and sipped her tea, luxuriating in the decadence of being spoiled.

When she finally decided to leave the tub, she dried off and dressed in the underclothes he'd left her. She was glad he'd laid those out for her instead of her nightgown. The day had been blistering hot and unless a breeze picked up, the night would be as well. She wrapped the towel over her shoulders, took up her dirty clothes, then stepped around the screen.

Jace sat at the table, naked to his waist and barefooted. "My turn." He grinned as he got up, then opened the fly of his pants and pushed them off his hips. Leah's feet were rooted to the floor. Jace's torso was all lean muscle with only a spattering of light brown chest hair. All of a sudden, she remembered the feel of him against her and realized she longed to feel him again. Her eyes lowered to his waist and down further to where his erection tented the loose material of his drawers.

His eyes darkened as he came near. "Did you

want to join me?" he bent forward and asked, his lips whispering against her cheek.

She shivered, her grip tightening on her towel. "No."

"Then maybe you could move aside and let me pass?"

Leah released her breath in a shaky exhalation. She sidestepped him and made a quick retreat from the kitchen, hurrying up the stairs to the safety of her bedroom.

A new trunk, long and flat, sat on the floor in the middle of her room. She came to a full stop and stared at it, wondering where it had come from. She set her clothes and towel aside and knelt in front of it. Releasing the catch, she opened the lid.

Inside, folded neatly, were dozens of beautiful undergarments made of lawn, cotton, satin, silk and lace in whites, beiges, and pastel colors of every hue. There were camisoles, drawers, chemises, nightgowns, and filmy robes. Leah lifted a pink silk night shift from the group, fingering the lace that edged the bodice. Never had she seen such fine work.

She heard Jace on the steps and turned to see him lean against the door jamb of her room. "Do you like them?"

"They are beautiful. Amazing. When did you buy them?"

"I ordered them when I took the sheriff in to Cheyenne. Before I knew you had left."

"How did you know my size?"

"I told the dressmaker that you were about this tall." He held out his hand even with his shoulder.

"Said you had a waist that was about this big." He made a circle with his thumbs and index fingers almost touching. "And that you had tits out to here." He held his hands a foot from his chest.

Leah couldn't stop the laugh that broke from her at his audacious grin. "Jace Gage! You didn't!"

He shrugged. His eyes grew serious. "I wasn't sure I'd ever be able to give them to you."

"Do you think they will fit?"

"Try them on."

Leah's heart began a heavy drumming, pushing heat out to every corner of her body. She took the shift over to the bed, then began unfastening the buttons of her camisole, every tiny one—while she faced Jace. She looked at him only once. His nostrils were flared, his pale eyes dark as he watched her hands. He grasped the ends of the towel that was draped over his neck in a white-knuckled grip. Leah got to the last button, then hesitated, afraid he would charge toward and take her into his arms. Afraid he wouldn't. She opened the old cotton top and drew it off her shoulders, venturing another glance at him. He hadn't moved, but his gaze lowered to her breasts. His lips parted.

She looked at the long shift and briefly thought about snatching it up to cover herself, but didn't want to ruin the effect of its smooth lines by wearing her drawers underneath. So she pulled the string loose and pushed them from her hips.

Jace sucked in a harsh breath as he followed the curve of her hips down to the dark triangle of hair at the top of her legs. Leah could barely breathe as she reached for the silk shift, praying it would fit and would cover her. She pulled it over her head. The cool material slipped over her skin as it fell into place. The light weight of the gown and the thin straps on her shoulders made her feel as if she were still bare. She looked at the lace of the bodice and saw the hard points of her nipples poke against the fabric.

"Come here," Jace rasped from his position at the doorway. Leah moved to stand before him. He ran the fingers of one hand down her face. Bending forward, he brushed his mouth against hers. "You are perfect. Beyond measure." He kissed her top lip, then her bottom lip, drawing each between his. He pulled back slightly to look into her eyes, and then his head twisted, his lips pressing against hers. He opened his jaw, the motion coaching hers to do the same. He still touched her with only one hand. His thumb beneath her chin angled her for his kiss. She wasn't afraid of this, wasn't afraid of him. She reached her tongue across the boundaries of their lips, across the threshold of his teeth, sliding it against his tongue. He groaned into her mouth.

"Leah," he whispered a long moment later as he searched her eyes. "I need to ask a favor." She took hold of his hand and kissed his palm. "Pack some of those underclothes for the trip to Cheyenne."

"I will. And you can watch me put them on."

Jace sucked in a sharp breath. "Oh, I'm gonna do a lot more than just watch you." He kissed her cheek. "Good night, sweetheart."

* * *

Leah brought her bedroll, saddlebags, and gun scabbard down the next morning. Jace was loading tarps and ropes into the wagon. He looked up at her and she smiled at him. She was happy, truly happy, for the first time in a very long while. Jace's gaze lowered to the first button of her shirt. Her grin widened, knowing he was wondering which new lacy top she wore today.

"Do you want me to saddle Blink? Or will you ride with me?" he asked.

She considered his question. If she rode with him, there would be no running—she'd never get anywhere on foot. But he'd said he loved her. He'd shown her it was true in so many ways, even not knowing whether she would return. It was her turn to take a step toward him. "I'll ride with you."

He nodded, the look in his eyes telling her he knew she was putting her trust in him. Cookie came around with a couple of filled canteens and a food basket. "Should tide you over for a few days. Here's the supplies list I need, along with a few things the boys are asking for."

They traveled south a few hours. When they neared the road that would take them to Hell's Gulch, Leah looked at Jace.

He caught her glance. "Audrey and Julian got married, while you were up the mountain."

"Was she happy?"

"Very. I think they are a good match. McCaid is good with the children. I have their address, if you'd like to write to her."

"I'd like that."

"She wouldn't believe you've gone to Cheyenne."

Leah looked at Jace, wondering if he'd heard of the times she and her mother had set out to leave Defiance, or what happened when the sheriff dragged them back home.

That night, they ate the meal she prepared from dried stew in silence. Or rather, she was silent while Jace chattered. She'd never been this far away from Defiance, not that she could remember. She hadn't been born in Defiance, but once she got there, she'd never left—except to go up the mountain. The further they went, the more tense she had become.

After the meal, Jace rinsed the dishes. She laid out her bedroll on the far side of the fire, then thought long and hard about where to place Jace's bedroll. In the end, she set his next to hers. When Jace returned, he looked at their bedrolls, then at her. He checked the horses, then came to settle down for the night, stretching out completely on his blanket. Leah lay on her back, her hands threaded together across her stomach. Waiting. Dreading. It was night. And they were alone. She was his wife. No one would fault him for anything he might do.

But he did nothing. She ventured a look at him. He looked at her and smiled. "Good night."

"Good night?"

"It's a common end-of-day phrase. It means close your eyes and go to sleep." She stared at him. He was making fun of her.

"Jace Gage. You know I'm wound as tight as a clock on Sunday. Don't you dare make fun of me."

His grin widened. "Some people stick an endearment at the end of the phrase." He settled back and put his hat over his head. "'Good night, darlin',' has a nice ring to it."

Leah forced a heavy sigh and tried to let sleep find her as she stared up at the stars, as she'd done every night while she was away. But this time she wasn't alone. She wouldn't have to be alone ever again, if she could believe him.

"Jace?"

"Mm-hmm?"

"What happened to your hands?"

He didn't immediately answer. He pushed his hat back and stared off into the distance. "When you wouldn't come back with me to Defiance, I was angry." He paused. "No, I was filled with rage. And pain. I wanted to flatten the town, wipe your memory from it. Before I'd finished tearing down the first shack, I'd worn through my gloves. I worked through the night. My hands were filled with splinters. By the next morning, I was well into the next house. It hurt, but the pain didn't come near to what I was feeling in my heart." He looked at her. "Aw, honey. Don't cry. It was stupid of me."

Leah couldn't speak. *You left a good man hurting back there,* Sager had said. "I can't help it. I did that to you. I caused you that pain." He lifted his arm and offered her his shoulder. She didn't have to be asked twice.

Jace wrapped his arm around her as she settled against his side. He rubbed her back, glad he finally had her in his arms.

* * *

They arrived in Cheyenne on the morning of the third day. Leah had never seen so many people in one place. Enormous crews of bricklayers stretched across city blocks. Hammers pounded a staccato beat. Construction crews shouted directions back and forth. Men tread frightening heights on scaffolds. A city was growing up out of the dry, treeless prairie even before her eyes.

The streets were filled with coaches and wagons, buggies and handcarts. People hurried about, shopping and carrying packages, ushering along slow-moving children. Women were dressed in fancy walking suits with matching bonnets and parasols. Men wore grand morning coats and beaver top hats. There were Indians and Chinamen and rough looking ranch hands of every size and color. And not a single woman wearing pants.

Jace pushed his hat back and sent her an appraising look. She gave him a smile. It was exciting to be here. She wished her mother could have seen this. Jace stopped the wagon in front of the Royal Overland Hotel. He lifted Leah down, then began to remove her gear. She swung her gun scabbard over one shoulder, her saddlebags over the other, and tucked her bedroll under one arm. Jace collected his gear and led her into the hotel.

Leah came to a full stop only a few feet into the space. The two-story lobby filled most of the lower floor. Marble panels as tall as a man lined the entire room and above those, beautifully carved mahogany panels went to the ceiling. Intricate mosaic work brought color to the floor. Enormous windows let in light that spilled over great potted palms. Several suites of plush crimson settees and armchairs were arranged on sprawling Persian carpets.

She followed Jace to the front desk, taking in everything around her. The doors to an elegant dining room were thrown wide, guarded by a sign that stood as a silent sentinel, warning: PROPER ATTIRE REQUIRED. PROSTITUTES WILL NOT BE ADMITTED. GUNS MUST BE LEFT AT FRONT DESK.

"Mr. Gage! How wonderful to see you again! Your room is, of course, ready," the man behind the front desk gushed. "I'll have your boy take your things to your room. Then he can drive your wagon to the livery."

"Thank you, Williams. I'll need the extra key for my wife." Jace pulled her forward. "This is Mrs. Gage."

The joy drained from the man's face as fast as a stage curtain covers a scene. His gaze moved over Leah from head to foot. His nostrils flared as he managed a stiff bow. "Mrs. Gage. Welcome."

Leah couldn't help smiling at him, imagining few women of her ilk were granted admittance to an establishment like this. She took the key he offered. "Thank you, Williams."

Jace took her arm and led her toward the stairs, which were carpeted in a rich floral pattern. The walls were covered in beige wallpaper with stylized sprawls of flowers flocked with green velvet. The opulence of the space was overwhelming.

At the landing to the first floor, Leah noticed that Jace's grin hadn't abated. He looked—happy. A porter hurried down the hall to open their door and set their things down. Gage pressed a coin into his palm, swapping it for the key as he passed them on his return to the lobby. She pulled back and frowned at him. "What's on your mind, Gage?"

His grin widened. "You. It gives me great joy to introduce you as my wife—even if it was only to the Major Domo. He's a force to be reckoned with and keeps this place running."

"Why do you keep a room here? You don't get to Cheyenne all that often, do you?" It seemed an extravagant waste of money.

"Honey, I own a third of this hotel." He started forward. She backed down the hall, trying to keep space between herself and the look in his eyes that stroked like cattails down her back. "You didn't think I spent all my ill-gotten gains on whiskey and women, did you?" He bent and scooped her up into his arms.

"Jace Gage! What are you doing?"

"Carrying my bride over the threshold. Something I should have done when you came home." When her eyes met his, all the humor was gone from them. "I'll remedy that when we get back."

He set her on her feet inside a parlor as richly appointed as the suites in the lobby below. A mirror, taller than a man and outlined with a heavily carved gilt frame, stood atop the black and white marble mantel. Jace took their things into the bedroom. Leah crossed her arms and followed him, feeling increasingly out of place. Beyond the bedroom was a washroom with a permanent claw-footed tub, a bowl and pitcher on a washstand, and a hidden necessary.

Her gaze swiveled back to the bed, a large,

brass behemoth. Involuntarily, her mind retrieved memories of the night they'd consummated their marriage. She remembered how he'd moved her body about, positioning her, using her like a tool for their combined pleasure. And the things he had done with his mouth . . .

She gripped her collar to keep from fanning at the heat in her face. He was watching her. "There's only one bed," she commented.

"We've slept together before." He came to her and lifted her hands. "Leah Morgan Gage, what happens next in our marriage is entirely up to you. We can lie next to each other and simply sleep, or we can spend the time making love. We can do one until you're ready for the other. Or you can leave. You own our future."

Leah Morgan Gage. Morgan was the name of her mother's adulterous lover. She was Leah *Kemp* Gage. What would Jace do when he found out? Fear cooled the heat in her cheeks. He must have been aware of the change in her, for he dropped her hands and stepped over to the window. Noise from the busy street below spilled into the room.

"I have to go see the marshal. Then I have parts to order for the mill and supplies to pick up."

"I'll go with you."

"I don't think you should—ordering supplies and getting some items for the mill isn't very interesting. I thought you might like to go shopping. I'll have Williams assign one of the porters to accompany you."

"I don't need a guard, Jace. I can take care of myself."

Jace sighed. "Leah, you know what I was, what I've done. You've seen that I don't come to you with a clean past. There very well could be someone with an axe to grind with me who might take it into his head that you'd make an easy target. We'll do things your way in the woods; please do them my way in town."

He pointed to the key she still gripped in her hand. "There ain't a door in this suite that I could lock that you can't unlock. And if you decide to leave, no one will stop you. You have my open account all over town. But if you go, ride fast outta here and expect to be followed." He moved closer to her. Lifting her chin, he looked into her eyes. "I've hung up my guns, Leah, but I would come out of retirement in a flash if anyone were a threat to you."

A few minutes later, Jace had secured an escort for Leah and they were on their way out of the lobby when a beautiful blond woman intercepted them. Felicity Conway.

"Jace Gage! They said you were back!" She rushed forward and took hold of his hands. Leah's hackles rose. "Oh, aren't you a sight for lonely eyes. And to think there's a nasty rumor circulating that you got married! Why, I can see it's not true. You're not wearing a ring."

Leah fingered her knife, thinking in two moves she could have the woman down and scalped. Then where would she be, without all that fine blond hair to go with her entirely too loud mouth?

Jace pulled free of Felicity's grip and wrapped a

hand about Leah's shoulder. "It's no rumor, Felicity. I married Leah."

"No!" Felicity looked from Jace to Leah and back. "You married the 'kid'? I should have known you'd prefer a boy."

"Felicity," Jace growled, his voice indicating he'd reached the end of his patience.

She looked at Leah. "Honey, you did in a few weeks what I failed to do in nearly three years—get this man off the marriage market. And worse, you ended the career of a brilliant hero."

"That's it!"

Felicity held up her hand, forestalling him. "Now don't be like that, Jace, darling. I know you mourn the fact that the stories of your exploits are no longer being written, but I'm done writing about legends." She smiled at Jace. "With you retired, there's none worth documenting anymore. I'm on to an even bigger project, one that's important to our entire country—one I need your wife for."

She slipped her arm through Leah's and drew her toward the front entrance. "You will excuse us, won't you, Jace, dear? I'm taking your wife for a quick luncheon and then a bit of shopping. She can't very well gad about town alone, can she?" She gave a throaty laugh and cast a look back at Jace, then said to Leah in a low voice that was loud enough for Jace to hear, "If there's one thing I do know, it's how to spend Jace Gage's money!"

Williams came to stand beside Jace as the two women left the building. He made a tsking sound and shook his head. "I think the Man upstairs hates you, Mr. Gage."

Jace laughed. Lifting his hat, he forked a hand through his hair. "I think they'll get along just fine. Leah had a hand on her knife, but she didn't use it." He looked at the porter who stood beside them in abject horror. "All the same—I think you'd better stay close in case there's trouble."

Chapter 26

"That was dreadful, Miss Conway."

"Oh, it was. And I do beg your pardon." She steered them around a delivery man who was carrying too many packages to see where he was going. "The problem is that he married you and not me."

"I don't see that as a problem."

"No, of course you don't. It's just that we were such legendary lovers around here." Leah gritted her teeth at the way Miss Conway dragged out the pronunciation of some of her words. Like legendary and lovers. "People were certain we would marry. And when they learn he chose a wild little mountain woman over me—well, I couldn't bear their pity. I had to make friends with you, else I'd never be able to lift my head about town again."

Leah frowned at the woman. "I'm not so sure I want to be friends, Miss Conway."

"Oh, never mind that now. I truly do need your help with my project. Here we are!" They stopped at a little restaurant that billed itself as an English tea house.

There were no signs outside warning about proper attire or guns or who could or couldn't enter, but one step into the restaurant and it was painfully obvious that it was an establishment for women of a certain social status—one far above Leah's. The room was not large and had only a center aisle. Felicity was leading the way through the tables out to a court-yard area in the back. The women were grouped by twos and threes at tables draped with lovely pink tablecloths. Floral tea sets in bone china of different colors and patterns graced each table, along with dainty plates and multi-tiered trays of small sand-wiches and treats.

As feminine as the space was, it was the women who were most foreign to Leah. They sat perched on the edge of their seats to accommodate enor-mous bustles of bows and ruffles and lace. They wore elaborate coiffures of braids and curls piled high atop their heads, capped with tiny hats topped with dried flowers or great straw contraptions with ribbons and whatnot. They were slim and perfectly shaped and looked utterly cool in their expensive silks and fine linen dresses.

To a woman, they all stopped to ogle Leah. She was painfully conscious of walking among them in her trail clothes. She was wearing an old hat Mal-colm had outgrown five years earlier. Her dusty hair hung halfway down her back in a thick, simple braid. Their razor-sharp gazes sliced over her from head to foot.

She straightened her back and lifted her chin,

thinking of other things she'd done that were more frightening than walking through this room. She'd once tracked a beaver to its dam and sat watching its antics until the sun was high. When she turned to leave, she realized she'd walked through a field littered with mating bull snakes, bunched and knotted in incomprehensible ways. To leave, she had to walk back through them to the trail. Though not poisonous, their bites could bring a nasty infection. She'd cursed the ignorance that had led her blindly through them to begin with, and wished it was still with her on her return trip. That was scarier than this.

She gripped the handle of her knife, taking strength from its stolid presence. The move must have seemed aggressive to the women, for they gasped and looked away, returning to hastily resumed conversations.

At last she and Felicity reached the back courtyard and were seated in the dappled sunshine beneath a portico. Potted plants were hung from the rafters, giving the courtyard a fresh garden feel. There must have been too much sunshine for the other ladies, however, for they were blissfully alone outside.

Felicity ordered a full complement of tea sandwiches, cakes, and scones along with a pot of Earl Grey tea. Leah's stomach rumbled in anticipation of the treats. It was a rare luxury to be served a meal, and rarer still not to have to wash dishes afterward. But she wasn't ready to let her guard down.

"What is your new project and how can I be of help, Miss Conway?"

"Do call me, Felicity," she said as she leaned forward, her face alight with excitement. "I'm writing a series of articles on the brave pioneer women who settle our frontier. I'm syndicated all over the East coast. Women can't get enough news of their western sisters. I'd like to do an article on you."

"But I'm not a pioneer. I didn't move here from somewhere else. I grew up in this territory."

"And that makes you extraordinary, because you know how to survive here. There's a dressmaker in town who is a close friend of mine. All my clothes are her creations. After luncheon, we'll go see her and have you made over as a proper young frontier wife. I will document your transformation—and interview you as the modiste works."

Leah leaned back in her seat, studying Jace's former lover in bemused silence, grateful beyond measure for the chance to have a few dresses and their proper accoutrements. "Well, if you can pull that off, then I'll be glad I didn't scalp you a few minutes ago."

Felicity threw back her head and gave a jovial belly laugh. Leah decided then and there that maybe she did like the woman.

Leah held her chin high and kept her shoulders back. She wanted to run across the street and hurry to see Jace, but the women beside her kept a sedate pace. Which was just as well, for the corset she wore made it impossible to take a deep breath, and she had to concentrate on walking on her tippy-toes so that the heels of her shoes didn't sink into the soft dirt of the road.

The dress she wore was a blue and white striped cotton with a tight fitting bodice and a square neckline with a lace edging. The skirt was of the same material, ruffled along the edges of a cutaway overskirt that was bunched, folded, and beribboned into a bustle in the back. The dress was a little shorter in length so that it did not drag on the ground, letting her cross the dirt road without ruining the fine garment. Every time she would look down to catch a glimpse of her magnificent high-heeled shoes, either Felicity or the modiste, Madame Delacroix, would jab an elbow into her ribs. She gripped her parasol even tighter as she tried to remember to hold herself in its shade.

Once inside the hotel, the women moved to one side of the door, out of the traffic area but where they might be close enough to see Jace's expression when he spotted her. They straightened the lace about her shoulders and fussed with the drape of her gown.

"Thank you for today. It was a very fun afternoon." She gave both Felicity and the modiste quick hugs.

"Hand your parasol and gloves to the porter, then walk toward the restaurant from that direction so that we can see Jace discover you." Felicity squeezed her hand. "Go on now, darling. And remember, he got the better of the two of us."

Jace had indeed been watching for her. And when he saw her, he didn't simply stand at his table and wait for her to enter, but crossed the room to greet her. He, too, had made a startling transformation. He was dressed in black tails, white vest and shirt, and a white silk tie. His golden brown hair had been trimmed so that it barely touched the top of his collar. He was clean-shaven, which only heightened the wolfish look he gave her.

When he reached her side, he stared at her with an intensity that made her feel as if she were an enigma to him, as if they two were the only ones in the whole hotel, as if he wanted to take her apart, piece by piece, and solve the riddle that she was.

He bowed over her hand. She remembered to dip a curtsy. A movement off to the side caught his attention. The girls. Leah couldn't tear her eyes from her husband to spare them a glance, but he did. He gave them a brief nod and, with the slight beginning of a grin, offered Leah his arm as he escorted her to their table.

"I wouldn't have thought my wife could be any more beautiful than she was when I last saw her this morning, but somehow my wild wood sprite has become a butterfly."

No sooner were they seated than the waiter stopped at their table. Jace ordered for them—a porterhouse steak for himself and a petite fillet mignon for her. Jace filled her glass with a fine red wine—a cabernet, the waiter had said. He lifted his glass and looked into her eyes. "Shall we toast our transformations?"

Leah touched her glass to his, then sipped her wine, feeling that dinner in this beautiful room was a fine cap to such an extraordinary day.

"Did you have fun today? I wasn't sure Felicity

would be good company—I thought you might need rescuing."

"It was amazing, Jace. I felt as pampered as a queen. Felicity had a photograph taken of me in my trail gear."

"A photograph?"

The tone in his voice made her think of the picture he had of his first wife. She smiled to distract him. "And she took a photograph of me in this dress. It took her maid hours to do my hair. And she did my nails. And Madame Delacroix's girls remade this dress for me from one they were preparing for another patron. They wanted me to take a fancy silk dress that was right for the opera, but I couldn't. I would never wear it again. This I could wear to church. It's beautiful, but practical. And I have new *everything*." She leaned forward and he did the same. "You should see my stockings. Drop your napkin and look under the table. I'll lift my skirt."

A flush of color rose beneath his swarthy skin. His crystalline blue eyes went dark. "Oh, I'm gonna see those stockings. But I'm not peeking at my wife's legs in this room. And if you feel a burning need to lift your skirts, perhaps we should take our meal upstairs?"

Leah bit her bottom lip. The heat beneath his words caused a stir within her. "I wouldn't say it's a burning need." She lifted her wine, glad her hand was steady. Their meal was served and they ate for a few minutes in silence.

"What did you do today?" Leah asked.

He shrugged. "I ordered my supplies. Picked up

some cigars." He looked at her. "Visited with the sheriff in jail."

Leah dropped her gaze, feeling dizzy suddenly. She hadn't thought of the sheriff behind bars, alive, yet waiting to die, hadn't let herself think of him at all, though she knew he was still held in jail here.

"His trial's been set for next month. They've been trying to get the location of his stash of stolen gold out of him, but haven't yet been successful."

She forced herself to meet his eyes. "And did he reveal his secrets to you?"

"Not all of them. Not the gold."

Leah's heart skipped two beats. He was watching her. He knew. He knew Kemp was her father. She tried to catch her breath, but the fiendish corset she wore gripped her ribs like a vise. She sat for a minute, trying to breathe. Her skin felt clammy and her hands went cold. She looked at Jace, who was watching her, his eyes concerned. Words wouldn't come out of her mouth. She shook her head and jumped to her feet, then hurried from the restaurant. When she reached the lobby, she gathered her skirt in her fists and jogged to the stairs.

Too late, she remembered the porter had left her key at the front desk. She had to run, had to *go*—it didn't matter where. When she reached the top of the stairs, she would keep on hurrying to somewhere—down the hall or up another flight. Someone was on the stairs below her. Jace. He took the steps three at a time. Passing her near the top, he hurried down the hall to unlock the door to their room and held it open for her.

She was breathing again, but in gasps, as if her lungs were half the size they needed to be. She began to rip at her dress, but her numb fingers couldn't work the hooks at the back of her dress.

"Jace, help me! I can't breathe—" Her ears were filled with a high pitched, keening sound like a severed telegraph wire.

Strong hands moved hers aside and made short work of the fasteners. And then he was pulling and tugging at her corset, loosening its ties. He pulled her back against him, an arm wrapped about her ribs. Her dress hung open and useless on her shoulders. A large, warm, calloused hand stroked her chest in slow, calming circles.

"Easy now, darlin'. I got you. Breathe slow and easy. Slower. One deep breath in. Let it go. Slowly."

The wild hum in her ears receded as she listened to him. She folded her arms over Jace's, holding onto him tightly. His lips were against her temple. "The door isn't locked, Leah. But in case you don't believe me, do you see where the key is?"

Leah looked at the table that flanked the closed door. The key was there, and so was her reticule.

"You can leave at any time. You are not a prisoner." His hand stilled on her chest as if measuring her heartbeat. "But if you stay, I have to warn you, we're having it out tonight, and it ain't gonna be a fair fight. There's not enough room for fear in your head and me in your heart."

Leah's chest grew tight again. She looked at the door. But Jace had resumed the soothing, slow strokes across her chest. And truth be told, she felt better in his arms than anywhere else in the world.

"Why did you run? Not now—a month ago. Why did you leave Defiance?"

"I panicked. I had to go."

"Why?"

"Everything changed, Jace. Everything. It was all over. My whole life was a lie."

"Tell me what happened."

"I-I can't."

Jace reached around her to the pile of her clothes that the porter had returned to the room earlier. Sitting on top was her belt with the knife sheath. Jace picked it up. Leah's mind flashed to the time the sheriff had forced her and her mother home after one of their attempts to leave town. She knew now her mother had been trying to escape him, but she hadn't understood that at the time. The sheriff had unbuckled his gunbelt before shoving her mother inside their house. He'd dropped the bolt on the door, but through the open window, she heard him hit her, leather against skin, over and over. And that was only the beginning.

"No, Jace, please. Please. I won't do it again. I won't run." The voice was hers, but it sounded like her mother's. She turned her face away, bracing for the first blow as broken, muted cries slammed against her clenched teeth.

"Honey, this is your belt. I'm gonna put it on you. Right like this. See?" The worn leather wrapped about her hips over her loosened dress like a hug from an old friend. Leah was trying to breathe again, but could only manage little gasps. Jace lifted her right hand and placed it around the hilt of the knife. "See? Everything's okay now. If you get scared, if I hurt you, you pull that knife." He held her for a moment, cupping his hand over hers on the knife hilt.

"I'm gonna lift you up, and we'll go sit on the sofa. And then you tell me what happened that day." He eased down and swept a hand beneath her knees, hoisting her up to his chest. "You all right? You see that I can't be hurting you while my arms are full with you. You got the advantage here I ain't armed."

He moved across the room and sat with her on the sofa. "Now you go ahead and start talking. I think my shoulders are strong enough to bear your fear." He smoothed a lock of hair from her face and looked into her eyes, his blue eyes worried. "And your pain."

Leah closed her eyes and wondered where to begin. "I'd spent the whole night in knots worrying about you when you left to go to Hell's Gulch. Then, first thing in the morning, the wagon came in with the dead and wounded, I searched for you, asked after you. And then I saw Blink." She tried to keep from crying, fearing if she started she would never stop. Her chin wavered, giving her away. "Your messenger told me that you were fine, then he said Malcolm had been killed." The tears did come then. "God, what Audrey's been through.

"I took Blink to Maddie's stable. That's where the sheriff found me." Her stomach tightened. She didn't want to tell him, didn't want to give life to a truth she hated. "The sheriff's my father, Jace. He was married to my mother. And everyone knew.

That's why no one stopped him when he forced us to marry. The man I thought was my father was my mother's adulterous lover. It was a lie. Everything about my life was a lie." She was nearly incoherent, she knew, for her words were spoken between gasps of breath. "He wouldn't let us leave Defiance. Twice my mother tried to get me away. Twice he forced us to return. He beat her with his gunbelt." She leaned forward to cover her face with her hands. "And then he raped her. I hated him. Everyone hated him. And he's my father."

Jace reached through her hands and lifted her face to him. His expression was harder than she'd ever seen it. "Did he touch you?"

"No. He never did." She wrapped her arms around his neck and let loose her sobs. He rubbed her back, stroked her hair, and bore her sorrow in silence. After a while, when she'd cried herself out, he kissed her temple and eased away from her. Leah folded herself into a ball and rested her head on her folded hands. When Jace returned, he brought a glass of water and a cool cloth for her face. He resettled himself with her legs across his lap and wrapped an arm about her shoulders.

"I don't know how you managed, Leah. A little girl in such a cruel town."

Leah drew a shaky breath. "I had the woods."

He stroked the corner of her jaw and kissed her forehead. "You were brave just now. You told me your secret and you didn't run."

"I didn't run from you then, Jace. I ran from me. I thought you would hate me. I hated me."

"How could I hate you? You're half of me. It

hurt when you left. I was afraid for you, afraid of my life without you."

Leah caught his hand and turned it palm upward. "After the sheriff confronted me, your brother-in-law came to me and told me you had killed his sister, said you had forced her to marry you. It was the last straw. I broke. And I ran."

Jace sighed. "I did kill her, Leah. But I didn't force her to marry me."

"I know. Sager told me the story when he came looking for me. I'm so sorry. About everything." Her thumb smoothed over his palm. "I hate it when I panic. I quit hearing. And my legs start running. And all I can seem to think is 'Go!'"

"It's an instinct that's saved your life, sweetheart. Maybe now, just maybe, you could think about running to me when you get scared?"

And that started her tears all over again. "I never had anyone I could run to."

Jace threaded his fingers through hers. His hand swallowed hers. "Leah, there's something I need to ask you." She sniffled and looked at him. "Will you marry me?"

"We are married."

"Married at the point of a gun isn't the way I want us to start our lives. I thought we could redo our vows in a proper ceremony in our church with the preacher."

"I'd like that, Jace. I will marry you!"

He laughed and dragged her into a tight embrace. "God, I love you, Leah."

Leah drew back. She took his face in her hands. "And I love you."

His hand moved up her arm, across her bare back, to cup her head as he sealed their love with a kiss. Nose to nose, chin to chin. She felt moisture on her thumbs and opened her eyes to see the tears on his face.

"All I ever wanted, ever, was to be a husband and a father. When I was young, I worked hard as an apprentice so that I could become a master cabinet maker and build my own life. Then the war came and destroyed everything it encountered like a great tornado, two-thousand miles wide.

"When I met Jenny, I thought she was the answer, the reprieve I needed. I thought I could make a life with her. I loved without questioning and married her in a whirlwind. Sager and Julian noticed what was happening before I did—the rebel unit of irregulars we were there to fight began to get the upper hand. They always knew where we were going to be and when. They said my wife was a spy. I didn't believe them. I went to confront her and found her in bed—with her husband. Her men strung me up. She held the rope while her husband beat me. Then Sager and Julian and the rest of our unit showed up. Sager cut me down and handed me one of his Colts. My right wrist was broken—they broke it on purpose not knowing I could shoot with either hand. I spotted her in the battle, saw her take up a rifle from a dead man and aim at Julian. Sager saw it too. We both shot at her.

"After that, it seemed I was only fit for killing. I hired out after the war. Being a gunfighter was never my plan. It just happened. It would have been my end if you hadn't come along." He smiled at her. "You saved my life, my brave little bundle of nerves."

She shoved his shoulder. "I'm not so little."

His gaze swept over her breasts, indecently revealed by her gaping bodice. "No, you're not." His grin shot heat into her belly. After a moment, his eyes turned somber again. "Honey, you asked before we left what I expect from you. I need only one thing—to know that you're gonna be in my life."

Leah smiled and wrapped her arms around his neck. "I love that freedom to choose. And I like our life in Defiance—if you do."

"I do."

"Do you think I could have a couple more dresses made? I'd like to wear something other than pants to church."

"You bet. Which reminds me . . . didn't you have some stockings to show me?"

Leah smiled and started to slip her hem up her calves.

"Not like that. Stand up,"

She got off his lap and moved a few feet away from the sofa. She lifted her skirt and showed him the embroidered flowers that decorated the outside of her calves. "Aren't they beautiful?"

"Amazing. Lift your skirts higher." Leah did as he requested, feeling warm beneath his heated gaze. She showed him her knees, then lower thighs, exposing the ruffled edges of her bloomers. He quietly regarded her legs, then dragged his eyes up to hers.

"Take your dress off."

Leah let the hem of her dress fall from her fists. She gripped and released the folds of the fabric reflexively, hesitating. She knew where this was going and the knowledge filled her with molten heat. She unbuckled her knife belt and let it drop. Jace stood up. She tensed, but he only moved around her to draw the curtains closed, in both the parlor and bedroom. The window was still open and now the sounds from the busy street below blew in with the breeze, a little muffled by the curtains. "I'm going to lock the door, but I'll leave the key in the lock. I hope you remember, if you feel like running, that you're going to be naked in a few minutes."

Back on the sofa, he crossed his legs and leaned his arms across the top of the sofa. Arching a bronze brow at her, he indicated she should continue.

Leah's hands shook as she reached to her shoulders and peeled the sleeves of her dress from her arms. It pooled about her feet in a soft whoosh. She pulled off her corset cover, too. It was shredded in the back, a victim of her recent panic.

"Sorry about that. We'll get you others. Take the corset off." Leah loosened the slack corset and drew it over her head. "Now the shift." Leah's lips parted. Jace watched the progress it made as she drew it up over her legs, her hips. When she dropped it on the floor, something flared in his eyes.

"Come here." Leah's heart was in her throat. He opened his legs, exposing a few inches of the sofa. "Put your foot here." She did as he ordered. He smiled up at her, then let his gaze move down her thigh and calf to her shoe, which he removed. He rolled her stocking down to her ankle, then removed it. She repeated the action with her other foot.

He came to his feet again. Standing large and clothed before her, he threaded the fingers of his right hand through her left and brought her palm up for a kiss. His head dipped toward hers. "Sweetheart, put your knife belt back on. This fight ain't over yet. And I'm not stopping till I win." His breath whispered against the side of her neck, below her ear.

Leah took hold of the sides of his black coat, but made no other move. "Jace, are you going to hurt me?"

He cupped her jaw with one hand and pressed his cheek to hers. She felt the pull of air as he drew in her scent. "Have I ever?"

She shook her head. "Then I don't need my knife."

He studied her eyes, perhaps measuring her strength. She straightened her shoulders, prepared for what would come next as he led her to one of the armchairs and had her sit. He pushed an ottoman in front of her, then sat down. He lifted her legs, settling her feet on his lap. "Do you trust me, Leah?"

She gripped the arms of her chair. And nodded. He smiled his half smile at her, his head tilted as he regarded her. He ran his hands up her calves to her knees and pushed her legs apart. He looked right at her dark curls revealed by the wide slit in her drawers. The hunger in his gaze stole her breath. She tried to wiggle free, but he gave her a warning look. "Don't close your knees."

Lifting each ankle, he settled one of her feet on his thigh and the other he cupped with his palms, bending, twisting, and massaging her foot with his thumbs until her entire body felt like warmed taffy, soft and boneless. He looked between her legs as he transferred his attention to her other foot.

"Jace, this is torture."

His eyes were hot with passion. "Mm-hmm."

When he was finished massaging her feet, he ran his hands up her legs, then rose to lightly kiss her lips. "I'll be right back."

Leah released a long, quiet breath of air as she set both feet on the ground and firmly locked her knees together. She watched him cross the room to a sideboard where he poured a glass of brandy. He turned and met her gaze as he sipped from the snifter. "Hold this for me," he asked, handing her the glass. "Like this—" He showed her how to cup the bowl of the glass in her hand. "It needs to be warmed."

He removed his coat and tossed it across the other chair. His vest soon followed. He untied his necktie and pulled it free, tossing it over his other clothes. He loosened his collar, then removed it, dropping it on the pile of his discarded clothes. Slowly, watching her, he unfastened the buttons of his shirt but left it hanging open as he returned to his spot on the ottoman.

Leah moistened her suddenly dry lips, nervous about what was to come. She was awkward and unschooled in the intimate practices of a husband and a wife. She sent a fast look at the door, noting the key still in the lock. The sight of an exit option was more calming than it should have been, after all they'd shared tonight. She looked at Jace, saw that he was watching her. The tension in his face made her jumpy.

He removed his boots and socks, then reached for the snifter, all the while watching her. He looked like a man sitting down to a feast, so intent was he on what was to come. Her whole body thrummed with tension, like something spring-loaded about to break free. He swirled the brandy about, watching the amber liquid splash up the sides of the glass. Sipping it, he held the liquid in his mouth briefly, heating it, then swallowed and handed it back to her.

He slowly pushed her legs apart. He wasn't smiling. Something dark and intense was in his eyes, in the hard edges of his mouth. He spread her thighs until they touched the arms of the chair. When he knelt before her, between her legs, Leah drew a ragged breath. Pulling her hips closer to the edge of the cushion, he leaned toward her, touching her mouth with his. His lips, firm and warm, paused against hers. When he opened his mouth, she did the same. His lips closed over her top lip, lingering, testing, then her bottom lip, before his head slanted and his mouth plundered hers.

Leah was breathing soft puffs of air when he drew back. She wanted to run to the door, wanted to pull him close. Neither of them spoke—there were no words that conveyed the emotions they battled. Fear and longing, surrender and freedom. And lust, so deep and burning a hum had begun again in her head.

Jace massaged her thighs. She caught her breath, fearing, wanting what was to come. His arms slipped under her knees, lifting them over his shoulders, opening her, exposing her dark triangle of hair to his face. Leah felt a rush of moisture there, and then his mouth was on her skin. The shock of it was exquisite. His tongue discovered her folds and hidden places, then dove inside of her. Leah cried out, her back arching involuntarily. The depth of her need frightened her. When he mouthed that sensitive nub, she tucked her heels into his back and pushed herself against his face.

He looked up at her and grinned. He took the snifter from her and tilted it so that he could dip two fingers into the brandy, then handed it back to her. Bending his fingers, he dribbled the liquid over her nether lips. It was warm, a hint of what was to come. He bent to lick the liquor from her skin, circling the center of her need with his tongue as his two fingers entered her, slowly, slowly, pausing, then withdrawing. He licked the sensitive folds of skin as his fingers penetrated her. Leah's body tightened as the storm gathered strength. She groaned, close to the breaking point.

He withdrew his fingers from her. Watching her, he put them in his mouth and sucked her essence from them. Then he leaned forward, bracing a hand on either side of the armchair. "I bind you to me, Leah Gage, with this and with your complete freedom to do as you wish, leave when you want, be what you desire."

Leah's body fought her. She couldn't make sense of his words. She needed release. Needed more. "No." She pushed against him, wanting him back where he'd been. Something cooled in his eyes, like water instantly frozen. Pain, there and gone before she was sure she'd seen it. He stood and retrieved the glass from her, then sat across from her on the sofa.

Leah's body screamed at his withdrawal. She was cold and alone, and she realized now that he'd misunderstood her intention. She looked at the door, curious that it no longer offered the freedom she sought. Only Jace did.

She got to her feet. Her lips thinned. She fought to make her bones feel less wobbly as she crossed the carpet to stand before Jace. "I can go if I want?"

His eyes hardened. He rested an arm across the back of the sofa and leisurely sipped his brandy, watching her. "The key's in the lock, though I reckon you should dress first. And be warned, I will follow you. At least until you're able to dodge me. I am compelled to see you safe, Leah Gage."

"I can do anything I want and you won't stop me?"

"Anything that doesn't cause you harm or involve being unfaithful."

She knelt between his splayed legs and rested her hands on his thighs. "Then I want to do to you what you did to me."

His eyes widened. He regarded her warily. He didn't answer, but when she reached forward to unfasten his trousers, he grabbed her wrist, stopping her. "You don't have to do this."

She met his gaze, held it until he released her. She unfastened his pants and took hold of his erect shaft, which reached nearly to his navel. She stroked a hand over it, then pointed it toward her mouth. Then she leaned forward and rubbed her closed lips against the length of him. "You're soft."

"The hell I am." Jace glared at her.

She smiled, enjoying learning about this side of him. She rubbed against him. At the stroke of her cheek, his member jumped in her hands. She flicked her tongue out, touching him with a tentative stroke. He drew a pin out of her hair, and then another, loosening the coiffure that had taken hours to assemble, letting her hair tumble about her shoulders.

Leah licked over the wide, round tip of his member, across the wet opening at the top. Jace's hands stilled in her hair and his eyes rolled shut. Her tongue caressed the long length of him. She sucked the tip, seeing from the way his nostrils flared that he enjoyed that sensation. She moved him deeper into her mouth, letting her tongue stroke the sensitive underside as he slid in and out of her mouth.

Suddenly he jerked out of her mouth. "Enough! I'll be no good to you if you keep that up." He leaned forward and, taking hold of her jaw, he kissed her, his tongue repeating the motion his penis had just performed.

Leah was still unfamiliar with the smooth feel of his lips against hers. Before she'd left, he'd had a moustache, which had been prickly when he kissed her. She wrapped her arms about his neck and tightened their embrace. The kiss was tender, now, lips to lips only.

"I was stunned when I saw you come to the restaurant tonight. My little huntress dressed like a civilized woman, in heels and fetching stockings, no less. Looking at you, no one would have known that you could out hunt, out camp, out track most men. I, alone in that room, knew it."

"The women were afraid of me at the tea room today. I guess I was a little scared of them too. I touched my knife and they gasped, Jace."

He laughed, his grin wide, his eyes alight. "I love you, my heathen wife."

"Heathen! That's the pot calling the kettle black. You had everyone in Defiance terrified of your arrival."

"You included?"

"Me most of all."

He swept an arm beneath her knees and lifted her into his arms. "You're not still afraid, are you? 'Cause, honey, I gotta tell you I'm about to end this fight." He carried her to the bedroom.

"It's been no fight at all."

"It wasn't between you and me. It was between your fear and your love." He set her on her feet by the bed, then lit a lamp. A movement across the room caught Leah's attention. It was their reflection in another huge mirror that leaned against the wall, standing almost floor to ceiling. Jace looked up and caught her staring at him. Something in his gaze made her feel like a hare heading right for a snare.

"So which is winning?" she asked.

He stood up to yank his shirt over his head and pushed his drawers and pants down. His penis swung free, engorged, veined and deep burgundy. "You can let me know in a little while." He stepped behind her and began unfastening each button on her camisole. He peeled the fabric from her arms and dropped it by his clothes. She didn't know which was more disturbing, the feel of his erection against the crease of her buttocks, or watching her husband reveal her nudity.

"Christ, you are something to see," he rasped against her ear. He stood behind her, his tanned hands on her pale ribs. She didn't stand higher than his shoulders. He cupped her breasts, lifting them, her erect nipples poking from between his fingers.

"These are what I saw the first day I met you. I knew I was in trouble then." Leah watched one hand release her breast and move down her ribs, to the tie of her drawers. He released the fine bow and pushed them down her hips to pool at her feet. His breathing grew harsh. He kissed her shoulder as his hand stroked across her belly, to her woman's curls and beyond to her secret place. "You're wet."

His voice, low and rough, stroked her senses even as his fingers slipped against her lower lips, in and out. He spread her legs with his foot, giving himself greater access. He moved his hand to her other breast, gently pinching and rolling her nipple between his thumb and forefinger. When his hand stroked that aching spot between her legs, she lurched involuntarily against him.

"Jace, I can't stand."

"Yes, you can. You can stand all the way through

it." To prove his point, his thumb worked that sensitive nub while he shoved two fingers into her channel. In seconds, her body was wracked with violent convulsions of pleasure. She gripped his arms, clinging through the waves of sensation crashing through her.

When it ended, Jace cupped her face, turning her for a kiss that mimicked what his fingers had done to her. His head twisted against her as his tongue entered her mouth. His eyes were open, meeting her gaze as he devoured her mouth. Her dark blue eyes had gone violet. He was lost to the madness he'd stirred within her.

He lifted her, pinning her against his chest, crushing her breasts between their bodies before setting her on the bed. Following her onto the soft mattress, he leaned over and took hold of her breasts. Supporting himself on his elbows, he suckled first one peak, then the other. He kissed the valley between her breasts, pressing the soft mounds against his cheeks. He rubbed the palm of his hand over a peaked nipple as he moved his face up her chest to her neck. Then he released her breasts to take hold of her face. She pulled him close. He shoved her legs apart with his knees and moved his dick against her opening. She moaned at the sensation. Her neck and face became flushed with hot blood.

In one swift, forceful motion, Jace seated himself in her sheath. Her orgasm hit instantly, her small inner muscles contracting, gripping him in spasms he could not fight. He shoved deep inside her, feeling his own peak crest. He released his seed, pumping himself inside her.

His face was buried in her neck. He lifted his head up to look at her. "You unman me, Leah." She was breathing heavily beneath him, body still writhing against his.

"Jace, I want more." Her fingers forked into his hair.

Her request gave new life to his erection. He grinned, feeling himself hardening again. "What made you think we were done?"

He rolled over onto his back, moving her to straddle him without ever leaving her body. A long, low, "Ohhh," slipped from her mouth with a sigh. She braced herself with a hand on his belly and pushed herself off his cock, then slowly slipped back down. He let her set the rhythm while he worked her tits. He sat up to suckle her. She changed her speed, riding him hard and fast, slipping up and down against his dick. It was torture holding back when her sheath was tight, throbbing, consuming him. One hand slipped down below, to manipulate her erect nub. He felt a corresponding squeeze of her muscles around his cock. She gripped his face, kissing him, thrusting her tongue against his, tasting him, owning him. She broke the kiss and took hold of his shoulders. Her nails stung his skin as the passion overtook her. And he was right there with her, spilling himself inside her slick warmth.

When the last of the aftershock eased from her, she collapsed on top of him. He wrapped his arms about her.

"I didn't know it could be done that way."

"That's only the beginning, my love."

Her face grew serious. "I sure wish I hadn't wasted so many weeks hiding in the mountains when I could have been with you—doing this."

Jace choked on a rough exhalation. "You will be the death of me, wife." He kissed her neck. "We'll have to make up for lost time."

Chapter 27

Leah turned to sit sideways on the wagon bench, curious about the man who had been trailing them for the last hour, on this, their second day out of Cheyenne.

"Rider coming."

Jace looked at her. "Do you recognize him?"

"No. But the sunlight on his badge tells me he's from the marshal's office."

"What color horse is he riding?"

"A roan."

Jace drew back on the reins and called to the horses, "Whoa—"

"Do you know him?"

Jace nodded, but there was a new tension in him, accentuated by the fact that he set the break and tied off the reins, freeing his hands.

They heard the approaching horse as it came alongside Jace. The man sitting astride the horse was neither short nor tall, young nor old. He lifted his hat as he nodded at Leah. "Mrs. Gage. Jace. Mind if I ride a piece with you?" When he set his hat back down, Leah became aware of his assessing gaze. She met his eyes, wondering what he was up to.

"Marshal," Jace returned the terse greeting. "Leah, this is Marshal Riggins."

"Pleasure to meet you, sir," Leah offered, disliking what she sensed in his hard eyes, though he did give her a polite nod.

"What brings you out this way?" Jace asked.

"I found out Sheriff Kemp's gonna try to break out of jail, and I expect he'll head up this way."

"Why are you here instead of stopping him?"

"I'm just taking care of business."

"Alone?"

"We'll talk in a little while. You about to make camp?"

"We are," Leah spoke up. "You're welcome to join us for supper."

"I'd like that, ma'am."

Jace took up the reins and called to the horses. Leah couldn't quiet her sense of dread. She knew, beyond any doubt, that Kemp would make it back to Defiance, that the peace she had found with Jace was about to be shattered. They neared the high ridge that marked the edge of the valley. They would reach Defiance late tomorrow morning.

Jace looked over her way, watched her, his face revealing nothing of his thoughts. A muscle worked in his jaw. He reached for her hand and kissed her knuckles. "I won't let anything happen to you, Leah. You've got nothing to fear. I give you my word on it. But if you want to run, you go. When you hear the bells, come back, okay?"

"No."

His jaw tensed. "No?"

"I can't lose you, Jace. I'm not leaving you to face this alone."

"Let's see how this plays out. I don't want you in any danger."

Leah moved closer to him on the wagon bench, touching him with the entire side of her leg. He wrapped an arm about her shoulders, calming her instinct to run.

At their camp a short while later, Jace and Riggins saw to the horses while Leah fetched wood and set pots of beans and bacon cooking.

"All right, Marshal. What's on your mind?" Jace asked when Leah was out of earshot.

"Your wife."

"What about her?" Jace silently cursed, feeling the present overlaid by the past. This was exactly how Julian and Sager had broached the issue of Jenny's betrayal.

"She's Kemp's daughter."

"That's old news, Riggins." Jace set out his and Leah's bedrolls.

"Well, I've been thinking. Didn't you wonder why Kemp let you marry Leah? You—the enemy? You were alone in Defiance. And weren't his men present? Man like Kemp never moves around without his cronies. They could have shot you in the back, but they didn't. Why?"

Well, damn it all to hell. He had been wondering that. Jace put his hands on his hips and faced Riggins. "Get to the point, and fast, Marshal."

"She's in it with her father. She knows where the gold is. She was to distract you from finding it."

Jace felt a cold sweat cover his body. His fists throbbed to connect with the marshal's teeth. He drew a few calming breaths, trying to work it through, trying to fit the pieces together. He'd heard much the same from Julian and Sager three years ago. And they'd been right about Jenny's ulterior motives.

"Any other man who dared say something like that would be eating those words right about now. Don't think your badge is any protection, Riggins. What proof do you have?"

"The sheriff and I have spent a lot of time together over the past month. He got to talking about a lot of things. He told me how using her was all part of his plan."

"The sheriff would say anything to delay his own hanging." Or to take Leah with him, forever under his control into the bowels of Hell. No, Jace had lived in her town, among her people, long enough to know that even if he doubted his own observations, he couldn't mistake their love for her. "Consider the source, Marshal. It's his word against mine."

Leah had never mentioned the sheriff's gold, other than the one time they were talking about it around Maddie's table. Hell, she'd even said the sheriff had probably hidden it at her house.

"You sayin' you vouch for your wife?"

He'd stake his life on Leah's innocence. "That's what I'm saying."

They broke off their discussion as Leah returned, arms full of kindling. She looked from Jace to Riggins, then back to Jace, and was astute enough to realize they'd been talking about her. He saw the color drain from her face, saw the shadows crowd her eyes, and knew the call to run was loud within her. He turned back to the tasks at hand; the fastest way to make her run was to corner her.

When supper was ready, Jace accepted a plate from Leah. "Who do you have working this with you, Marshal?" he asked, curious if Lambert had a role in the drama that was soon to unfold.

Riggins frowned down at his plate. "I sent Murdock and Atkins ahead to Defiance."

"Jack Atkins?" Jace asked. The marshal nodded. "What's Lambert doing?"

"He's breaking the sheriff out of jail."

"With your permission?"

"Hell, no. I've known for a while he's every bit the sidewinder you claimed. But I don't know if he's the only dirty gun in my employ. I don't know who else might be in it with him. I've got to let this disaster play out, catch them in the act."

"You can trust Atkins. He's a straight shooter. If you need someone at your back, he's your man. Murdock, I don't know anything about. You're sure they're headed for Defiance?"

Riggins nodded. "I overheard him negotiating Lambert's cut with him."

"You got someone trailing them?"

Riggins slowly grinned. "Roy Bancroft."

Jace nodded. "Well, you've got two trustworthy men. Sounds like Murdock is the one to watch. Do Atkins and Bancroft know your plan?"

"They do. In the morning, I'm riding into Defiance." He met Jace's gaze. "I could use another gun."

Jace nodded. "I'll swing by the house for a horse and my gear. I'll get into town shortly behind you."

* * *

Leah considered their bedrolls lying out next to each other on one side of the fire. Marshal Riggins was stretched out on the opposite side of the fire, his hands clasped across his stomach, his hat on his head. Rhythmic snores indicated he was already asleep. Leah set a couple of pieces of green wood on the fire, knowing they would smoke and pop, giving her and Jace a bit of privacy from the marshal.

She looked at Jace and he at her. He said nothing, silently offering her her pick of bedrolls. Last night she'd slept between him and the fire. Tonight, she chose the outer bedroll, putting Jace between her and the marshal. She lay on her back, aware of everything around her—the crickets, the breeze in the aspens and pines. The man lying next to her.

No doubt he thought she was close to running, but some problems you couldn't run from. Her father was such a problem. Joseph had told her once about a grizzly that came out of hibernation mean and hungry. He'd stalked the occupants of the small mining village until the great rivers fully thawed and the fish runs began, mauling ten people over two years. Bullets didn't stop him, didn't even slow him down.

Joseph visited the village one year when the bear came. The villagers were hiding in a dugout at the back of the town's supply depot, waiting for the madness to pass. Joseph had set a trap for the beast, hanging a beef haunch off a low overhang in front of the store. At twilight, the grizzly came, huffing, sniffing for humans. He found the beef and ripped it down off its tether. Joseph, who had been lying in wait on the low overhang, jumped onto his back and sawed into his neck, cutting through winter thick fur as he fought to sever the monster's artery. The grizzly stood on his hind legs, roaring, twisting and lurching till his artery was hit, and his blood ran out.

"Honey, sometimes you got to kill the beast, 'cause it's gonna come for you again and again, just to make your life a living hell." Joseph's words came back to her now, as if he sat at her campfire. He'd told her that story the day he'd brought her down the mountain with a broken leg. And he'd given his necklace of bear claws and teeth to her mother. She'd never seen him again.

Leah knew what she had to do. She was done running.

Chapter 28

They reached the house at mid-day. The marshal had left their camp ahead of them that morning, wanting to get situated before the others arrived. Jace lifted her down. Some of his men came out to take the wagon and get the horses settled. Jace ordered one of them to saddle a horse for him. She called for Blink to be brought around as well.

Jace glared at her. "You are not coming with me."

"You will not win that battle, Cage." She went up to her room. At the back of her top drawer was Joseph's necklace. She put it on, feeling as if the old trapper was right there with her. She took up her cartridge belt, transferred her knife sheath to it, then retrieved a box of cartridges and her rifle and went back downstairs.

Jace was in the kitchen. His gunbelt, bandoliers, rifle, and Colts were on the table. He met her eyes, then dropped his gaze to her necklace, her belt, and rifle scabbard. His hand paused midway, holding a cartridge before the open rifle chamber. "No."

"I have the absolute freedom to do as I choose."

Jace glared at her. "Not if it causes you harm." A muscle ticked at the corner of his jaw. He stared blindly at the desk. His nostrils flared. She could feel his temper gaining momentum. He set his rifle down, then came toward her, his long stride covering the space in only two steps. She was proud of herself for not flinching when he stopped nearly on top of her feet, forcing her to arch her neck to look up at him.

"This ain't a game, Leah. Anyone who gets between the sheriff and his gold is gonna die."

"I've dealt with Kemp most of my life. I will not be bullied—by him or by you."

Jace took her rifle scabbard and leaned it against a nearby chair. He faced her again and closed the distance between them, using his own body to push her back against the wall where he locked his hands flat against the plaster and glared down at her. "If something happens to you, what the hell am I gonna do?"

Leah tried to read his face, but could see only anger in his eyes. Was it possible that what she saw was fear for her, for them? "Probably the same thing I would do if something happened to you. Hurt every second of every hour for the rest of my life."

He sucked in a sharp breath, then bent his head, pressed his lips to hers in a kiss that might be their last. She wanted to move against him, deepen the kiss even as she wanted to stay as they were forever, softly touching, yearning.

When his lips parted, hers followed suit, and she opened herself to him. He gently touched his tongue to hers. His body tightened, his breathing stilled, as if he waited, resisting. And then his arms crushed her to him and his mouth twisted against hers. He broke the kiss to press his lips to the corner of her mouth, then across her lips to the other corner. His hand at the back of her head held her immobile while he paused. She wondered if he was memorizing everything about the way their lips felt against each other. She was. His breathing was rapid now, as was hers.

He kissed her again, his mouth open, his tongue searching, sliding against hers. His hand came around to the front of her stomach. He tugged her trousers free of the cartridge belt. He popped the top button of her fly open and slipped his hand inside her pants. The sensation was exquisite, flooding her with moisture. She moaned against his mouth. He rubbed the opening of her feminine folds, instantly finding that sensitive spot, pressing her cotton drawers against her skin. His strokes set flame to her passion. She kicked off her boots and ripped open the remaining buttons on her fly, then shoved her pants off her legs. He freed himself from his pants, opening them enough to release his erection. Then his hands were at her buttocks, lifting her, positioning her, spreading her legs around his hips as he thrust into her through the slit in her drawers.

She tightened her legs around him and wrapped her arms about his neck. His mouth was open against her cheek. He hadn't shaved since Cheyenne and the bristles of his beard scraped her skin. She was aware of every place their bodies touched, the stroke of him inside her. He moved her over his shaft as if she weighed no more than a stack of dishes.

She could feel her passion coiling, tightening, drawing near. She bucked against him. Again and again. He leaned her back against the wall and freed a hand to tease her—there. She broke free. A cry ripped from her as she surrendered completely to him, to their passion, to her love. He pressed his forehead to hers as his body slammed into hers. With a groan, he sheathed himself to his ballocks, holding her as he spent himself deep inside her.

For a long moment, neither could speak. Her heart felt two sizes too big within her chest. She pulled back, desperate to tell him how much she loved him. But his eyes had gone cold, as if a wall had shot up between them, though they were still physically joined.

She pushed him away, pulling herself free and dropping to her own feet. She drew on her pants, tucked in her shirt, and settled her belt over her waist again as he righted his own clothes. He moved back to the desk and finished loading his rifle. She watched as he pulled his bandoliers on, strapped on his gunbelt, then took up his hat. She picked up her scabbard and headed for the door—but not quite fast enough. He grabbed the waist of her pants, halting her.

"You stay behind me and follow my directions," he ordered in a harsh voice. "Got that? No heroics. If you can't do as I say, I will tie you up and leave you here."

"Then we got ourselves a dilemma, cowboy. Kemp is my father, my problem. I'll deal with him."

"Leah, I will yield to you in everything that you do better than me, like fishing and hunting and tracking and baking—just about everything but gunplay. Yield to me in this."

"This is not 'play,' Gage. I have the right to protect you from the fiend who is my father."

Jace's face took on a hard edge. "Yield to me, Leah." He would not budge, and they were wasting precious time.

Leah took his face in her hands. "I love you too much to see you hurt."

"Sweetheart, you may not have noticed, but you aren't alone anymore. Let me protect you."

She sighed. And surrendered. "Let's get this over with."

Their horses were hitched outside. One of the hands was there and Jace briefly filled him in, ordering him and the others to stay at the mill. Leah followed him down the drive.

"You do know I'm not a cowboy— " he asked her as they turned onto the road toward Defiance.

Leah smiled at him. "It's a common phrase. It
me and I love you more than I thought I would ever have the luck to experience." The look he gave her made her toes curl in her boots.

An hour later, they were riding into Defiance. The old tension was back in Jace. He held the reins with his right hand, giving the false impression that he'd be slow to draw. Riding next to him, Leah saw him scan the streets and buildings from the distant ridge where they'd stopped. Heading down into town, they moved to the east and came up behind her old house, under the cover of a stand of shrubby cottonwoods. Murdock was there, rifle at the ready. Jace asked where Riggins and Atkins were. The marshal's man pointed to Leah's wood pile, then nodded over to the shack. Jace could see neither man.

A wagon was pulled up outside of Leah's old home. Reverend Adamson stood beside the front steps, his hands in the air. The sheriff had removed a panel beneath the steps and was retrieving small, heavy bags which he and one of the marshal's men carried to the wagon.

The gold had been at her house the whole time. Just as she'd suspected.

Watching them was painful. Leah had seen—and heard—enough. She slipped her rifle from the scabbard, discarding the worn leather sheath.

Jace caught her. He didn't like moving forward with Murdock at their backs. "I reckon it's futile to ask you to wait here?" She nodded. He made a face, shaking his head. "Then stay behind me." They pushed through the bushes and moved out into the open.

The sheriff looked over at them. The afternoon was hot, and sweat matted strands of thinning hair to his face and colored dark patches beneath his armpits. Leah went cold.

"Drop your guns," Kemp ordered, his pistol drawn.

"I don't think so. How about you drop yours?" Jace countered. "The marshal's here, Kemp. You're out gunned."

Leah cocked her rifle and pointed it at Kemp as she stepped around Jace's back. "You kept your gold at my house. *My house.* You used us, Mother and me."

Kemp laughed as Lambert picked up another bag to carry to the wagon. "Of course I did. What the hell else did I need you for?"

"That's why you would never let us leave town, why you would never let any man court Mother."

Kemp spun and faced her, eyes blazing. "I didn't let anyone near her because she was my wife! The whore. She was a runner like you. She tried to get my brother to take her away barely three days into our marriage." Despite the fact that Jace was nearly blocking her, Leah felt Kemp's gaze slice through her. "You're most likely his by-blow."

Leah fingered the trigger. "Your brother—what was his name?"

"Joseph." Kemp watched, waited for her reaction.

Leah's knees almost buckled. Bile rose in her throat as waves of hot and cold washed through her. "You killed Joseph."

"The men I sent could never find him in the woods. He knew I'd shoot him if I ever saw him again, but he walked into town as bold as you please. He still loved Mary. He was coming for her, when he brought you back with that broken leg. You, I didn't care about, but Mary was mine. I used you to keep your ma in line. But she said she was going to leave last winter, once and for all, said I couldn't stop her. But I did stop her."

Leah gasped, remembered her mother's sudden illness. Sally and Maddie hadn't let her help prepare her mother for the funeral, and Leah now knew why—she would have seen the bruises. "You killed her, too." They had lied about that as well, Maddie and Jim and Sally. Leah's world began to spin. Her grip tightened on her rifle as she vowed the sheriff would never survive this day.

"I didn't mean to. She wouldn't listen. She was going to leave me. Hell, the bitch left me anyway when she died. At least you were still here, still useful to me. I used you to distract Gage, keep him from looking for the gold." The sheriff chuckled. "He buried that goddamned wolf of yours right next to it. The gold was inches from his shovel and he never knew it."

Kemp's image began to jump and waver as her eyes filled with liquid. She struggled to absorb the impact of his words, the truth that he had killed two people she loved very much, her mother and Joseph.

Lambert had stayed near the wagon after dropping his last bundle into the back. He now moved slowly toward the front of the wagon. Leah saw his furtive movements, but before she could call attention to him, a man came out of the trees behind them.

"Drop your guns, Gage. You too, girl." Jace didn't move, but Leah tossed her rifle to the ground. She cast a quick look over her shoulder, realizing it wasn't likely that the man would let them go.

Riggins, who stood behind the stack of firewood, shouted, "Lambert's getting away!" Lambert slapped the reins, whipping the horses into a gallop. The marshal fired his pistol and missed, then ran between the reverend's house and the church to fire at Lambert's retreating form.

At once, the tense stand-off broke. Kemp fired, and Jace's gun discharged almost simultaneously. More shots were fired down the street, but Leah wasn't paying attention. She pulled her knife, flipped it to grip the tip of the blade, then turned and released it, sending it flying into the shoulder of the man behind them. The man's gun discharged harmlessly into the ground as he dropped his pistol to rip the knife out of his shoulder. He looked at her with bloody intent, pain draining the color from his face. She crouched to retrieve her rifle as another deputy stepped out of the woods holding a gun on the man she'd just knifed.

"Drop it, Murdock, else you'll be dead before you throw it." Murdock tossed her knife into the dirt between them. "You hurt, Mr. Gage?"

Leah spun around. Kemp's body lay face down in her old herb garden. Jace was holstering his gun. Her gaze flashed over him, checking him from head to toe. He looked from her to the man behind her, seeing her knife half buried in the dirt. He retrieved Murdock's gun and pulled her knife free. A muscle bunched in his jaw as he wiped it clean on his thigh, then handed it to her, hilt first.

"I'm fine, Bancroft." Jace nodded at his gun. "Thanks."

Maddie rushed out of her house, crossing to the reverend. Jim and Sally hurried down the street as the wagon returned, driven by a deputy who sat astride one of the lead horses. Lambert's prone body was draped across the front bench. Riggins clapped the deputy on the back when he dismounted. "Well done, Atkins! That was some quick shootin' and quicker thinkin', stopping the wagon the way you did."

Atkins gave a reluctant grin. "Figured if they managed to get past all of you, they still would have to get past me."

The men moved Kemp and Lambert's bodies to the back of the wagon and loaded the rest of the gold into it. Then they gathered up the extra horses and their prisoner, and drove back into town, toward the undertaker.

Just like that, the entire nightmare was over.

An uncomfortable numbness slipped over Leah, slowly, like a fog creeps into town. She couldn't move, couldn't speak. She shut her eyes, heard the silence that she could summon at will. She thought of the mountain woods and the secret places that she knew, the places Joseph had known too. Was he her father? He was more of a father to her than Kemp had ever been.

The wind stirred the leaves of the cottonwoods behind her, blew against her skin.

When she opened her eyes, Jace was there, silent, watching. She was sad. She was furious. She sucked in a harsh breath, as emotions that had lived like parasites in her soul now broke free. "I've had a bead on him a hundred times. I could have killed him, for a hundred valid reasons, but I didn't. I let it come to this." She thought of the life her mother had lived, knew Kemp had been the cause of the mysterious injuries that always happened when she'd been out hunting.

"The only good thing that man ever did was make me marry you." She folded her arms about herself. Her tears were coming fast. She swiped at her face, trying to focus on him, dreading what she would see in his eyes—the look he might give a favorite horse before shooting it. "Say something, Gage."

His lips moved, but no words came out. He stopped. The muscle at the corner of his jaw bunched and released. "You didn't run."

"No"—she shook her head—"no, I didn't. I can't run when you're in trouble. I have the right to defend you, and any children we might have, and the mill. And I will make use of that right."

"You forgot one person in that list." His words, spoken in a quiet voice, contrasted with the fierce look in his eyes. "*You*. You have the right to defend yourself. Always."

She blinked. And nodded. "I should have protected my mother. I should have done better by her." And then Jace was there, wrapped around her, holding her against his body in a tight hug. And the rest of her tears came in an ugly wash of snorts and sobs.

He rubbed her back. "You cry it out. God knows you've earned it."

Someone pressed a handkerchief into her hand. She heard the reverend tell Jace they were going over to Maddie's. She stood with Jace a long time after her tears were spent. Gradually the pounding in her head receded enough that she could hear his heartbeat.

It was over. He was safe. She was safe. She wiped

her eyes and blew her nose, then ventured a look at him. He was smiling. "Don't look at me."

He laughed. "Don't look at you! Don't look at the very best thing in my life?"

"I'm a wreck."

"You're a brave wreck. You didn't run, just now. You were scared and angry. But you faced your father. I was trying not to feel what I knew I would if you ran, trying to believe that if you left, you'd be back."

"You said I could run to you."

He nodded and pulled her into another hug. "Leah, I know that Maddie and the Kesslers hid things from you. They did it out of love—and fear. Kemp had a stranglehold on everyone. I hope you can forgive them. They're the only family we have, you and I."

"I know." She dipped her head against his chest and wrapped her arms around his waist. "I do forgive them. It's over, Jace—the nightmare we were living."

Jace pressed a kiss to the top of her head. "Maddie's got some coffee on. Let's go get a cup. Then I'd like to go home and make love to my wife in our bed, in our room, in our home." A smile broke through the shadows on his face. "And this time, I will carry you across the threshold."

She smiled up at him. "I don't need coffee."

He laughed and led her around her old vegetable garden. "Neither do I, but everyone wants to make sure you're okay. Just one thing, honey—" Jace squeezed her hand and sent her a warm grin. "Drink fast."

Epilogue

Leah pulled a tray of fresh rolls out of the oven and set them on the warming tray. Jace had gone into town for some supplies and was due back in time for supper. October had been a mild month, but she knew the weather wouldn't hold long and had sent him to fetch the supplies she liked to have on hand before the winter storms made roads impassable.

Right on cue, Jace came up the porch at the back door. "Leah—can you give me a hand unloading?" he called through the open kitchen door.

Leah wiped her hands on her apron and went outside. The afternoon already had a cool bite to it. She stepped off the porch and came to an abrupt halt as she stared down at the small, black furry animal sitting by Jace's boots. He had bright yellow eyes, huge pointy ears, an enormous snout, and long legs. A wolf pup. Leah dropped to her knees, hoping he wouldn't be afraid of her. He sat where he was for a moment, his head tilted. After a minute, he lifted his head and barked a string of funny little yaps, not quite able to howl. And then he launched himself at Leah, jumping to lick at her.

She laughed and held his little face for a kiss, thinking this pup must have been exactly what Wolf looked like when he was little. And whole.

"Where did you find him, Gage?"

"Sager sent him down. Apparently, one of his supply wagons was followed home by a stray dog— a stray that had spent some time being friendly with Wolf. All the other pups came out looking like normal dogs. But this one, the runt of the litter, was all Wolf. Rachel had to work long and hard to keep him alive, but she knew you needed to have him."

Leah felt tears warm her face. She wiped them away. "You mean he really is Wolf's pup?"

"Strange, isn't it?"

"What should I call him?"

Jace pushed his hat back on his head. "A wise person I once knew said every living thing has a name, you just have to be quiet and listen to hear it. I did that very thing coming home from town."

"What did he tell you his name was?"

"Well, it was a long, complicated thing, full of love and hugs and nights being chased off the bed. There wasn't a human equivalent, so I was thinking we might call him Wolfson."

Leah flashed a smile at him. "Wolfson it is. Though I suspect the baby will call him Wolfie."

Jace went utterly still. "What did you say?"

Leah came to her feet and made her way around the pup. "You heard me, cowboy."

Jace let out a whoop and swung her up into his arms. "Honey, you just made me the happiest man alive."

Did you miss the other titles in the
Men of Defiance series?
Start from the beginning!

RACHEL AND THE HIRED GUN

When Rachel Douglas left her aunt's house in Virginia for the wilds of the Dakota Territory, she knew the journey would be long and arduous. But she didn't realize that she has been summoned west to be used as a pawn in a ranch war with her father's neighbor—or that her fierce, sudden attraction to Sager, her father's hired gun, would put her heart and her life in jeopardy. Seducing Rachel and feeding a bitter feud between the two ranches was Sager's plan of vengeance against those who slaughtered his foster Shoshone family. Instead, Rachel's guileless mix of courage and vulnerability touches the conscience he thought he'd buried long ago, and draws them both into a passion without rules, without limits one that will change their destinies forever . . .

Audrey and the Maverick

In Elaine Levine's stunning novel of the American West, a proud rancher and a determined young woman are drawn together in the lawless town of Defiance.

Virginia financier Julian McCaid has put his troubled past behind him. His plans for the future don't include Audrey Sheridan, the extraordinary frontier woman he met just once. But it's because of her that he's come to the Dakota Territory to investigate problems at his ranch. And it's all the more surprising when he discovers she isn't the innocent he believed. Now nothing but her complete surrender will purge her from his soul.

If it weren't for the children she cares for in her makeshift orphanage, Audrey would have left Defiance long ago. Now the sheriff is blackmailing her to distract the man who might derail his corrupt schemes—a man who can offer Audrey not just protection, but a passion bold enough to make them claim their place in this harsh and beautiful land . . .